THE QUIET WIFE

BY J.M. CANNON

The Quiet Wife

TABLE OF CONTENTS

OUT OF THE WOODS

It drove me crazy. It had snowed twice this year and both times someone had found a mysterious set of footprints coming from the woods. I was outside, a quarter mile from my house in the woods, staring down with a frown at a large set of tracks. I knew there was an old story that started off similar to this, but I couldn't remember its name.

The story went something like this: a farmer finds a strange set of footsteps in the snow. The prints come out of the woods and stop at his back door, but when he searches his home, it's empty.

That night he goes to the village pub and complains about the footprints, but his friends laugh at his worry and assure him he's safe. And while his wood stove is seen smoking for the rest of the week, he and his family aren't seen again until they are found murdered in their beds.

The story is German, and the name of the case is likely some mouthful of that language I couldn't hope to pronounce. That's probably why I had so much trouble remembering it.

But it was a silly thing to be hung up on. I was only distracting myself from uncomfortable questions. Like what the hell was anybody doing outside in a storm? It had only just stopped snowing. A blizzard had dropped nineteen inches in the last fourteen hours, whipping the world into a whiteout.

Which begged the question: Why were the footsteps I stared at so steady? They didn't waver or trip. They plowed through the snow. Someone had walked a quarter mile through the woods in a whiteout. Night or day, it wouldn't have mattered, they simply would not have been able to *see*.

In the clearing outside the forest, the steps were hard to identify as human. They were too deep and blown over. But there was less wind in the woods and there the steps showed clearly. They were boot prints the size of clown shoes. I made an oval of my mouth and blew out a cloud of breath. I frowned again. The footsteps were so confident. So straight.

Still, it was a weird thing to worry about. It's funny how the brain can dribble and dance around disturbing facts. Maybe it was shock, but it took time to dawn on me why I even thought of that German story to begin with. It was because the prints seemed to appear from nowhere in the middle of the meadow and then lead directly to the back door of my house, and stopped.

Yet my house was empty. I was certain it was. My pants were grey with dust to prove it. I had searched the crawlspace. The attic. Everywhere. And there was no one. Nothing. Either someone went out my back door and walked backward through a blizzard and then vanished where they stood, or...

Again, that wasn't what I should've been worried about. It was Leah Miller's words that my mind had been ignoring. Jack had said she'd talked about a lone set of footsteps that crossed her yard and stopped at her back door.

I took a deep breath. The kind that burns your lungs with cold.

I looked between the trees. Down the ridge in the distance, I could see a sliver of my house. My vision blurred as my eyes welled with tears of fear. Who came blind through a blizzard to my home? And where were they now? They could be somewhere hidden. Another place in the walls I'd yet to discover.

I could see two windows on the second floor of my house. They glowed orange against the bluing dusk. It was too far to tell, but I felt like someone was watching me. The funny thing was all I could think about was what had led me to this moment—my stubbornness, my insecurity. But it felt like I was missing something now. Why did it feel like I had been coaxed to come here to this creepy housing development in the woods?

Why did it feel like everything started at that goddamned party?

SAN DIEGO, NINE WEEKS EARLIER

My life had gotten to the point where there was little that could compete with my bed and a book come 10pm. I never wanted it to be like that, but it's funny how pleasures change. Crisp, cool sheets on freshly shaven legs... a novel. A deep, uninterrupted sleep only to wake with the sun. I was happy I had those things, because, at thirty-six, my hangovers had become Cat 5 hurricanes. But to be fair I was a little drunk as I thought all that. Oh well.

It was 2am and I sat on the back patio. While people laughed and chatted in their seats around me, I was in my own head thinking of home. Maybe because I was so far from it. Or more likely because nobody at the party liked me and even at my own house, they weren't shy to show it.

My husband, Howard, and I had decided to host a party, but it had wound down by this hour. Sheryl Caper got so drunk she fell asleep on a pool chair and the Wheeler's left after Melissa grew tired of Rick staring at one of the caterer's chest's all night, but I wasn't stressed about any of that.

It was my sister who left me on edge. She's the kind of family that makes you wonder if you were adopted or switched at birth.

But I was stuck with her because I was a sucker for that word: family. Family First. Family over everything. Blood is thicker than water. I'd been berated with that mindset since birth. But I'm convinced those sayings were invented by Italians trying to run bloodline mafias. I'm not sure it meant to stay close to your mean aunt or narcissistic sister who has hurt you one too many times, but alas. I was a sucker for that talk, and I gave in. Always.

So, when Bea needed money for a lawyer because her healing crystal business was caught selling quartz instead of the minerals advertised, I came to her rescue.

3

I regretted it when I wrote the check and I regretted it even more when Beatrice called me afterwards to ask about our will. She was curious because "Even if we didn't have any kids it was always best to keep the money in the family." I pictured her getting cold feet about the call, and then her husband, Randy, recited some Michael Jordan quote about how you miss 100% of the shots you don't take, and she dialed.

I could tell people at the party sensed that my sister and I didn't get along. They were happy to be friendly with her as a dig at me. They wouldn't know her long enough to figure out that Bea was 8th grade mean. She's the kind of woman who told you she liked your dress and then mouthed to a friend over her shoulder how ugly it is— "I mean how could she *possibly* think I thought her outfit looked good."

I wanted to tell everyone the truth. She doesn't actually like your dress. That smile isn't even genuine. Look! Did you see that? The way she tightens her lips as if she's sorry for you. It's her tell. She's pretending to be nice, you idiots! The Bea you see is manufactured. A mirage.

But I kept my mouth shut. I'd just seem sour if I said anything, so I knocked back the rest of my wine. Things had gone smoothly enough. My best friend, Miranda, saved me by insisting I hire caterers. Still, the idea of hosting a catered party in Pacific Beach, San Diego would forever be alien to me. I didn't grow up with money. Any of it. I'm from a place that one ritzy tech wife referred to as "Wow, bum fuck nowhere."

It was all a little surreal. The party, the people. The glamor. And the occasion? Howard had finally sold his software business. Of course, it's why Bea had called about the will. We weren't ever planning on it, but Howard and I were wealthy now. There were balloons that spelled out the amount Newton Tech had sold for strung on the far side of the pool.

87000000

Eighty-seven million dollars. Howard was a bit gassed but still on top of the world. And I excused the ego stroking of the balloons because I was also a little proud and it wasn't his idea anyway.

When he drinks his cheeks burn blushed, and they were alight that night. I smiled, thinking how lucky I was that my geeky husband was also so handsome with his perpetual stubble and brow-line glasses. He'd been smiling all night and my heart was light from seeing it. We'd had a rough patch from the stress Howard endured from selling the business, but the party seemed to be an exhale from all of that.

At the least I hoped the feeling of victory would stick. His sleeves were rolled up, and he rested his chin on his fist. I couldn't stop staring at the veins running down his forearm like vines. I was fantasizing about that fist unfurling its long fingers and grasping my neck. It was partly why I'd been so damn quiet. We hadn't had sex in more than a month, but that would change. Tonight.

Miranda held my hand under the table—something she liked to do when she'd been drinking a lot. I was grateful to have her. When hating me became trendy in the techy SoCal clique, I was surprised to see Miranda become my defender. In the last two months, we became twice as close. She swung her head drunkenly over to me. "You should just...go." I met her eye and smiled, confused.

"What?"

"Go. Buy a boat. But not a monstrous white plastic yacht. I don't care if Howard has the money. Buy a beautiful sailboat. Teak. And just go," she slurred as she extended out her arm in a gesture of escape.

"Maybe we'd do that for a bit." I bounced her hand in mine. "But reality always sets in."

"No." She shook her head violently. I had to be careful not to make her disagree too much. When Miranda was drunk, which was often, she'd sometimes shake her head so strongly that she'd give herself the spins.

"There is no reality for the young and the pretty and, most importantly, the rich. You're free. You're done. You won. Bon Voyage."

I smiled and shook my head. "I don't know about that."

"You should think about it. You've had a horrible year. All of Howard's bullshit is finally done and you two now finally have a chance to..." She nudged my ribs. "Rekindle. And wouldn't it be nice to get away from here? To get away from all these people? They're staring at you when you're not looking. Do you know that? They didn't like you because of where you're from, and then after what happened in LA..."

"I don't want to talk about that right now." I took my hand from hers.

"Sorry." Her eyes narrowed soberly. I could tell she was frustrated with herself, but her self-awareness was usually lost to her after just a couple of drinks. "Sorry, it's just like if Sheryl hadn't passed out, I would've punched her. She literally *flared* her nostrils at you when you weren't looking. Like you're something that stinks. Maybe I'll push her in the pool. Everyone will assume she just fell."

Miranda gripped her chair's arms to stand and I grabbed her wrist laughing. "It's okay. Sit down. She might wet herself. We can watch from here."

Miranda's eyes lit up and I realized I had given her a lightbulb idea. She gestured to a glass of water with her eyes and leaned into me and whispered, "Why wait on fate? We can make it look like she did. Create a diversion, and I'll dump some water on her crotch."

She set her forehead on my shoulder and rocked with laughter. I glanced down the table and met Howard's eye for a moment. He was staring at the two of us intently and looked away instead of acknowledging my gaze. He nodded too zealously in response to something that was being said to him and I knew he was faking interest. I knew he was thinking of *me.*

"I think it's best," I said as I plucked the glass of water off the table, "If you *drink* this instead."

"Fine." Miranda took the glass from me and chugged the water like beer. When she was done, her shoulders rose as if she was going to burp, but she held up a finger and exhaled instead. "But think about it. Really. I would kill to have that kind of cash. I'd just... sail off into the sunset. Goodbye. But it's not like I don't ever want to see you again. You'd meet me in Panama."

"Oh please," I scoffed. Miranda was getting ridiculous. Even after the sale of Howard's company I didn't think we were going to be anything but a few million dollars richer than she was. She was old money, trust-fund rich. The kind of person I didn't think I'd ever get along with if I was being honest. "Aren't you set for several lifetimes?"

She shrugged, "It was never a lumpsum. My money trickles out once a month. I guess..." her thoughts trailed off with a hiss. "Never mind. Just the idea of getting all that money at once. I'm just saying it must make you want to do something. Hell, it makes *me* want to do something. I'm okay living vicariously through you, though."

A phone began to ring loudly.

Howard pushed back from the table and pulled his cell from his pocket. "Sorry, everyone. This is hopefully one of the last times I'll have to take 2am calls from China." There was a murmur of laughter as Howard stepped inside.

"So," said Miranda. "Get out of here." She picked up a glass of wine that I wasn't sure was hers and drained it. "I would if I were you. Isn't there something intoxicating about a fresh start?"

I looked around and my heart jumped when I realized every other person at the party was staring at me. Their heads whipped away when I tried to meet their eyes. I cupped my elbows in my palms and withdrew from the world. How foolish I was, if only for a few hours, to not have preferred my bed to people.

"A fresh start," I repeated the cliché with some sarcasm.

Miranda found my hand again and gave it a squeeze. "Think about it."

COPE

The morning after the party I sat with my feet in the pool. Typically, nights were reserved for my deep thinking, but my thoughts from the party had bled into the day. I was at a cusp in my life. Every life has before and after events. Deaths, divorces, mostly bad things where when you look back at a memory you might calculate where it was in relation to one of those grisly yardsticks of life. That was before dad died. Before he left me.

I hoped I was going to finally have a *good* before and after. Howard was done with sixty-hour weeks, and we were going to live the life we always wanted. We weren't even forty. While youth may be wasted on the young, wealth is wasted on the old. We were fortunate enough to turn the tables.

But we weren't off to a good start. We didn't even have sex after the party. By the time everyone had left at 4am, we were both practically asleep by the time we were alone. Maybe we did have to leave San Diego for a fresh start. I was sick of people's eyes burning judgmentally into my back. It would be a hard sell to Howard. He'd fallen in love with an average of 266 sunny days a year and didn't have a pressing feeling to leave. But I felt like Miranda was right because for the second time in my life I really felt like I had to go. The first was when I was still a kid.

I was bullied for everything growing up. My face, my clothes, my name. Instead of Katie, I had nicknames that weren't meant to be cool or nice. Personally, I liked the two chops of my full name, Katie Cope. But bullies can make fun of anything, especially when you're not that talkative, and I was quickly named Quiet Katie.

The funny part is that my sister Bea was the one who started it. She was in the grade above me, popular, prettier and envious of my normal name. So, if she had to be Bea, I didn't get to be just Katie.

I have a theory that bullies are more common in boring places. I was from Langdon, North Dakota; a flat, farm town of 2,000 people. The boys there seemed to be able to entertain themselves better than us girls. They'd blow stuff up. Do pull-up contests on the farm sprinklers. Maybe I'm just saying that because the boys mostly left me alone. The girls of Langdon were not as kind.

But I was an easy target, an ugly kid. It was like my body ballooned at thirteen with all the fat and nutrients I'd need throughout puberty and I slowly deflated as I grew taller. But when the fat receded like flood waters it left me pretty—or so I was told.

I looked at my reflection in the pool. I had healthy, auburn hair and eyes like two dark chocolates. But I'm happy I wasn't always clear-skinned and doe-eyed. I'm a better person knowing what the world really thinks of homely, overweight girls.

It wasn't a hard decision to leave North Dakota after high school. I went to college in Chicago. The stage was set for my past to be forgotten when Bea decided to follow me. She didn't even get into college there. But Bea's one of those hypercompetitive siblings and the idea of her little sister making it in the big city while she wasted away in Langdon was too much for her to stomach.

Bea refused to admit she was copying me. One day at dinner, the July before I moved, she simply told me and my parents that she was moving to Chicago. She said it like it was her own thing. Her own adventure. Like I didn't just get accepted into college there a few months prior. My parents awkwardly congratulated Beatrice on her plans, unsure if it was a joke or not. But I knew that if it were up to her, I would never have anything in this world to myself. And just like that, I had a shadow.

Luckily in Chicago I was able to *find* a sister. My brain was on boys when I first moved there, and I didn't expect a girl to be the one who swept me off my feet. During my first semester at college, I sat next to another shy girl in my English comp class.

For weeks we didn't say much other than "hi" until one day she passed me a doodle of the professor where his droopy, mustached face was put onto a dolphin. It was so random and well-drawn that I laughed until the professor stopped lecturing. My new friend said it looked like I needed some cheering up that day, and I've loved her ever since.

I try to picture her smile at least once a day. It's a nice thing to remember about someone, after all. When she smiled, with her baby face and blushed cheeks, you'd feel your lips smiling, too. It was *actually* contagious. But now, I wasn't smiling anymore. The memory of Claire was a before and after stronger than any other in my life. I pictured a body in the woods, a skeleton grown over with lichen, and I pulled my feet from the pool.

ESCAPE

The doorbell rang around 10am. I had a hard time learning not to help the help. We had a cleaning service scheduled that morning, but I had still made sure to get the heavy messes. Whenever the cleaners came, I couldn't be there. I always had the feeling of not knowing what to do with my hands but with my entire body. Should I read in a chair? Retreat to my room? Lounging by the pool seemed too decadent. I typically just left. Outside of being served at restaurants, I wasn't very good at being waited on. It made me uncomfortable. I let the cleaners inside and then went to my bedroom to change.

Miranda wanted to meet me for a hangover Americano anyway. It was a good reason to get out of the house. But there were storm clouds in the distance coming over the water, a rare sight for San Diego in October. I grabbed an umbrella from the hall closet and went out the front door.

The café we were meeting at was a ten-minute walk and I'm glad I didn't drink any more than I did. The dark clouds weren't close enough to block out the sun and the bright white beaches and seagull squall took on a more hellish form when hungover. I usually found them both beautiful, but I could tell I was growing sick of sunny San Diego.

When I got to the café, Miranda was seated inside, sunglasses still on, a steaming mug in front of her. I loved her hungover housewife aesthetic. She was seated at a table facing the beach and didn't notice me at the counter ordering. It was only when I pulled out a chair that she turned her head quickly in surprise.

"How are you so sneaky?"

"I think maybe you're still just a little tipsy."

"I'd better be. I had two mimosas for breakfast," she pointed at her mug on its saucer. "I started without you. But don't worry, I'll get another."

"That's okay."

We drank our coffees in silence for a little while, the way best friends can. I set my drink down and watched the surf break on the shore. "Do you remember what you said last night? That stuff about getting out of here."

Even under the big sunglasses, I could see her brow raise. "I wasn't completely wasted."

"I know. I've just been thinking about it even before you even brought it up last night. Now that Newton is sold, there's nothing keeping us here. You're pretty much my only close friend. Everyone else is busy having babies."

"Like you're not about to get busy making babies, too."

There were some things I kept from Miranda, like how Howard didn't really want to have kids. He wasn't vehemently opposed, but he would stare in horror when a kid was having a tantrum in public. I loved Howard, but he was easily embarrassed. A bit insecure about himself. He was the kind of guy who thought it was an affront to his masculinity to use an exclamation point in a text. There was no doubt a misbehaving kid would make him blush.

Bea's boys don't help my case with Howard. Her twins, Brayden and Braxton, were more than a handful. I tried to tell Howard that's because Bea lets them do whatever they want. Eat whatever they want. *Say* whatever they want. At seven, they already cursed like sailors. Sometimes it was cute, but most of the time, it was disturbing.

We actually tried for kids before the business deal started, but after six cycles we still didn't conceive. Afraid of tests telling us stuff we didn't want to hear, we forgot about it while Howard was selling his business. We'd probably start trying again for a first, but only if we got our marriage back on track. And in my mind that meant leaving San Diego.

"Maybe we'll start a family soon," was all I said. I didn't want to get personal this morning.

"So, why are you hung up on what I said last night—are you thinking of moving?" She didn't let me speak. Miranda took her sunglasses off and looked me in the eye. "Because I was drunk last night when I said all that, but there was some truth to it. Things have felt extra fake here lately. You're the only friend I have that makes me feel like I can say what I really think," she looked sad then, even guilty, but she blinked several times as if to clear her head. "When did the West Coast become so passive-aggressive?"

"I hear ya."

"Shit. I know it's even worse for you. I didn't mean to make this about me."

"You didn't. And people aren't even passive-aggressive to me anymore. Mostly just aggressive. Which, thankfully, I can handle." I laughed.

Miranda set her elbows on the table and leaned forward. "I've been thinking of moving. I know what you're thinking, Mrs. South Dakota. Another fleeing Californian looking to ruin the housing market of a flyover state. But don't forget, girl, I'm from Dallas."

I had stopped trying to correct her that I was from *North* Dakota. Somehow the fact could never stick. "Where are you thinking of moving?"

"A couple places... but mainly just one. Have you heard of Philip Pope?"

"No."

"He's an architect and a real estate developer and something of a futurist. He's building these new housing developments. All of them are off the grid, except with internet and toilet paper and a community."

Miranda was always looking for the next thing to center her soul. Last year, it was a $5,000 retreat to do psychedelics under supervision in the Peruvian jungle. A couple of months ago, it was a $1000 online course on spirituality. They were always pricy fads that didn't amount to much of a lifestyle change. She had never extended me an invitation to join her before, and I was glad. The hallucinogen retreat sounded like the premise of a horror movie. I figured this was just the next new thing when she spun her phone so I could see the screen. There was a slideshow playing slowly. A picture of a glacial lake faded to a gorgeous shot of an outdoor hot tub in a snowstorm. The next picture was a palm tree beach. A hammock was stretched between two trees. The headline read: "Get away, stay in touch."

"There are two developments. One's on its own private cove in Puerto Rico but not finished yet and the other's in the Rockies... Montana or Colorado. Somewhere way up in the mountains, I can't remember." The beach shot switched to a picture of a mountain, not tall enough to have a timberline, furred with coniferous trees.

Colorado, I thought. I bit my lip. Suddenly I struggled to focus. But thankfully, the slideshow continued. The forest disappeared and my memories with it. It switched to a picture of a tall man in a checkered suit and a hardhat. He stood in the middle of a group of smiling developers. They all clutched blueprint rolls under their arms. Miranda turned the phone back to face her. "Isn't he something? I think he looks like a more handsome Jeff Goldblum."

"The man in the suit, that's Philip?"

"Yeah, you should look him up when you get home. He has these seminars on the importance of the neighborhood. How part of the reason we're all unhappy is because we've abandoned the way we were supposed to live with one another. Abandoned community. Anyway, I know I'm the eccentric friend. I just thought I'd share. Howard would never go for this kind of thing, anyway, would he?"

I smiled and shook my head. "No. But I can imagine some of the names he'd pick for Philip."

"Oh, what? Snake oil salesmen? Charlatan?"

"Douchebag, probably."

"He should lighten up a little. Have some fun. I'm just picturing Howard logging into his online bank the day he gets all that money and getting excited looking at what bonds he's going to buy."

I spat up my coffee a little. Just the other day Howard had come to me with bright eyes to show me a list of Triple A bonds that would net us a fixed 4.7% return a year. He was becoming a little bland in his middle age.

"Howard just plays it safe. It's a pro and a con."

Miranda set her phone on the table. "I don't expect you two to move across the country on a whim. But if you did, I'd come with you."

"Why this housing development? Why not just buy a cabin by Lake Tahoe?"

"Because these developments aren't just houses in the middle of nowhere. They have their own market, hiking trails, and strangers who grow to become your neighbors. Neighbors who are like us. People that moved there to get away from this bullshit."

"That's a good point," I lied. Gossip and pettiness were inescapable and the kind of people with the money to join some futurist's housing development were probably bringing baggage. At the very least, the residents would be more East or West Coast money—the same people I was trying to get away from. But Miranda was my friend, and I didn't like to rock the boat. I nodded along. Quiet Katie.

"It does sound... like it would be good for me."

"Good for both of us. And your marriage. I'm sick of all the construction and the *speed* of this place. I leave for a week, and when I come back, another twenty-story apartment building has popped up and another twenty something blonde is jogging down my street wearing *nothing*. Do girls even go to college anymore? I mean, where do they get the *money*?"

Miranda took a sip of her coffee and I just shook my head. When Howard's business started taking off and we moved from Chicago, I was afraid I'd become someone else because of the money. But there I was, San Diego. With the sun and the sand and a million dollars to own just 1,000 square feet of it. But thankfully, paying ten dollars for a latte still made me cringe.

"It's an interesting idea," I said.

"Right?! I know you'd probably have to wait until Howard had the cash. But we've got one life and don't try to tell me we couldn't be living it better."

The truth was Howard already had the cash. He'd sold plenty of stock to private investors over the years but kept it in bonds like everything else. "What's the name of the development company?"

"The Eden Project."

I held my lips tight again. Better not to lie but men who promised utopia scared the piss out of me.

CLOUDBURST

I spent the walk home tangled in the past. Thrown back to a cold November night in Chicago. Before Miranda and I even said our goodbyes at the café, I was pretty much checked out. When Miranda mentioned Colorado, I was destined to remember. Some things *always* made me think of Claire. Say "the Rockies" or "Colorado" or even "camping," and the memory of the last time we were together begins to play in my brain. It's a tape I cannot stop.

November 2008. That election and recession year. Yet it was when the world still felt normal. Claire and I stumbled back into her apartment together. It was cold, but we'd been at jungle hot bars all night and I slid the window open, shed off my jacket, shirt and bra, and held onto the frame above my head. The crisp breeze hit my sweaty pits, my previously imprisoned breasts, and I groaned in sweet relief. Claire had gone into the kitchen but returned quickly and nudged my back with something.

"You *have* to try this," I said without turning from the window.

"No, no, no. Not now. We have business."

I heard a tin cap crack, and when I looked over my shoulder, Claire was pouring herself a glass full of freezing vodka.

"No way." I brought my arms down to my sides and shook my head. "I'm still at that point where I can be alive in the morning."

Claire licked her lips nervously. She was one of those desperate drinkers for whom panic sets in if the party ends early. It wasn't about a fun night out. It was about escape. "I'm not sobering up just to fall asleep. Come on. Keep me company, please?" she whined. "It's the last time I see you for like eight days. I think that'll be a record since we met."

It was junior year, and Claire was going home for Thanksgiving. All the way to Salt Lake City. It would've been a bit of a betrayal if I called it a night.

"Only so there's less booze for you." I extended my hand for a glass.

"Yes," she hissed triumphantly and knocked my glass so hard with a cheers that some of the liquor rolled up the side and onto her hand. She licked it clean like a cat and laughed. At some point, I ended up on the corduroy couch while Claire was scrolling through an iPod. "I'm not sure I can do any more music," I said.

She leaned back with her lips pouted. "Oh, come on. It's almost three in the morning, what else do you want to do?"

"Talk." I closed my eyes and wiggled my shoulders into the cushions. "Talk ourselves to sleep."

She turned off the music and we were both quiet for a minute. I was nearly asleep when Claire spoke again. "Whenever that window is open, I think of jumping out of it."

It took me a moment to blink myself awake and process what she'd said. "Jesus. Fuck, Claire. Here..." I started to stand. "I'll shut it."

"No." She held out a hand to stop me and I leaned on the edge of the couch, now very much awake.

"Don't say stuff like that," I said.

"Don't tell you the truth?"

"I didn't mean that."

"That was kinda bitchy of me. Sorry. I'm just saying," Claire looked towards the window and watched the curtains flutter in the freezing wind. "Whenever that window is open, I think of leaping the six stories down to Bissell Street. But don't worry, I know I can't. It's not that I don't have the balls, though. It's my mom, my dad, my sister. They're the kind of people who think everything is their fault. I'd rather they be victims. The kind of people who blame the world. But they'd never forgive themselves if I jumped."

Claire had always been depressed, but she'd never shared her thoughts on suicide before. I shifted uncomfortably. "You also might not die. Six stories? It's possible you just break every bone in your body and poop in a bag forever." I cringed internally. I didn't know what to say. I was just trying to keep it light. Keep it comfortable.

She tilted her head to her shoulder. "I'd plan to dive headfirst, but I guess shit can happen."

I exhaled a laugh and ran my hands down my thighs. "You don't actually want to die—do you?"

"I don't want to live. But if there was a button I could push to just not exist I'd slam it in a heartbeat. It's this body that's the problem," she grabbed her gut. "One hundred and seventy-five pounds of stink to dispose of. And the pain of my family... Suicide just isn't simple. If it were, I'd be gone." I watched her push her tongue against the back of her two front teeth. "Long," she paused. "Gone."

I thought of what to say but bludgeoned any attempt at language my brain could make by finishing the vodka that sat at my feet. All the things I could've said... All the things I could've done. But I didn't even stand up to wrap an arm around her. I just fucking sat there and said, "That sucks."

She sighed. "I can't help but wonder about all the young men and women who go into the wilderness alone and never come out. It's assumed they're lost but it's what I would do. Say I'm going for a hike and then wander off the trail. Jump off a cliff into thick forest. I could kill myself if my family never knew. It's actually what got me into hiking. I established a pattern. Sometimes I go off into the woods and one day I might never come out. It happens."

The subject of mental health was a very private one where I was raised and my background in the boonies didn't prepare me for this kind of conversation. I sat there silent, twenty years old, just a girl, but still old enough to know better. Old enough to know to *say* something. *She's pleading for help. She's telling you.*

"They'd never find me. If I chose the right place to hike, I'd be as gone as if I were at the bottom of the ocean," And then, in what was maybe a metaphor for the depression she'd let consume her, she said the last words I ever remember her saying, "Do you have any idea how deep you could go into the woods, if you knew you never had to come out?"

I don't think I even responded. I just drank the rest of my vodka and the night faded out. Two days later, her car was found at a trailhead about an hour from Denver. She had been on her way home to Salt Lake City, driving west on I-80, when she texted her mom that she was going to detour to hike in the Rockies.

I don't like to think it was premeditated. But I knew it was. That night she was telling me exactly how she was going to take her own life and I said nothing about it. I still like to think she caught a glimpse of the distant mountains from the interstate and saw the forests black and endless, and felt the pull of eternity. Chose death on a whim.

I blame myself anyway. Claire and I had agreed we were like sisters and she was so certain she didn't want to hurt her family. She was sure she wouldn't kill herself and leave them with the guilt. But she told me. She told me *everything*. And then she vanished just like she'd said she would. After what she had told me, how could I ever believe something else happened to her on that hike?

The only person I ever told about that night with Claire was Howard. He had said what he was supposed to. That it wasn't my fault. That there was nothing I could've done. But it never felt genuine. Of course, I could've done something.

I was taken from the past by a cold drop of rain. I watched it race down my arm and off my thumb to drop again to the ground. I could hear the rain coming behind me, a torrent pattering up the pavement fast. I didn't turn around. I didn't open my umbrella. I just stopped walking and closed my eyes as the cloudburst wet my hair and shoulders and stained my clothing darker shades of everything.

21

I focused on nothing but what I felt. Cold, fresh, tickled. A wet world with the warm smell of damp pavement filling my lungs. But steps were clapping toward me, and I opened my eyes as a woman weaved past, scampering with her head tucked to her chest.

Ahead, an old couple, Asian tourists, stood on the corner in the rain. They surveyed up and down the street. They must've been waiting for a rideshare. I watched the husband wrap his arm around his wife and stoop over her to try to keep her dry.

I walked the rest of the way to them and caught their eye. I offered out my unopened umbrella. They both looked at me like I was crazy. "I was about to buy a new one anyway." I pointed at a clothing store a few businesses down. "Please, take it." I'm not sure they understood, so I shrugged and smiled wide. "I have lots of them."

The woman reached out and took it gently, but as soon as she opened it, she smiled, wide and genuinely. It was the kind of thankful smile that makes you wonder if we really do things out of the kindness of our hearts since it felt so damn good to see.

"Thank you." She nodded at me and then her husband smiled, too.

"Yes, thank you."

"Enjoy San Diego. It doesn't usually rain. I promise."

I walked to the clothing store next door. I was the only one inside apart from a girl behind the counter, and she was almost comically distant from the door. She waved, and I waved back.

A few steps later I met myself in a full-length mirror. My features were paler. Cold and wet. My big brown eyes stared back at me. Even with my button nose, when I got wet I looked a bit witchy. My brown hair would turn lank and blackish and my cheeks lost their flush. While I looked at myself the counter girl crept up silently and I jolted as she said hello.

"I'm sorry," she said. "Can I help you with anything?" I turned to look out the window and saw that the couple had been picked up from the corner. "An umbrella, maybe? I think we actually have a few."

"No," I said. "That's ok, thank you." I walked past her, out the door, and back into the rain.

THE EDEN PROJECT

When I got home any evidence of a party was gone, apart from the ample leftover booze and food that filled the fridge. I had a nutritious and high-class lunch of party leftovers (cheese) and I walked through the house silently in my socks. Howard was gone along with his running shoes. He typically likes to outrun a hangover. Something I'm sure would make me vomit. I got into bed and opened my laptop. I bit my lip and watched the cursor blink in the search bar for a moment before I typed, "Philip Pope."

Back before San Diego, I was an investigative journalist in Chicago. Or I suppose more of an assistant to one. Most of our stories came to us through tips from a spurred client or pissed-off employee and the more senior journalists got the stories while I did research and writing.

I wasn't cutthroat or social enough to climb the ranks. Now my journalism was more of a hobby. One of my old colleagues started her own online magazine and I'd write pieces for her every now and then. Nothing new or incendiary. Stuff like reviews for television series and sourdough starter kits. Sad, sure, but I liked it. I liked writing alone at my laptop. I liked being content that I wasn't going to change the world. This is my little life and I'm doing just fine, thank you. But sometimes, something still itched, especially as Howard grew more and more successful. I wanted to prove myself. And uncovering something headline worthy was a fantasy of mine that never died.

There were plenty of search results for Philip Pope. He was important enough to have a short bio pop up. The internet's consensus was that Philip and his ideas were far past their prime. I found some old Forbes articles about him but nothing remarkable.

He seemed to be just another man who made a career out of ideas rather than action. The media ate his type up, I should know. It made for the perfect story when there was no real news. The only thing he actually accomplished was resurrecting an old library in Quebec City to international applause. But the genius of the postmodern monstrosity he'd turned it into was lost on me.

After that, he coasted on nothing but grand ideas for creating different kinds of communities. There was one for a circular city with nothing but green space in the middle. Another was for an island in the pacific that would follow the North Equatorial current. Cabo in the winter, Tokyo in the summer. *Wait until he hears about cruise ships*, I thought.

He was made semi-famous by bored publications desperate for clickbait. A Reuters release from three years ago was more my speed; it read that he'd filed for personal bankruptcy.

I ended up on the web page Miranda had shown. I clicked around until I ended up on the page where it outlined the Eden Project. It was certainly tamer than his other ideas.

The Eden Project was just as she'd said: A series of housing developments in the United States that promised a connection to community like no other. The idea was isolation, but of course with satellite internet, fresh farmed food and neighbors that were not too near nor too far.

Only one development was finished. It was in Colorado in a place called Carson's Pass. It was forty minutes from the closest airport, an hour from Aspen and it bordered the White River National Forest. When Miranda had first told me about this place, I figured it would be a stone's throw from Denver or Boulder, but it was far more secluded than I thought. I backed out of the page and the next link down caught my eye:

"Phillip Pope interviewed in connection to the disappearance of the McMann Family"

I opened the page and narrowed my eyes as I read.

"Rachel McMann and her twin daughters, age four, vanished while living in the ambitious beta project for a new way of urban living, the Paradise of the Palisades. The imaginative apartment building was constructed following the plans of eccentric architect Phillip Pope and was funded by the city of San Francisco as a possible solution to homelessness.

Now demolished, The Paradise of the Palisades was a twenty-unit apartment complex that was touted as part-shelter, part-rehabilitation center.

Pope was never initially involved in the investigation, but after the structure was torn down in 2021, he was contacted by the San Francisco County Sheriff's Office."

This was strange. I had seen the Paradise of the Palisades mentioned in other articles. They said the project failed after a lack of funding from the city, that it was never even started. Same as all of Pope's other ideas. It was just another headline grabber. I hadn't seen anything about the McMann family.

I put Rachel McMann into the search bar. There were a couple of links about a disappearance, but when I clicked on them, I got the same 404 message every time:

The page you are looking for no longer exists

All I could find was the article I had just read and a short Wikipedia page about the disappearances. But the wiki article didn't mention more than what I'd already read. But there was no mention of Philip Pope being questioned by the police. I scrolled to the bottom to see when the page was last edited. It was just a couple days ago. I leaned back from the screen and frowned. Someone was scrubbing the page.

I searched, "Phillip Pope disappearances."

I found another unsettling article. This one was by some small local news site in Canada. It was a brief piece about how an occupant of a home designed by Philip Pope had found secret passages in her walls. She said she found a hidden space, just big enough for someone to stand in, behind the wall that her bed was pushed against. The woman was named Amanda Bryan.

I googled the name, and my heart started beating faster.

I found article after article about her disappearance. Much like Rachel McMann, all the pieces were on strange small news sites. Nothing mainstream. Amanda was a cold case largely forgotten, it seemed. She went to take the trash out after dinner and never came back in. That was it. Gone. No trace and no leads. I wondered how none of it was ever linked by a journalist. Maybe because there was so little online. Philip Pope and the McMann disappearances and now Amanda Bryan. There was a connection. But was anyone looking into this? It seemed like whoever wrote the piece about Philip Pope being questioned by the police in San Francisco seemed to think so.

The front door slammed, and I flinched. I easily scared myself with internet mysteries at midnight, but I rarely got jumpy when the sun was still shining.

I heard the fridge open. A can's top went crack-pop.

I closed the laptop and went towards the kitchen. I trailed my fingers on the cool wall as I walked, picturing tunnels behind them, and spaces large enough for a man to look out of. It was obvious that someone had missed something about Philip Pope. But there was a bigger question on my mind: Was this the kind of investigative story I had been looking for?

SAN CLEMENTE

I came into the kitchen just as Howard brought a can of tomato juice from his mouth and crushed it in his fist. His eyes were haggard, and he panted, exhausted. "Salt. God, my body needs salt. Electrolytes." He opened the fridge and pawed around until he brought out a sports drink.

I leaned on the door frame and admired him. He always ran without sunscreen. Up and down the beach in the blazing heat. He was red, tan, tall, and wet with sweat. "You look good, sweaty. Especially for drinking like a college kid last night."

"Never. Again. Ugh. Where were you this morning?"

"I was with Miranda. She wanted to get coffee."

"I thought she'd still be sleeping it off."

"She's awake and alive, surprisingly."

"What did she want to see you so early for?" He walked to the sink, cupped cold water in his hands and laved it over his face.

"Oh, she's got one of her ideas again. But it's not drugs this time."

"That's no fun."

"She has a simpler idea. Maybe it's growth, but she just wants to move."

He turned off the faucet and smiled. "Is it *really* that simple?"

"Well, no. She wants to move to some weirdo's commune."

"Ah, there it is."

"It's an interesting idea," I said testing the waters to see how he felt about moving. "I can't blame her. It would be nice to have a change of scenery."

"Everyone's so gung-ho about moving these days. What's wrong with laying down roots?"

"Right?" I said in agreement. But really, I needed to get the hell out of San Diego. I had made mistakes and the roots were poisoned in Pacific Beach.

28

"Maybe you could quit writing those review articles now," said Howard.

"What?"

"You know, now that money's never going to be an issue, I don't see why you're writing those things. You don't seem happy doing it and they don't have much of an audience. No offense."

I was definitely offended, but I didn't want to get defensive about my work. It was never about the money. I got paid peanuts. It was about my readers. While I didn't have much of an audience, I still had one. That was a more difficult thing than Howard realized. I composed myself but he spoke again before I could. "Anyway, I just want you to be doing what you want in life. We made it." He tapped my butt as he walked by. I knew what he really meant: *He* made it.

When Howard was in the shower, I eyed my laptop on the bed. I didn't know what to think of Philip Pope. On the one hand, he seemed like a charlatan with no real power and nothing but failed ideas, but on the other, it's nearly impossible to remove something permanently from the internet. And it seemed like he had.

For the disappearances of an entire family to have nothing online but a single article and a tiny wiki page was perhaps as impressive as any of his architectural ideas. I thought about all the "page not found" messages I had come across. You had to have serious money and connections to get something removed from the internet. You had to *know* people. Even then, it was hardly a guarantee whatever you wanted would be gone. The internet has a way with permanence.

I opened my computer and went back to the first article I had found about Philip being questioned in relation to the McMann's. There was a little bubble with a picture of the journalist who wrote it. Her name was Amy Myer, a young brunette. I had no other leads. If I wanted to know more, she was my best bet. In her bio picture she smiled with a golden doodle in her arms. There was a beach in the background and the sun was setting over the water. I clicked the link that said, "contact" and my hands hovered over the keys as the cursor blinked in the textbox. I couldn't help but think I was just pretending to be a real journalist.

Sometimes the imposter syndrome hit hard. I sighed and shook it off. In the internet age, anyone with a computer and an inkling of an idea can be a journalist. I actually had formal training to be one. I knew I shouldn't feel like a fool.

I sent Amy a brief message asking if she knew where I could get any more information on the McMann disappearances. I didn't give my last name and I didn't mention that I used to be a journalist. I shut my laptop the second I hit send as if I'd nervously texted a crush. But I realized I had made a mistake. There was no incentive for Amy to respond to me. I had to give her a lead. Something worth her time. I opened my laptop again and sent a second message saying that I was interested because I was thinking of buying a place in one of the Eden Projects. It was only a half lie, I told myself. I came back to the computer twenty minutes later and she had already responded.

"Hey Katie! Thanks for reaching out. I'm actually working on a bigger piece on Philip Pope and would be very interested in working with you if you plan to live at one of his developments. Have you applied yet?"

I was conflicted about whether to tell her I was a journalist or not. If I acted like a would-be resident, who had grown weary of Philip Pope after some googling, she probably wouldn't tell me everything. She knew if she did, she'd probably scare me away. But I didn't want her to think I'd try to steal her story. However, good journalists want to work together. I risked radio silence on her end and decided to tell the truth.

"Do you think he had something to do with those disappearances? To be honest, I used to be a journalist myself. A friend of mine is thinking of moving to one of the developments. That's how I found out about it and now I'm curious about the Eden Project too, but not for the same reasons as she is..."

I watched my inbox nervously for several minutes before a reply came.

"Ok, you could really help me out Katie. I would kill to get into one of those developments. What are the odds you actually get a place there? Sorry to be so forward. It's just very exclusive is all."

The more I thought about it, the more ridiculous I felt. I wasn't really going to move. Or was I? The place in Colorado, Carson's Pass, did look incredible from the pictures. Even if it turned out there was nothing more to this story, it might be a nice break. A good, quiet place to live. It would be low-risk, high-reward. I felt nervous butterflies in my stomach as I typed. I realized maybe I should shut my mind up and listen to my gut more often because I felt more alive and curious than I had in ages. I typed, *"If I really wanted to get in, I'm sure I could. Do you really think there's an interesting story there?"*

I wiggled my feet as I waited. I was *excited*. I had forgotten what that even felt like.

She responded, *"I'm biased, but I think I have the beginnings of something big. I don't want to message it here. I don't even really feel comfortable calling. Do you mind telling me your full name?"*

I was one of those journalists who dreamt of getting a story where I didn't even feel comfortable calling. With that single line, she got me.

"My name's Katie Cope. I see your website is based in SF. I'm down in San Diego. Do you write locally?"

A quick response, *"Yes! I'm actually in LA now. Would you like to meet somewhere halfway?"*

I paused before I typed. I could feel my pulse in my fingertips. Disappearances. Houses with hidden compartments. To hell with reviewing the new Game of Thrones spinoff, I wanted to do this.

"Say where!"

"Meet me in San Clemente."

MISTAKES

I woke with the sunrise the day I was meeting with Amy. Howard was newly unemployed, so to speak. Part of the sale contract was that he'd be available to train the new owners of his business. But they hadn't called much, and I could tell he was bothered. He'd been playing video games late on his computer more and more. But that morning, I noticed he'd gotten up before I even woke.

I had a nervous pit in my stomach while I got dressed. I'd considered that maybe Amy wasn't who she said she was. We had only chatted on the internet and the news site she worked for was a small outfit. They only had three writers and some of the articles on their home page were months old. I tried finding her on Instagram but had no luck. In the end I made sure we were meeting somewhere public. I found Howard in the kitchen thumbing through his phone while eating a bowl of cereal.

"Good to see you up at a decent hour again."

"Hey, there's nothing indecent about 10am," he mumbled as he looked back to his phone. "Many brilliant men were late risers."

"Uh-huh." I wanted to tease him about whether those men were killing aliens in video games at those late hours, but I wasn't confident it would be taken well. Our relationship still felt like it was on a razor's edge sometimes.

He set down his phone and yawned. "Where are you off to all dressed up?"

"I'm not dressed up, am I?"

He shrugged, and I looked down at my outfit. Howard's idea of dressed up was anything more than jeans and a t-shirt. I used to find it cute, but as we got older, it was something that I wished he'd grow out of. "I'm getting coffee with a friend." I knew he wouldn't ask which one.

"Well, have fun. I'll be..." He gestured in either direction. "Here."

"Getting a little stir-crazy, are we? Maybe you should take up surfing."

"In what world am I remotely cool enough to surf?"

I kissed his forehead and walked towards the front door. "This one. Believe it or not."

"I don't trust you."

"You should," I said, and he waved me off with a grin.

I blew him a kiss as I shut the front door. I felt bad about not telling him where I was going. I thought maybe I was jumping the gun, but if Amy did have a serious story, Howard would never move anywhere under the circumstances. I had to keep him in the dark. He thought I had a chip on my shoulder. That I should just forget when it came to my failed journalism career. I thought he might be right, but the problem was that he was patronizing about it. He'd think I was playing detective. When I got in the car, I realized it didn't matter. The odds of this going any further after I met with Amy felt very slim. I pulled out of the driveway and was soon trudging through the traffic as I headed north on I-5.

Sometimes it was a pretty drive, but mostly, it made me realize that the beauty of any place is lost in bumper-to-bumper traffic. The ocean glistened like one giant jewel, and in a symbolic slight to SoCal, I moved my sun visor to block the sight of the sea.

The last time I drove to LA, a before and after moment was just a few hours away. I made a mistake. I suppose it was why I was driving north again in the first place. It was the reason I felt like we needed to move.

Have you ever watched your spouse become another person? It's not fun. It fills you with doubt, and that old adage sings in your mind: *people change*. When you marry someone, you want to believe that the person you chose to spend the rest of your life with will be static. Consistent. Your rock. And Howard has been mine, for the most part. But when he was in the throes of trying to get a deal done, he changed. He was selling the business and he wanted me to be the invisible wife. Clean up his office. Wash his sheets. And it was done without so much as a "thanks" because I had let it become expected.

During that time, he was so irritable he'd erupt on me for so much as talking about my day for too long. He was busy, trying to set us up for the future. For forever. But business deals take time. It wasn't like he'd sell the company in a month. So, we decided to take a break. And not just time apart. We put our relationship and our obligations to each other on hold.

He was so busy when I brought it up all I got was an "ok." No argument. No discussion. It seemed like he was happy to be rid of me for a couple months—one less distraction. When it came to the ground rules around seeing other people all he said to me was, "Don't fall in love." That little comment took my breath away. I had hoped the idea of me being intimate with another man would be enough for him to change his mind and start acting like a better husband.

During that time, I went to LA to attend a boozy barbeque that was put on by the magazine I worked for. And I hate this cliché, but that night I met someone who paid attention to me. You don't know how good that really feels until your supposedly significant other can't be bothered to talk to you.

It was the perfect storm because during this time I also had the dangerous realization of how young I was. I knew that when I was seventy, I'd shake my head with regret at all the time I spent fretting about my age when I was really still just a kid. Thirty-six and I thought I was old. What a joke. In a sundress with tan skin, blushed cheeks and wedges, I wasn't just young, I was hot.

You see where this is going. His name was Ryan. I'm not sure if it matters what he looked like, but I'd like to plead its relevance to the jury that he was tall, dark and handsome. He didn't work for the same magazine. He ran his own media company and was just there to network until I shook his hand with a flirty twinkle in my eye. The barbeque was at a rooftop bar and feeling young and dumb and full of free cocktails, we ducked into a room where spare chairs and patio equipment were stored.

Kissing a man on the same night I met him, a little drunk, with the Hollywood sign in the distance made me feel more interesting. Like there were more layers to my little life and my story was still unfolding. Not already told, and predictable to the end. I wasn't looking for a new partner. I wasn't looking for love on his lips but a taste of all the other lives I could've lived. And I'd be lying to say it wasn't intoxicating to see, if not just for a second, all the other Katies there could be.

But someone had seen us wander off, and when we returned to the party I was met with smirks and dirty looks. Word spreads fast, and while he was single, I was a slut.

So, it was my fault everyone hated me. It's not like Howard and I announced our break on Facebook. No one knew we were temporarily separated. Word spread before I could get back to San Diego and when Howard's friends found out and told him he was humiliated. I didn't see him for three days. And while he'd forgiven me, and even apologized for how cold he'd been, the problem was that it made getting out of San Diego much trickier. It was the reason I felt guilty. Why would he leave a place he loves for mistakes that I made?

Ryan, on the other hand, didn't play the part of being a one-time regret. He was one of those "hey" guys. He texted me a "hey" once a week. I hadn't responded to his last five "hey's," and I wanted to shake him by the collar and say, "Hey! Take the fucking hint!"

Eventually, I had to block his number. I'd never done that before, but I understood then the appeal. It had a satisfying feeling of finality to it. This was *over*.

SCRUBBED

It was around 10:30 when I pulled into the parking lot of the coffee shop in San Clemente. Right away, I saw who I assumed to be Amy. She was seated outside under the sunshade with a folder on her table and a black tube container at her feet. I nearly stumbled when I was halfway to her. Up close, she bore a striking resemblance to Claire. I had to steady my breath before I got any closer. "Hi, Amy?"

She looked up surprised. "Yeah! Katie, hi! So nice to meet you." She stood and gave me a hug. She smelled like cigarettes and my heart hurt then. Their facial resemblance was close—not uncanny, but Claire smoked, too. There's nothing like scent for nostalgia to sink its teeth into.

"It's nice to meet you, too!" I said.

We talked about traffic for far too long and I felt awkward like I was on a first date. I was leading her on, I thought. After all, what were the odds I do something like move across the country to chase some story?

She took a long sip of coffee and cleared her throat. "So," she reached down and set a blue folder on the table. "You want the scoop?"

I shifted nervously. "I'd love it."

"So, you know about Philip Pope, his background, and the disappearances tied to him?"

"Yeah, I've tried searching more about the McMann case. And I'm not sure even you know this, but I found this article about Amanda Bryan..."

"Oh, I know. How she mentioned there were passages built into her walls and not long after she goes public, she disappears without a trace? Just a coincidence that Philip Pope built the place. At least that's what the media thinks."

"Right? I can hardly find anything on these cases. Especially the McManns. It's like they've been—"

36

"Wiped. Well, they have. Take a look at this." She held out her phone and I squinted to read the page. It was a society article. A wedding announcement on an ancient-looking webpage that read:

"Mary-Ann Pope and George Barlow tie the knot at The Plaza"

"I'm sorry," I said. "I don't know what to make of this."

"Does the name Barlow ring a bell?"

It did, but I couldn't put my finger on it. I blushed, somewhat embarrassed. "Sort of."

"The Barlows are like the American Murdochs. They own the other half of the media in this country and guess what? Mary-Ann is Philip's older sister. And George Barlow is the billionaire James's grandson. Philip Pope is related by marriage to the fucking Barlows."

The picture was beginning to form. "Is that how you think he's scrubbing the internet?"

"There's no other way. Do you know what it takes to remove nearly everything about the disappearances of a mom and both her little girls from the internet?"

"Money."

"Yeah, tons of it. And connections with Google don't hurt either."

"What about your article? That won't be removed."

She smirked and turned her phone back to her. When she turned it back so I could see the screen, I saw a message I'd become all too familiar with the last few days.

"The page you are looking for no longer exists"

"What is this?"

"It's the article I wrote last week. The one you read and contacted me about. Gone already. My boss got a cease-and-desist letter from the Barlow Media Corporation. It's been pulled."

"But that's news alone! Why would a giant media conglomerate want to can your article?"

"I asked the same question to my boss, even though I knew the answer. He told me that if I write a negative article on Barlow Corp, I'm a fucking pariah. Oh, and not to him but to the bigwigs in the media." She opened the folder and took out a laminated newspaper article. She turned it and pushed it toward me. It was a San Francisco Chronicle article about the McManns.

"Questions still linger over security at Paradise of the Palisades."

"Are these articles not archived online?"

"Nope. Scrubbed. I had to go to the fucking library and page through every newspaper for the first half of 2006 to find these. And whenever I tried to put one of these up online on my little blog? Boom. Gone. Their bots must scan the web for certain terms. McMann, disappearance. That kind of stuff. The web hosting service shut me down after a few days, probably after getting a cease-and-desist."

"Isn't there somewhere you could publish an article about them taking stuff down?"

"Proving they're scrubbing things is the harder part. Evidence of cease-and-desist letters are one thing but it's a whole other matter to prove they have bots and connections with Google."

"I could try bringing this story to my boss. She might know someone who would take it."

"I doubt it. This is all speculation. We need hard proof. When I called the sheriff's office to try and find out why Philip Pope was questioned again about the McManns, they wouldn't say why. But think about it, they questioned him after the building was torn down. What do you think they found?"

"Passages?"

"Exactly, something like what Amanda Bryan complained about before she went missing. But who's your boss?" Amy perked up. "I didn't know you were still actively a journalist."

"I mean, I'm not really. It's part-time, pop culture pieces. I'm with The Meridian."

"Oh, sure." She raised her brow, and I could tell she was only pretending to have heard of them. "I'm going to sound a little greedy here, Katie, but I need this story. I'm one more rent raise from being priced out of LA entirely."

"Of course!" I shot out my hands. "I would never take this story, I just meant—"

"I know, don't worry about it. I just want you to know it's why I haven't sold this to anybody. But I would work with you if you could help me out. I've been stuck for weeks. So, can I ask you something?"

"Sure."

"Would you still live at Philip's new development knowing all you do now?"

"I mean—"

She cut me off again and spoke quickly. "I don't think you'd be in as much danger as you think."

"Yeah?"

"I've been thinking of reasons for the disappearances. The McMann family is easy, right? Homeless. Vulnerable. One woman and two girls that no one will really miss. Sex trafficking, it has to be."

I bit my lip. "Yeah, that makes sense."

"And Amanda. She told the press about the passages she found in her home and mentioned Philip by name. That's what got her in trouble. Not only that, Amanda and Philip Pope used to work together. At a firm called Country Construction in Canada. She was an executive while he was employed temporally as an architect. They fucking knew each other."

I was far more impressed than I thought I'd be. Amy may work for a small outfit, but she didn't seem like an amateur.

"Maybe Pope took a liking to Amanda and was all too happy to design her home himself. One he could watch her in."

"I thought that, too. But here's what's going to make this story big. Don't ask how I got this." She set her coffee on an empty table next to us and opened the black tube that had been at her feet. She pulled out a blueprint and unrolled it on the table.

"Amanda Bryan's home was a beta product. It wasn't some unique one-time project by Philip Pope. Country Construction has built dozens of homes around Canada using the same design. Do you see this space?"

I squinted at the blueprints. There were multiple floors overlayed on the one page, and they were crossed with dozens of lines and little numbers. The whole thing looked like a kind of geometric mandarin.

"I can't really..."

"I know. After I got my hands on this, I had to take a blueprint reading course on YouTube before I could even make sense of it. But this space here..." Amy pointed to a little square beneath what looked like stairs. "It's doorless. Void space. There doesn't appear to be a way into it."

There was a tiny square within the room that her finger moved to next. "But this little guy in the floor *is* a door but it doesn't lead anywhere in these blueprints."

"What is it then? Some kind of secret way out?"

"I think it's a secret way in."

I leaned back in my chair with a frown and Amy rolled up the prints. "I think Amanda knew about it at first. About the design that is. But something went wrong, she grew a conscience or got cut out of a deal and ratted to the media."

"A deal?"

Amy smiled shyly. I could tell she was embarrassed by whatever she was going to say next. "Now, I don't have proof, but it's possible they were designing homes they could kidnap people from. All I have to go off is the human trafficking angle."

I leaned back and paused for a moment. "And this place in Colorado, do you think the homes are designed the same way?"

"I don't think yours would be. A quarter of the homes in Carson's Pass are affordable housing. He's going to let the employees stay in them, the grocers and groundskeepers. From what I can tell from the pictures those are the ones that are similar to this design." She tapped the blueprint. "But if you could get into them and find tunnels, anything, we'd have at least *some* evidence. Philip will be living in Carson's Pass, too. You could see what he's like. If we're serious about this and you can get your hands on some concrete evidence, we could get someone mainstream to pick up this story."

I looked at the laminated articles on the table. Amy had something here. This wasn't a game and I almost felt guilty for agreeing to meet with her. I was in it. I was presented for the first time in my life with the possibility of scratching my journalistic itch.

As if reading my mind Amy leaned forward. "I know I'm young, but I've been around the block, Katie. I know it when I see it, and this has the makings of a big story. Book deal, Pulitzer shit. Can I count on you?"

DRINKS

Amy had an answer to every one of my questions. It was clear this case had lived in her head for weeks or more. She said that before I'd reached out to her, she was planning to fly to Canada to try and get into one of the homes designed by Philip Pope. She was going to risk breaking and entering in a foreign country for potential evidence. I wasn't surprised. She was determined, and I assumed she'd obtained the set of blueprints by somewhat sketchy means.

She gave me the number of a burner phone she was using and told me to take as much time as I needed to think it over. When I got back in my car, I sat behind the wheel in silence. Amy was smart, confident and sure that she had something. I knew if I went to Colorado, to Carson's Pass, it wasn't just some whimsical move across the country on a hunch. There was a story here.

The problem was I wasn't single. I couldn't go alone, and my marriage couldn't take another break. Not only that, but Miranda would want to come with me. But if she or Howard knew what Amy had just told me, they wouldn't move in a million years. If anything, they'd probably try to convince me not to go.

I drove back to San Diego, thinking. I couldn't lie to them. But I'd be lying if I said I didn't *want* to. I figured they'd be fine if they came to Carson's Pass. Like Amy said, we'd probably all be safe.

Every person who had disappeared was a woman so Howard would be okay, presumably. And if this was human trafficking, they'd target the affordable homes. Not the rich ones. That's just reality. I realized the idea of Carson's Pass might be to funnel in desperate employees who needed housing and a job, then only hire the young and vulnerable ones... I shivered.

I knew I had to tell Miranda at least some of the truth. There was no way around it. My conscience wouldn't be able to stand it if I didn't. But for some reason, I didn't feel like Howard had to know. It wouldn't even be another lie. It was a simple omission. I didn't want to look like an idiot in his eyes and come back home empty-handed if it didn't work out.

When I got home, I stayed in the car in the driveway, thinking. I decided I was doing it. I texted Miranda to come over for drinks that night and planned to tell her I'd join The Eden Project. But only if I could get Howard on board. It wasn't fair to Amy for me to tell Miranda the truth about why I was interested, but I was the one doing her a favor. Amy's story couldn't go any further without me. If it wasn't for me reaching out and agreeing to help her, she might have already been imprisoned in Canada.

*

I was lighting candles under our little Gazebo when Miranda knocked at the tall side gate.

"It's unlocked!"

"Um. My hands are a bit full!"

I briskly walked over and unlatched it. As it swung wide Miranda was smiling with a wine bottle in each hand. "I couldn't decide between the two so..." She stepped past me. "Porque no los dos?"

"Oh, you shouldn't have. I mean it. We have so much left over from the party."

She got to work with a corkscrew immediately. "Hm. Well I hear the stuff ages well." I shook my head with a smile. "So, I have to ask... is there an occasion? When's the last time I was over here for just drinks?"

If she knew the answer to that question she wouldn't have asked. The last time she was over for drinks was when I got home from LA after my fling with Ryan when Howard and I had been fighting. I changed the subject before she might remember.

"I kind of have some news."

"Yeah? Please don't tell me you're pregnant. I can't be the only odd one out." She suddenly perked up from pouring her wine. "Unless, of course, you are! In which case that's amazing!"

I laughed. "I'm not pregnant."

"Oh, thank god."

"I've been doing a lot of thinking about where to move... if we were to. I think this Eden Project looks really interesting."

"Shut up," she said, her mouth hanging open. "You're a terrible liar. Are you really interested?"

"Well, maybe not for the right reasons."

She raised a single eyebrow. I didn't have that level of control over my face, and it was a gesture I was always envious of. "I have to be honest, I had cooled on the idea of moving there. You're right. Why not just get a house on Lake Tahoe? But if you're up for it I'm one hundred percent on board! But tell me," she brought the wine to her lips and spoke into her glass before she drank, "What are your *wrong* reasons?"

I picked my thumbnail and smirked at how ridiculous I was about to sound. "This is based on a bit of speculation, but I think this Philip Pope guy is involved in human trafficking. Or something of the sort."

She wore a shocked, incredulous smile. "Did you just invite me over to fuck with me?"

"I'm serious. I reached out to a journalist who's doing a big piece on him. She doesn't have the money to move there herself and she needs someone on the inside. I told her I'd try."

"Who are they trafficking?"

I hadn't intended to, but I told Miranda everything Amy had told me. By the time I was done, we'd each had most of a bottle. Miranda was splayed on a lounge chair. The back of her hand sat dramatically on her forehead like she was some flushed, Victorian woman in a heatwave.

"I'm coming with you," she said suddenly as if hit by inspiration. "I'm going. I'm serious."

"It's ok if you don't feel that way in the morning."

She pivoted so her feet were on the ground and leaned forward. "I *won't*," she started to laugh. "I'm not leaving my best friend with freaks and sex traffickers."

"But what do you think about telling Howard?"

"Or not telling Howard..."

I held my breath nervously. "That's what I was leaning towards."

"You know my take. He needs to live a little. Just say you want to go for the winter. It's a beautiful place to spend it anyway." She pointed at me suddenly. "And make sure he knows there's internet."

"What if it's a hard no?"

She twirled her hand drunkenly. "Something something about crossing bridges when you come to them. You're persuasive. He doesn't exactly use the amenities of where he lives anyway. He just spends his time inside." She looked past me to the house. "Online, playing video games, right? He loves to ski, sell him on that! Honestly, Katie, look at me and tell me you don't think you can get him to move there for a few months."

"I know. That's not it. It's that I feel like I should tell him the truth."

"But then he wouldn't go." I sighed and Miranda took her wine glass from where it rested on the ground. "So, stop worrying about Howard and worry about getting abducted and sold to Saudi Arabia, instead."

"If you're really okay with coming with, I think it would help if you led the way. It would just make more sense if you bought a place there first. Being that you brought the idea up, you know?"

She paused and scratched her chin. For a second I thought I'd called her bluff.

"What the hell. I can always sell."

I leaned back, a tinge of butterflies fluttering again in my stomach. I had a feeling that took a minute to place: Shame.

Miranda sensed my unease. "What's on your mind?"

"I should be asking Howard where *he* wants to live. Not manipulating him and deciding for us."

"Okay, you know my thoughts. You were on a *break*. And he knew what that meant. He's just pissed he was too busy to tell his friends you two were taking some time apart and he got caught looking like an idiot when you… exercised your freedoms."

"Nice euphemism."

"Look, you shouldn't feel shame about that. You're human. Even when you're in a relationship you're sometimes going to want to jump into bed with someone just because they're a fresh face. To deny ourselves that in the name of monogamy is… I don't know… either too bad or a sacrifice that makes us better people. But don't beat yourself up. You even had a hall pass."

"I know," I said, but I wasn't sure that's what I even felt ashamed about. It was more that I felt like I should be tied to some place at this point in my life. I was thirty-six and I could move anywhere. No kids. No real job. No friend group to worry about. And while people dream of that kind of freedom, now that I had it, I couldn't help but feel like a bum. The money didn't matter, it almost amplified the guilt. At this age, I should have obligations. I should be stuck somewhere. I have always been one to want what I don't have. I once thought of that as a character flaw before realizing it's probably just biology, and that the grass looking greener is just evolution's way to always keep us moving.

But screw the guilt. I wasn't moving for pleasure, or for soul-searching. We weren't buying a beach bungalow in Aruba. I was working on something. I was going to reveal a conspiracy. This was strictly business, and I was going to make the world a better place. And maybe I'd prove myself of being a capable journalist in the process.

POWERS OF PERSUASION

Miranda put in an application to the Eden Project just a week after she'd come over for drinks. She was accepted within twenty-four hours, which was a weight off my shoulders. I figured Howard and I would be able to secure a place just fine. Apparently, the project didn't have many applicants.

It was a Friday night, and Howard and I were cooking dinner when I first touched on the subject of leaving San Diego. "I think we should move," I blurted sloppily.

Howard stopped slicing an onion. He tried not to smile but failed and grinned as he gestured at the house around us. "A mansion in San Diego not good enough?"

"You know that's not the problem."

"Well, what is the problem? I'd like to hear it from you."

"I just wanted to have a discussion. Not a fight."

"Is this about where Miranda is heading? That commune you mentioned?"

"It's not a commune, and to be honest..." I hesitated but the truth came out. "There's more to it than that," I realized I couldn't lie to him. I was relieved in that moment to see what I wasn't capable of. But Howard would think I was a fool if I mentioned human trafficking. "I've been talking to this journalist. The guy who runs the thing, who'll be living there too, he's sketchy. She's making a case against him—fraud, embezzlement. White-collar shit." Ok, maybe I could lie a little. "She wants me there on the inside. She can't afford to live there herself."

Howard tilted his head back in surprise. "You want to move there for a journalism project?"

"Kind of. But I mean, yes. I'd be trying to uncover something there. Something potentially serious."

He turned away from me to hide what I assumed was a smirk. Howard lived in a software world of men where women just weren't as capable in his mind. Howard's sexism wasn't hateful, it was belittling. Although he never said it, he simply thought women were weaker and sometimes it made me stew. He walked over to me briskly and kissed me. "You should've led with that. Of course. God, I'd love to see you working on something that lights up your eyes for once. I was almost going to give you an intervention after I read 'eleven trending one-pot recipes for lazy days.'"

I blushed and looked away. "You read that?"

"Babe, I read *everything* you write."

"No. Oh, please. Tell me you don't," I started laughing and shaking my head.

"If you think you have something serious. Something better. Chase it. Let's go."

"Are you serious?"

"Only if we don't have to sell this place. And only if I don't have to be there all the time."

I felt more uneasy then. It seemed like Howard's idea was to stay in San Diego. "Sure, that's fine. But I think they want commitment. It's the community of the future," I said sarcastically. "They're not going to want to accept anyone who looks like they'll half-ass it. You should stay there with me for a bit."

"I won't leave you hanging. I'm just saying, what're they going to do if we don't make it a primary home? Evict us? Aren't they essentially just an HOA anyway?"

"Yeah, we'd own the property."

"And where is this place?"

"It's called Carson's Pass, Colorado. It's by White River National Forest, not that far from Aspen, actually. You could ski!"

He squinted for a moment and suddenly he wasn't as excited as I had hoped. It was like he was chewing on something I had said. But he seemed to shake it off. "Ah, what the hell. Ok."

"Just like that? It's really ok? Don't you want to read the website?"

"Hell, don't even show me a picture of the place. Excuse me this, but I have to indulge the ego sometimes." He wrapped his arms around my shoulders. "Do you know how *fucking* rich we are now?" I rolled my eyes and he laughed as he planted a kiss on my forehead. Life is often what you least expect, and just like that, it was settled. I put in our application that night.

CARSON'S PASS

It was easier than I thought it would be. I expected a phone call or some vetting process, but suspiciously there was nothing of the sort. Our application was simply accepted, and we were granted access to a page to purchase a home. It was apparent that the development wasn't garnering the enthusiasm it had hoped to. Out of ten houses, six were still available.

Philip Pope's interviews and clickbait headlines were all in the past. There was nothing on Forbes or Fortune about The Eden Project. It was probably a bit more difficult post-bankruptcy to get good press. But I was happy about that. If the development had been posted everywhere Howard and I probably wouldn't have gotten in.

Despite there being six homes, there were only two sets of pictures. It took me a minute to realize there were only two designs. Probably five homes of each one. This was valuable information. Amy would love this. It would make it easy to see if there was anything peculiar about the home builds. Tunnels, void rooms, god knows what. I just had to make sure Miranda and I picked different designs. There weren't many differences between the two—they were roughly the same square footage, 3,000 and 3,500 and both styles of homes were classic cabin-chic.

They were all dark wood, red rugs and moose-head mounts over fireplaces the size of sedans. A masculine aesthetic. I wouldn't be staying long enough to do any redecorating, but I thought it still looked like a cozy place to spend winter nights.

I didn't have access to view what the affordable homes would look like. It made sense. We had applied as residents not employees. Luckily, I imagined they were having trouble filling those, too. They were probably sitting empty, isolated in the woods. It couldn't be difficult to sneak into one.

The more I thought about it the more I realized we likely wouldn't be there long. Get in, find the hidden passages, take pictures, get out. Amy thought photos would be enough evidence to get published by a serious paper. She said they were new construction, so there'd be no passing the blame onto some defunct and forgotten developer.

The place itself, Carson's Pass, was beautiful. The development was built off of an old logging road and bordered 2.3 million acres of national forest. There were two dozen miles of private hiking trails (not like I'd be doing much walking alone in the woods) and three glacial lakes each with breathtaking views of the surrounding mountains. The website had almost sold me to the point where I was excited to move there for the geography alone.

We chose the option to have the place furnished. It may be all leather and bear-skin rugs but there was no way I was going to spend the time it took to furnish a 3,000-square-foot house, and we weren't taking that many things from San Diego with us.

The process was surprisingly simple. Howard found a realtor, and a virtual assistant named Jessica that worked for The Eden Project helped us along the way. I didn't lift a finger. It was simple as that. I guess the ease of purchasing was supposed to be part of the allure. The Eden Project was built to be used by the blight of every housing market in America: rich people who were comfortable buying a million-dollar home they'd only seen pictures of online.

After a brief video call with Miranda to decide which house we'd each pick, we were practically done. We decided Howard and I would take the bigger of the two designs while Miranda would purchase the still large 3,000-square-footer. I stretched out on the leather couch that was cool from the air conditioning while Howard was in the kitchen making us mojitos. When he came back, he handed me a drink and then clanked it with his.

"To second homes. And for you, second jobs," he said with a smile and drank.

"Cheers," I said. I was too nervous to smile. If nothing came of this, I'd feel like a fool, but we were buying real estate. It wasn't a stock that could go to zero and it wouldn't be hard to sell when the time came.

My phone buzzed with the ping of a text notification. I had just texted Jessica our decision on which home we'd get, but the message was from Philip Pope.

"Uh oh,"

"What?" Howard plopped down next to me and looked over my shoulder.

"A really long text message from our friend," I started to read it aloud.

To Howard and Katie,

I am so delighted that you have chosen to make Carson's Pass your new home. We live in a world where urbanity and anonymity are almost synonymous. Community has been forgotten and we have suffered for it, spiritually. It is not the way we were intended to live.

You have chosen to live in a place that's flipping the neighborhood on its head. A place that promises to bring back the basic structure of oneness that people are meant to feel when they live with one another. I think you'll find, at least I truly hope, that you have just made one of the best decisions of your life.

Yours,

Philip M Pope

"Man, can you picture the hippies and trust-funders we'll have for neighbors?" said Howard.

"They'll probably be nice people. Maybe a little spiritual for your tastes but have an open mind."

"Maybe. But I hate kale. And rock climbing, and I'm not interested in eating things that aren't supposed to be vegan but are."

"Like what?"

"Ice cream." Howard leaned back, and his face was deadly serious. "I'm not fucking with vegan ice cream."

"Ok babe. Deal." I patted his chest reassuringly. "You don't have to fuck with vegan ice cream." I found myself smiling, finally. But that quickly changed. I was interrupted as my phone vibrated on the coffee table. I flipped it over to read the caller ID. It was Bea.

"Great timing," said Howard. "You're not really going to answer that?"

"It's 8:30. I should. She doesn't call this late." I accepted the call and put the phone to my ear. "Hey, Bea."

"Shut up! That's not a solution! I'm not a teacher!" Bea yelled so loud to someone in the background that I flinched away from the phone.

"Told you so," said Howard. I got off the couch and started walking out of earshot of him.

"Bea," I said, irritated. "What's up?"

"Oh, hey!" she said as if she forgot she'd been calling me. "I'm just handling some things at home. The boy's school is trying to kick them out now. Expulsion. When's the last time you heard of seven-year-olds getting expelled? This modern world."

"Oh, jeez. What happened?"

"Well, Brayden put thumbtacks on this little girl's chair. Just as a joke. I mean he's *seven*. He doesn't know any better. Anyway, she had to go to the hospital," she said the word hospital like it was an annoyance. "To get some tetris shot or something. I don't know exactly what she needed, but her parents were being dramatic. The school said they've had enough. They just don't let boys be boys anymore. They want them medicated and staring at a screen seven hours a day."

"But why do they want Braxton gone?"

"Oh. You won't believe it. Apparently, because when this little girl stood up squealing, he called her 'bloody butt' and got the whole class chanting it. But honestly, that's just the character trait of a leader. And Braxton has *always* been a leader. I swear that's why they want to get rid of them. My boys pose a threat to their order."

My face was scrunched against my palm. I was unamused. "Bea, I think you have a—"

She cut me off, "So, I'm calling because there's this middle school opening up next year. It's for like the uber-wealthy. They teach leadership and it's the kind of place where you make lifelong connections."

"Ah-huh," I said. I was afraid of where this was going.

"But third grade starts at $30,000 a year… each."

"Bea, I don't think we would be comfortable doing that."

"But you didn't even ask Howard. You mean *you* aren't comfortable. If it's a no from you, just say that. Don't pussyfoot."

Her request seemed so absurd that for once in my life I didn't even hesitate with her. "It's a no. That's a mountain of money for middle school. If one of the boys got into an expensive college and needed tuition help then I'm sure—"

But Bea didn't let me finish. "Some people would jump at the opportunity to help their nephews. Especially someone who's *childless* themselves. I knew you'd fucking say no. I knew it. Don't say you've ever rescued me, Katie."

"I've got to go, Bea," I said, but she'd already hung up.

INTO THE WILD (COLD) YONDER

Two weeks later, we were on a plane to Colorado where fall was in full swing. I had lost my winter skin to seventy-degree Decembers, but it felt good to be back where it got cold. It was November, and the mountains already had snow on their shoulders, but the ground was still nude. The grass stood tan, brittle and drought-dry.

We did something we'd never done before and flew private. There were no direct flights to Gypsum, Colorado, so Howard chartered us one. If I'm being honest, it was one wealthy indulgence my conscience was silent on. But I didn't hate airports. I actually liked them when they weren't crowded. There was something calming about a quiet airport with the entire world just a ticket away. Sometimes I pictured changing my flight at the last second to go somewhere new.

I never would but it's about the thought. Like flirting with an attractive member of the opposite sex when you're married. It's fun to think about. Different. But I suppose I can't make that comparison anymore. I took that ticket.

I was happy we chartered a jet for other reasons. Mainly because I was nervous about checking a firearm on a commercial flight. When I went off to college my dad, being the small-town man that he was, insisted I had something to protect myself with in the big city. He got me a small, silver pistol that fit snugly in my palm. I never carried it around. I hadn't even opened its plastic case in years. But I kept it because I felt like if I ever got rid of it then of course I'd end up in a situation wishing I hadn't. The world loves its irony.

Sitting next to Howard for a two-hour flight was as close as I'd been to him for weeks. We still hadn't had sex. I'd tried a couple times. Not too hard, I only hinted. I wanted him to initiate it. To want me. There was a time when I did a full-nude photoshoot for Howard—I got a tripod, a timing app for

55

pictures, everything. Now I felt like I was in a dead bedroom. It didn't help that our California king was so damn big it was hard to touch him at night without army-crawling across the thing, and I didn't want to seem desperate. The ball was in his court.

A black SUV was on the runway ready to take us to Carson's Pass. Philip had provided a chauffeur service to and from the airport. It was good enough for now. At some point, one of us would fly back to San Diego to bring back a car, but neither of us felt like driving a thousand miles here. Especially when there was the chance that this place was so strange that we'd turn right around. Besides, if things got too sketchy and we wanted to leave, Miranda had a car, after all.

She'd got to Carson's Pass two days prior and had been talking it up. She sent me a few pictures of her house and texted me that she almost hopes Philip Pope doesn't turn out to be a sex trafficker so she could stay here permanently. I wasn't sure she even believed me when I told her what Amy had shown me. I couldn't sleep alone in this place, but Miranda seemed perfectly fine. But I didn't think much of it. That's just the type of person she was—the opposite of a worrier.

As we drove out of Gypsum and into the mountains, I actually began to feel excited. The trees, the space. The smell. I thought I could see myself living here, too. What a refreshing change from the sun and the sand.

In the distance, branching off the road, a long stretch of gravel went up into the woods. "What's that?" I asked.

"Huh," Howard looked at me and then followed my gaze. "It might be for runaway trucks. Probably when this was still used for logging."

The driver turned to us. "That is a runaway ramp now, but it used to be the main road into Carson's Pass. Your house is probably just at the top of it. But this mountain is all protected land now, and when the logging stopped no one was allowed to repave it."

"So, how do we get there now?"

"The long way. We wrap around in a horseshoe. It takes about another fifteen minutes to get there from here."

"Jeez," said Howard. "You think they'd pay to get a permit."

"Protected land." The driver looked at Howard in the rearview. "It can't be bought."

Several minutes later, a roadhouse bar came into view. It had an unlit neon sign that read: Fool's Gold. The driver put on his blinker and I frowned, thinking we were going to the bar, but instead we pulled onto a dirt road just before the bar. For the next few minutes, we began to ascend steeply while bumping along on the rutted dirt road. My ears popped somewhat painfully, and I pinched my nose and blew but they stayed plugged.

"You okay, Great Plains girl?" Howard smiled at me teasingly.

"I'm fine." I was becoming nervous. Although it was early afternoon the darkness under the pine canopy was that of dusk. A blackening forest. Maybe the last thing Claire ever saw before she tied a rope around a branch. Put the loop around her neck. *Stop.* I squeezed my eyes shut to block out the thought.

There were other reasons to stress. I was here to investigate a dangerous man. This was not a game or a new place to live. It was a job, and a risky one at that. I bobbed my leg several times a second until Howard reached out his hand and set it on my thigh. He said, as if reading my mind, "If we don't like it here, we're gone. We don't even have to even stay a day."

I knew he was really saying that if I felt like it was too much, I could bail. And he didn't even know why I was really here. My stress faded some then. I was determined to be strong. I sat back straight and discreetly took a deep breath. "I'll like it," I turned to Howard. "This will be home, at least for a while."

"Ok." We both turned to face out the windshield. The road was beginning to crest, and the woods on either side of the SUV stopped. We came to a clearing, although it was almost too big to be called that. I could count six houses right away. They were mostly hidden, each nestled behind their own patch of pines for privacy.

"You two are just a little further down this road," said the driver. "Up on the right there." He pointed and I could see a bit of a house through the trees.

Carson's Pass was even prettier than the pictures. It was astounding. And like Fjord towns or villages in the Alps, it gave me a feeling that this was how to live. Not with nature tucked away under aprons of asphalt but stretching into the sky. The driver turned right, and after a hundred or so feet, we saw our new house. It sat Lincoln-logged and looming at the end of a driveway. A man was standing in front of the stairs in a long overcoat. He gave a little wave as the SUV came to a stop.

"Is that...?"

I was trying to figure it out myself. He looked like the Philip Pope I'd seen in pictures but a few years older. His hair was more white than grey, and I figured he was between fifty-five and sixty.

"Yeah, it has to be him." I put on a polite smile and opened the car door.

"Hullo!" said Philip. "Welcome!" I stepped out and Philip held the door the rest of the way open for me.

"Hi there! Katie," I said as I extended my hand.

He took it and gave me a firm shake. "Philip Pope, pleasure to meet you. I hope you had a great flight in." Philip had a long beak-like nose and close-set eyes. He looked regal, with the fierce face of a bald eagle.

"The flight was perfect." Howard stepped from the other side of the SUV and they shook hands. "It's beautiful here."

Philip released Howard's hand and gestured at the mountains. "That's the idea. I just thought I'd introduce myself real quick. And." he pulled a set of keys out of both his pant pockets, "let you in! There are three keys," he explained as he handed a set to each of us. "The gold one is for the garage. Silver one opens both doors, front and back. And wider silver opens the shed in back. Not much reason to keep anything locked around here, though. Again, that's kind of the idea." He smiled.

"Thank you."

"I know you've already done the virtual tour. I'd be happy to give another, but I know how fun it can be exploring the nooks and crannies of a new place for the first time as a couple alone. Makes it feel more like your own place. I don't want to intrude."

"Oh, you wouldn't be intruding," said Howard. "But I'm with you. I think we're up for some exploring on our own."

"Great! The market is at the end of the road and they should have everything you need to fill the cupboards. Ah, there really is so much to tell you! There's a pamphlet on the counter that will answer most of your questions, but just come meet us when you're settled in. We're having a fire at the community garden. Though I suppose it's less of a garden this time of year."

"Oh, who's we?"

"Everyone! Don't be alarmed but it *is* a welcoming party. We're trying to build a close community here so it's important to know your neighbors."

"Of course," Howard cleared his throat and said plainly, "that's part of why we're here, too."

Philip widened his eyes like maybe he didn't really care why we were here as long as we had money. "All the houses here have a trail that leads to the garden. Yours starts there." He pointed to a path of black gravel that poked out from between the trees. "It's about a quarter mile till you get there. Once you hear a bubbling brook, it's just another minute or so."

"This is incredible, thank you so much. We're so happy to be here," I said.

"Thank you! And if you like it here tell your friends! The more the merrier."

"I'm sure we will," Howard said and shook Philip's hand again.

"Well, enjoy! And I'll see you shortly," he started walking but paused. "And I'm sorry about that little noise," he said as he pointed in the air. I hadn't heard anything before, but now I did notice a distant grumble in the air. "We had a bit of trouble with the electricity for one of the houses and we have a generator running in the meantime. It's a little noisy at times. We should hopefully have that fixed this week."

"I hardly noticed. Don't worry about it," I said.

"Right, see you soon." Philip smiled and walked towards the gravel path.

The driver placed our bags on the steps, took Howard's tip and got back in the SUV. "Shall we?" Howard put his hand on the doorknob but didn't open it. I paused and turned over my shoulder to look after Philip, but he'd already disappeared down the path and into the trees.

WARM ORANGE SQUARES

The inside of our house didn't smell like a cabin. There was no hint of pine sap or old wood. It was all very clean. The décor was as rustic as the pictures, however. In the living room we were both startled by an enormous bear skin rug that was laid in front of the fireplace.

Howard set his bag down and laughed. "This is ridiculous, isn't it?"

I was running my hand along the wall, already looking for some sign of a secret entrance. An outline of a square. The scar of Sawzall. But nothing stuck out right away. I was being silly. It was a 3,500-square-foot house. It would take time to find something I could show Amy.

"What is?" I asked, "This place, or moving here?"

"Everything."

"We can always go back to San Diego if you like."

Howard sighed. "Oh, it's fine. I'll survive." I couldn't help but notice how he bit his lip uncertainly as he said it.

We explored the rest of the house skeptically as if we hadn't already bought it. The bedrooms were well lit with big windows looking out to the mountains and the kitchen had glistening granite countertops and new appliances. The dining room and first floor bedroom of the house still smelled like new construction. The strong scent of wood dust and paint were assailing.

After I unpacked my suitcase and freshened up, we headed out the door to the garden. Miranda had already texted me asking when I'd be there, and I didn't want to keep everybody waiting long, first impressions being important and all. It felt like an obnoxious obligation—we'd only just gotten here, but community was what this place was supposedly about. I wondered how many events like this I'd be expected to attend. I pictured game night, community hikes, painful crap like that.

But thankfully, there was nothing in the application stipulating that I had to be a social butterfly.

When we reached the start of the gravel path to the garden, Howard stopped suddenly and bent over to kiss me. It felt like it had been a long time since he'd done something like that. My eyes wetted and I had to look away from him.

"I forgot how fun it is to do new things with you," he said and started walking again, swinging our arms in synch to our strides. "Thanks for dragging me out of San Diego."

I kissed his cheek, blinking rapidly to rid my eyes of their blur. "Don't mention it. Just don't go back right away when it gets colder and starts to snow."

He chuckled. "Well, I'm not a snowshoer or ice-fisher..."

"You have skiing. I'm sure there's a place within an hour from here."

"Yeah..." he lingered on the word. "But that upstairs den? Got any plans for it?"

"Oh, not really. What are you thinking, video games with a view?"

He smirked. "If that's alright?"

I realized I should search that room first before Howard moved his big desk into it. "That's alright."

We zig-zagged through the pines, listening to the wind whoosh through their needles. In just a few minutes we heard the babbling brook and saw a small stream trickling alongside the path.

"Do you think our welcoming party will be in robes?" said Howard jokingly. I rolled my eyes, but Howard went on. "I bet they'll be roasting a toddler over the fire."

"Shush! We're almost there. I'm sure they're just hippie types. This isn't Epstein's island."

"Mhmm. Don't look at me all crazy when you find out we're eating two-year-old little Timmy for dinner." I gently nudged his ribs with my elbow. I smelled woodsmoke and when we turned the next corner, there were several people sitting around a bonfire. I paused until Howard gently ushered me on.

We were met with hearty hello's and I saw Miranda on the far side of the fire. She beamed, set down her mug and queued behind the others to greet us.

It was lots of smiles, handshaking and names I immediately forgot. I was about to count to see how many people there were in total when Philip said, "Welcome the ninth and tenth residents of Carson's Pass!"

Miranda stepped to me first and we hugged. I looked across her shoulder to Philip. I realized we hadn't mentioned we knew each other in the application process, and I blanched, afraid that I broke the rules. "I'm sorry we didn't say anything in the application but we're good friends."

"Oh, why didn't you? That's wonderful! There's no rule about knowing each other beforehand. Did you think there was?"

There was something in his tone that felt fake. It was like he was pretending to be surprised but was a horrible actor. I had to be careful not to let my face show my skepticism and I widened my smile.

"We just honestly forgot," said Miranda.

"Well, I'll make it very clear on the website from now on. Friends encouraged!"

For the next ten minutes, Miranda introduced Howard and me to the other residents. We were told there were three couples and only one had kids.

But one of the couples, the Millers, weren't at the bonfire yet. There were the Larsons, an older hippie couple. The husband, David, had a gritty Rasputin appearance. Bushy beard and shoulder-length hair, both graying and unkempt. His wife, Jodie, was dressed in bright wools. She had lavender gloves, a rainbow hat and a lemon-colored coat. They were nice enough, but when I talked to them, they stared into my eyes so intently it was like they were trying to read my soul.

I was happy when Philip guided the next couple toward us. Jane and Miles McCarthy were a quiet California couple. They wore expensive parkas, and both had thick, cared-for hair. They were both surprisingly shy and talked softly. There were long gaps between our small talk and Jane spoke so quietly that I had to lean forward to hear her. When we parted Howard widened his eyes—an expression that said *yikes.*

Jessica came over next for a quick hello. Howard and the realtor had worked with her when we bought the house, but I'd never spoken with her. She was much younger than I had expected. Early twenties. Her hair was platinum blond and she held her phone in her hand. She looked like one of those women that was always busy. Skinny latte in one hand, iPhone in the other.

The other residents so far weren't my type. They were all a little off. If this was a speed dating event it was clear that we didn't click with the two couples so far. Miranda, Howard and I formed a tight trio the way people who know only each other at a party will.

"The people are... interesting," said Miranda. "But I love my house. I could stay here indefinitely." She leaned forward and lowered her voice, "I'm almost hoping your story on Philip doesn't pan out. I want to live here."

I smirked. "We'll see." While Miranda had loose lips, I had faith she could keep my secret from Howard—that I was investigating Philip for much more heinous crimes than I had told him about. She was isolated here. And the two of them weren't close. The three of us were quiet for a moment and I noticed an older man sitting alone by the bonfire.

"Who's that?" I gestured with a nod.

"Just another resident. He's not very social." Miranda leaned forward and whispered, "I think he's one of those men who thinks they're outdoorsy but doesn't like doing much but chopping wood. This place is good for those types. It's Walden meets satellite internet."

I laughed. It didn't seem like the kind of thing Miranda would say. Maybe she'd heard it from Howard. He was always reading old literature, but his expression didn't convey that she'd stolen his joke.

We wandered to a wooden table lined with danishes, donuts and stainless-steel dispensers of coffee and hot chocolate. Howard and I took our time stirring the sugar into our coffees.

There were two teens sitting on a bench to our left, laughing and having more fun than the rest of us. They were both blond, the girl more than the boy. I noticed that the boy's cheeks looked powdered and soft. He was wearing foundation, but the rest of his look—Khaki pants and a quarter-zip sweater—was very heterosexual.

"Let me guess," I said while walking over to them. "One of you invented a cryptocurrency?"

The boy laughed while the girl looked slightly nervous. "Those are our parents." He pointed to the quiet couple who were now staring peacefully into the fire. "We're the McCarthys. Pardon my parents if they haven't said hello, they're stoned."

"No, they're not. Shut up, Aiden."

The kid shrugged. "I'm Aiden, and this is Kenna. We're twins but, I'm the oldest."

"No." Kenna glared at him teasingly. "We agreed to this and you can't even remember. *I'm* the oldest."

"Ok, fine. By like thirty seconds, maybe."

Howard cleared his throat. "What're you doing for school here?"

"Oh, same old. We've always been homeschooled. If you can call it that." He imitated a fatherly voice. "Read this son. Read this daughter. Is Ernest Hemingway's style genius or was he just too drunk to write anything but short sentences?"

"Homeschooled," I said. "Is that hard on you, socially?"

"No, we wouldn't have it any other way," said Kenna. "Our parents raised us on a sailboat in the Caribbean. We thought they were criminals or something. Tax evaders, I don't know. Turns out, they're just crazy."

"Wow," I said. "I couldn't picture that."

"Yeah. It was alright. Sucks always having temporary friends. We were in Nepal for a few years while they taught

English and now," Kenna looked over our heads to the mountains, "We're here."

"Why they'd choose this place?"

Kenna and Aiden glanced at each other and Kenna shrugged. She stretched the corners of her lips down as if to say *I don't know*. Aiden turned back to us. "I think they just wanted friends."

We talked to them for a bit longer, but the third couple had appeared and were taking my attention. They were younger, late twenties or so, and the woman was beautiful. She laughed while the man whispered into her ear. They reminded me of the early days of love. That can't keep their hands off each other because they can't believe they got this lucky, love.

"The Miller couple."

I looked up. Philip stared at them while he spoke to me. "Leah and Ted Miller. Aren't they cute? You should say hello. I know it looks like they're in their own little world but they're quite friendly." I could tell by the way he said it that he thought the Millers were more normal than the others.

"I will," I said. Philip nodded and walked off. But I never did say hello. Before I could, I watched them whispering to each other, and they snuck off from the bonfire without goodbyes, I assumed to screw with a mountain view.

*

I put the investigation on hold while we settled in the first day. Miranda came over for drinks later and the three of us had more than a few. It was almost midnight when she left. I walked her back home through the woods. It was a similar distance as our house was to the garden—a quarter mile or so, but in the other direction. The trail went behind a house that Miranda pointed out belonged to the McCarthys. I noticed a slight purr as I passed and realized this was the house with the generator. It was much bigger than ours and nothing like either of the house models I'd seen on the website. I guess not all the homes here were built in the same style. All the blinds were drawn and dark on the ground floor, but the second-story windows glowed warm and orange against the black night.

Miranda invited me inside to tour her new place, but I said I was too tired. Really, I was a little afraid. I had to walk back alone now. But thankfully, the alcohol and the moonlight made the woods far less frightening. When I passed the McCarthy house again, I saw movement in one of the upstairs windows. It was the twin girl, Kenna. She was looking out the window and I thought for a second she could see me, but it was obvious she was examining her reflection in the glass.

I saw her bedroom door open behind her and she looked over her shoulder. Aiden came in. He looked both ways into the hall and then shut the door gently. I smiled. How nice to have a sibling you got along with. Someone to share the world with since birth. But then I gave a little gasp as he pushed her against the wall and set his hands on her shoulders. And my mouth hung open dumbly as I watched them start to kiss.

BEHIND CLOSED DOORS

The next morning, I ate my breakfast with a furrowed brow. They weren't eating children, but Howard was right to assume that the kind of people to move to a place like this, and even their kids, would be strange.

I wasn't a peeping tom. I didn't stick around to watch last night. I stared, entranced for a few seconds. It was long enough to get the picture that they weren't stopping at first base, and then I walked on, head at my feet.

Howard had been sleeping when I got home, which was disappointing in a couple of ways. First, I'd hoped he'd wait for his wife to get back from a walk in the woods before feeling comfortable enough to sleep. Second, I wanted desperately to tell him what I saw. But he'd been drinking, and I didn't hold it against him. When he came down that morning, I was practically prancing around to tell someone. He was filling a glass of water at the sink. When it was full, he held it up to the light and scrunched his lips.

I could see little motes floating in it. "I'm sure it's fine," I said. "The pamphlet says it's spring water. Probably fresher water than you've ever had."

"That's what I'm concerned about. My body is so used to tap water teeming with chemicals that I'll probably go through withdrawals." He knocked the glass back and chugged it.

"Wanna know what I saw last night?"

He sighed and wiped his lips. "Cult shit?"

"Kinda. I don't know. I saw those twins..."

"Staring at you from the woods?"

"No. Kissing in their bedroom."

Howard erupted. "I told you! What did I tell you? It's a bunch of weirdos. Their parents probably taught them."

"Gross." I shook my head. "And you didn't guess incest."

"Yeah, but you even just said it's kinda culty. There's a word for that..." he squinted searching his brain. "Twincest! You saw twincest. My god."

"Should we... tell their parents?"

"You're kidding? Sure, if you want to get an invite to the bedroom. I bet the parents know."

"Maybe." I remembered the quiet parents, Jane and Miles. They certainly seemed strange.

"They're almost eighteen, right? It may be illegal, but they can do what they want. They'd probably kill you if they knew that you saw them, anyway."

"Yeah. They were trying to be secretive about it."

"Katie, seriously. Don't tell a couple you've barely met that you saw their kids screwing."

"I'm not going to. But I'm not telling Miranda, either. She'd mention it somehow."

"Good idea. God." Howard put his hands on his hips. "You're sure it wasn't just like a, 'love ya, goodnight, sis' kiss?"

"Oh, I'm sure."

"Fuck."

"Right?"

"Well, what do you want to do today? Want to do a little roleplay, twin sister?"

"Ugh. Don't even joke."

"I can't help it."

I stretched my arms towards the ceiling. "We don't have much to unpack. I'm going to explore. Get to know the house a little more. Maybe go on a hike."

"Nice, I'm going to set up my gaming room. Moving truck gets here at..." He looked at his naked wrist as if he wore a watch and let his arm flop to his side. "Shit. Have you seen my watch?"

"Bathroom counter."

"Thanks. Moving truck gets here at ten, right?"

We had a small moving truck coming here that had some of our things from San Diego, creature comforts so we could still feel somewhat at home.

"They're going to be an hour or so late, they texted this morning."

"Ok, I might do some calisthenics in the garage. I need to sweat out this booze."

"Have fun. I won't go anywhere before the movers get here."

Howard drank another glass of water and shook his head with a smirk. "Twincest," he said in disbelief and went upstairs to change.

Last night before Miranda had come over, I had searched the upstairs den, but it seemed to be a perfectly normal room. Nothing about the construction of the house so far had caught my eye. This morning I was going to search from bottom to top, starting in the basement and finishing in the attic.

I even brought a stud finder, per Amy's recommendation, to see if there were any discrepancies in how the walls are built. But I wasn't excited to start my search. Before I saw the McCarthy kids kiss, I was almost content to let this investigative project slip my mind. At least for a little bit. Howard seemed happy, like getting away and coming here was actually good for us. Ever since he kissed me and took my hand on the way to the garden, I felt giddy. Howard hates holding hands, but knew I liked it. It was a sweet gesture, meant to reassure me of *us*. It said we were a married couple, and we were still in this together. No matter what. He's not very vocal and his actions have always spoken louder than his words.

But now it's possible I'd be hightailing it out of here before the movers were even done getting our boxes out of the truck. If I found some dark, dank tunnel mazing through our walls I wasn't sleeping here another night. I would take pictures for Amy and split.

The basement was far less lovely than the rest of the home. It was dark and partly unfinished. But it was ten degrees cooler down there, a blessing for my little hangover. The air itself was so cold on my cheeks it reminded me of late college, post-Claire, when I'd crawl to the bathroom cripplingly hungover and press my face against the icy tile. Sweet relief.

I futzed with the stud finder. I had never used one before and Howard wouldn't be much help since he wasn't a tool man. Not to mention he didn't know what I was doing. *Hey, honey*, I thought, *Can you help me work this thing? By the way, I'm looking for secret sex trafficking tunnels. Sorry I didn't mention it earlier.*

I didn't think I'd be a wife that was so okay with lying to her husband, but it all felt easy to justify. I couldn't be here if I told the truth. I was able to forget the thought as the little plastic box beeped in two different tones and when I ran it against the wall, it sang when it found a stud.

I didn't have a tape measurer on me, but I could tell by eyeing the space between beeps that it was built uniform. Nothing was out of the ordinary, but I wish I had a reference. It was quite possible that the house in Canada where Amanda Bryan lived was built the same way. But it didn't mean there wasn't something in this wall.

I got down on all fours and traced the trim that ran around the wall. I was crawling slowly like a giant baby when I froze. In the trim, just below an outlet, a tiny line formed a square in the wall. It was easy to notice if you were looking for it, but you wouldn't be able to see it if you were standing.

While the square didn't seem to be big enough for anybody to crawl through it was a start. I placed my hands against the outline and pushed. It didn't budge. If it was some kind of door it probably opened outwards anyway. I knocked on it gently and then knocked on the rest of the wall. The little square sounded hollower.

My heart began to pound. Was it this easy? I suppose Philip Pope was probably not used to having residents that were suspicious about passages in his walls. If I didn't know about his past, I could've lived and died here and never even noticed this slight square outline. And even if I did see it, I wouldn't have thought anything of it. But now I had a problem. I wasn't going to just break the wall in. I could drill a hole. Find some kind of thin camera to stick inside. Suddenly I realized it was probably simpler. The square was set directly under an electrical outlet.

I stood up and looked around. I needed a screwdriver. When Howard and I walked through the house yesterday, I saw a little shop in the concrete boiler room. There was a workbench with old tools on pegs and a string light bulb that swung wildly when you pulled it on.

I went to the boiler room, turned on the drunk and bobbing light and found a short screwdriver with a fat handle. I had the face plate off the outlet not a minute later. I stuck my hand in, searching for some kind of switch, and voila: I lifted a little piece of metal acting as a lock and the square section of wall fell open like a trap door.

"Yes!" My fear was replaced with ego. I felt a kind of genius pride, the kind good reporters must feel when they make a break. It hadn't been twenty minutes since I walked downstairs, and I had already found something. With the panel open, there was nothing but a black square in the wall. My fear quickly funneled back. My imagination pictured someone staring back at me from the dark. I quickly turned on my phone's flashlight and held it up.

It wasn't a tunnel. I could see the back of the sub-wall just two feet in. It was just a hidden compartment in the wall. At the bottom was a furry gray rectangle. A shoebox, I realized, covered in dust. I turned my face away while I brushed it off and waited till the startled dust had settled before reaching back in to take it out. Weird, I thought. There was more dust on the box than on the floor of the little compartment. Maybe the box had been moved at some point.

When I had it on the floor in front of me, I paused for a moment feeling my pulse flutter in my neck. Anything could be in this box. Gold bricks. A human head. If this was evidence of some string of crimes maybe, I shouldn't even open it.

I flung the box open quickly, giving no more time for my doubts. It was full of what looked like paper and sitting on top was a glossy picture portrait of a girl. It had one of those banal blurry backgrounds of school photos. I realized it was likely a yearbook picture. The girl was probably a junior or senior in high school.

I picked it up and frowned. Underneath was another photo. This one wasn't from a yearbook, but it was another headshot. It was a perfect portrait photo. The kind, I realized, you might give to the police if they asked for a picture to circulate for a missing person. The box wasn't full of papers but portraits of young women looking their best.

A pipe banged somewhere in the boiler room and I shot my head over my shoulder. It was just the house making noise. I paused and breathed, thinking of what to do next. I was almost certain these had to be missing girls. I flipped through the pictures faster and faster until halfway through the stack I stopped. I held my breath in disbelief. Because staring up at me from the dusty box was a smiling portrait of Claire.

ALL GIRLS

It had been over a decade since I'd seen a picture of Claire, but her face was so ever-present in my mind there wasn't a feature of her face I didn't remember. I ran my thumb across the picture, across her round childish cheeks and contagious smile.

I had to stay calm. It could just be a coincidence. It was possible all these girls were just missing persons in Colorado and that whoever collected the pictures was interested in disappearances. I had never mentioned to the police and search teams that Claire was suicidal. That would've made the truth that I failed her more real to me. I kept my mouth shut, and as far as the world was concerned, Claire was a missing person. I was the only one she left a hint with.

I counted and there were forty-six pictures in the box. The era of the photos ranged from what looked like the late 90s to present day. I figured the pictures were probably just collected by some weirdo fascinated with missing person's cases. Afterall, there were more of those than serial killers. But I didn't believe that. My heartrate was rising. I spun around, my peach fuzz prickling on end as I felt like someone was watching me.

I tossed the shoebox back, closed the hidden compartment and double-timed it up the stairs. I'd learned to listen to my gut, even if it made me look like an idiot. At the top of the stairs, I jolted with a gasp as I ran into Howard.

He frowned. "Hey, what's up?"

"Oh, god," I said and put a hand on my chest catching my breath. "Nothing, sorry I thought you were still in the garage."

"No, the movers are here." He looked me over for a minute. I was out of breath and didn't meet his eyes. "Are you sure nothing's up? I know you think I'm unobservant and all but... you seem a bit bothered."

"I don't think you're *unobservant*." I leaned forward and kissed him quickly. "But maybe a little observationally challenged."

"Ah huh. I won't disagree, but I was just wondering."

"Thanks for asking. But I'm fine. Really."

"Ok. You can tell me anything, you know?" He gave my shoulder a squeeze, but it felt too late to backtrack. I was in this hole of lies. I watched his back guiltily as he walked to the door. I was given another opportunity to tell the truth to Howard, but my mouth stayed shut. Everything just felt so fragile. So fake. I felt like our relationship needed to be wrapped in bubble wrap, so I shrugged off his questions. And now I couldn't stop lying.

*

The moving truck had brought with it the kinds of things that made our house feel homier. Our good coffee maker, my favorite bedding and a solid chunk of my wardrobe and toiletries. When most of everything was put away, I noticed our winter clothes box was missing. We only had the sweaters and coats we had come here in. I went to find Howard in the upstairs den. I opened the door and he spun in his swivel chair, tapping his fingertips together from pinky to index like Doctor Evil.

"Can I help you?"

"You brought that monstrosity?" I nodded at the chair he sat in. It was black and race-car red.

"Hey, you can't worry about my posture and complain about the gaming chair."

"It's just so giant." I stepped forward and ran my hands over his shoulders. I looked past his dual computer monitors to the mountains. "You've got quite the set-up."

"So long..." He spun back to face the desk in his chair. "San Diego." He drummed the desk happily. "You know what? This was a great idea."

"What?"

"Moving here. I'm with Miranda. I almost hope our friend isn't a fraudster. Hell, maybe I'll buy the place from the bank if he is."

"You actually like it?"

"Hey, I mean the incest is a little weird, but I'm having fun. This is different. It's not like us to just get up and go."

"Well, I'm glad you like it here. It's fun to be doing things with you again."

Howard swiveled in the chair. "Hey, by way, have you seen my winter clothes box? I left it in the garage back in San Diego for the movers to take. It was right by your coat box."

"No, and I haven't seen my coat box either." Howard glared at me. It was a look of judgment I'd come to know well. "What?" I fired back.

"This kind of shit is your responsibility, Katie. Now I'm in Colo-fucking-rado with nothing but a light coat and it's supposed to snow in two days."

"Howard, come on," I said pleadingly. "It wouldn't be a real move if something didn't get screwed up."

"What a cop-out. You really think you can break the financial crime case of the decade when you can't so much as pack our clothes? You were supposed to bring them."

I didn't want to fight, especially so soon after we'd gotten here. Howard was looking to blow up on me. I didn't even forget anything. The boxes were by our other things and marked to be taken. I said what I'd unfortunately had to say to every man I've ever dated. "I'm not your mother."

"I'm not asking you to be." He stood up as if to remind me how much he towered over me. "I'm just asking you to keep your shit together."

I spun on my heel and left the room.

That afternoon, I pulled five of the portraits from the shoebox and sat on my bed reverse image searching them. My assumption was right, three of the photos got matches and the google image results were all news articles on the girls as missing persons.

Again, a cold feeling of pride peaked above my fear. I was doing this, and so far, I was doing it well. I sat cross-legged. The side of my thumb was pink and a little pruned from biting it nervously. While I was good at finding the pieces, I wasn't great at putting them together. I couldn't see a solid connection between them.

One of the girls from the few pictures I got results for hadn't even gone missing in Colorado. Grace Lewis, a college sophomore, was last seen in Topeka, Kansas. I realized this was a good thing. Whoever kept these photos didn't just do so because of an obsession with missing girls in Colorado. There was something else tying them all together, not just geography.

But I knew I had to get these photos to Amy. I'd done my job thus far and two sets of eyes were better than one. Forty-six missing girls. Figuring this out would take a war room like in the movies with black coffee, corkboards and thumbtacks traced together with string.

I looked up from my computer screen and out the window. The sky was overcast, and the pines were so bunched in their thousands that the forest looked black. There were parts of these woods that people had surely never even stepped foot in. Claire, I thought. Are you in there?

TOUCH

That night, I sat in the living room on my computer trying to match names to the rest of the photos, but I didn't have much luck. Reverse image searching was extremely unreliable. I'd need Amy to access a missing person's database. I heard Howard come out of the den and I quickly hid the pictures and opened a new browser tab.

"Hey." He came behind me and set his hands over my shoulders. "I just wanted to apologize for earlier. Genuinely. Sometimes I remember... what happened a few months ago. And it puts me in a mood."

He was talking about when I slept with Ryan. He had never said that out loud before and I felt so guilty then. Like everything was my fault. But maybe I shouldn't feel that way because his words still echoed in my head, "Just don't fall in love."

"I love you," he said. "I want to be with you."

I kissed his palm. "I want to be with you, too." He gently stroked my cheek in silence for a minute. Eventually, he moved his strong hands on my shoulders and began to rub them. I felt some of my stress escape as he dug into my muscles. I let my head go heavy and flop around. I was slightly smiling, enjoying the massage for several minutes when I felt his breath on my ear lobe and then his lips on my neck.

My eyes flew open. This was finally happening. It had been so long, and our relationship had been so strained that my stomach had nervous butterflies. It was funny how my needs commanded me, and forty-six missing girls suddenly slipped from my mind.

He lifted my shirt off my head and grasped my breast in one hand and my neck in the other. Howard wasn't good with tools, but he was still good with his hands. The men I'd been with before him would strum strum strum like folk artists or finger me like I'd asked them to scratch an itch. But Howard was professional. Serious about his work. His touch started soft, light, and searching, before it gradually became rougher. An orchestra building up to a crescendo. He applied pressure to his fingertips with his big hand wrapped around my nape and my groin buzzed. He slid around the couch so he faced me and took my lower lip between his forefinger and thumb.

"I think it's time I brought you to the bedroom."

I nodded submissively and he held my hand as he led the way upstairs. He unbuttoned my jeans and gently pushed me onto the bed. Then he grabbed my pants at the pelvis and hefted them over my hips and ankles. With one hand holding me down by my neck and the other between my legs, he made short work of my first orgasm. It'd been so long that I giggled as I watched stars swirl across my vision.

I perked up on my elbows to look at him and saw that he was still fully clothed. I felt a little vulnerable, embarrassed even, but when I saw the angry lust in his eyes, I realized that was his point. We were typically mutual partners in bed, but it seemed he wanted me more than he usually did. I laid my head back, happy to submit.

When my legs calmed down, he turned me hard by the shoulder so I was on my stomach. Howard was strong built and had the ability to make me feel weightless and I gasped, panting as he arranged me like a doll. He was being rougher than usual. He stuck his arm between my legs and pressed his palm against my belly, lifting me so I was on my knees and elbows. I swayed my bottom at him teasingly and let out a sharp little cry as he spanked me with a loud slap.

I heard him behind me fumbling with his fly and after his fingers rubbed me wetter I was suddenly filled. He pressed into me hard with his first stroke so my face rubbed against the bedding. Howard was a symphony conductor. Not a jackhammer. It was part of why I married him. His strokes varied in length, power and depth. He knew how to drive me wild with just the first inch of him. But tonight, he was a one-note band.

He was making a point by fucking me hard. I just took it and put the sheets in my mouth so my moans were muffled like a good girl, just as he wanted. It was different, but I was open to the change of pace. His animalistic anger and hard strokes drove me wild. I was a lucky girl; penetration was all it took for me cum, and soon, my legs were buckling again.

He finished quickly after and slid from me. I spat out the sheets and looked over my shoulder as I heard a door shut. He had already gone to the bathroom without a word. My desire began to fade quickly—I felt used. I had the sudden craving to be clothed and wrapped a sheet around my shoulders. I looked at the closed bathroom door and felt silly as a tear tickled my cheek. It wasn't that I was in any pain, it was the realization of how much work we still had to do.

IN CODE

The next afternoon, Howard and I walked to the food market for the first time to fill the fridge. There was a number we could call and give our grocery list to and they'd all be delivered in a half hour, but that didn't feel very communal to me.

I thought of the night before while we walked. I knew that Howard's inconsistent behavior of the last months stemmed from Ryan, and the thought that he hadn't been the last man inside me is what probably made him quiet last night. Whatever it was, I wasn't sure it was a good idea to bring it up. Howard was high-strung, short-fused, and more time, not words, was the best thing for us.

The market was at the end of the road that we'd driven in on, just past the garden. It was a part of Carson's Pass we've yet to see. There weren't any houses back here. Just the food market and what looked like the start of some hiking trails.

Howard held the door for me, and I stepped inside. A redheaded girl, twenty-two or so, swept an already spotless floor and a boy about the same age came to the counter. Seeing the girl made me blanch. I should sound the alarm, I thought. Get these people out of here. Kenna and this girl were both the prime age of the other missing girls I'd found in the box.

"Hey!" said the boy at the counter. "How're you folks?"

"Great!" said Howard. "We haven't been by yet so we're just getting all the essentials."

"Alright. If there's anything you'd find in the supermarket that you can't find here let me know and we can have it here in an hour."

"Sounds great, thanks."

I said nothing. I just smiled tightly and turned my gaze to the girl with the broom. But she spun away when I tried to meet her eye.

Howard and I both picked up little wood baskets and started gathering the basics: sugar, coffee, eggs, spices, produce. I realized while filling my basket that I'd have to alter my shopping style if I were carrying everything back home by hand.

When we set our baskets on the counter the boy started ringing everything up. "Find everything?"

"Yeah," I said and looked behind me. There were far too many groceries for ten residents and just a handful of employees. "What do you do with the food you don't sell?"

He raised his head up from scanning. "To be honest we're still trying to find out the perfect amount of food to keep stocked. We're trying to minimize waste, obviously."

"Sure."

"So, where are you folks from?"

Howard smirked. "I'm sure you could guess."

The kid nodded. "Oh yeah. Well guess what, I'm from California, too. I'm an actor or at least..." he blushed, embarrassed. "I was trying to be. Obviously, things didn't work out."

"Oh cool, how'd you end up here?"

"I'm from Denver. I was going to move back and was looking at jobs in Colorado when I found this gig. Let me tell you, I may have to live away from civilization for a few weeks at a time, but it won't be long until I have enough saved to move back to LA and give it another go."

"This job pays well?" I asked.

He widened his eyes, nodding. "Oh yeah. It's technically remote. I mean I haven't left Carson's Pass since I started last month. There's no reason to. There's no nightlife to check out in Gypsum, ya know?"

"I bet," I said.

He finished packing our paper bags and pushed them across the counter. "What are your names?"

"I'm Katie, and this is Howard."

"Well, it's nice to meet you two. I'm Jacob. If you ever need anything ordered give me a call and I can have it brought right over to you."

We hefted our bags, cradling the bulging bottoms. "Thanks, Jacob," I said.

Outside, I slipped my free hand into Howard's. I was still trying to hold onto the honeymoon phase of Carson's Pass, but with the box of girls and my marital strife as ripe as ever, the excitement was gone. Anxiety seeped from my stomach as I watched the clouds slice in two as they slid over the mountaintops.

*

Amy texted me a few hours later and I needed a minute to sit and think before I responded. I stared at the text on my lock screen.

Amy 12m ago:

"Hey, hope you're well! I know you're busy, but I REALLY need your help. I twisted my ankle the other week and can't run any errands. I could really use your in-person help."

I knew the message was code. "In-person help" probably meant whatever she had to say, she didn't think she could say it over the phone. I thought she was being paranoid by not calling. Did she really want me to fly back across the country for a conversation? I sighed. At least I had a reason to go back. I could pick up our winter clothing that the movers forgot and bring back a car. But I wouldn't mention I would be seeing Amy. Howard would probably smirk if I told him I was going back home to drop off some evidence I'd found. I knew he thought I was just playing detective, but I couldn't blame him. I never proved myself as a journalist. I wanted my success here to shock him.

I went upstairs to the den. Howard stared intently at the screen playing some first-person shooter. I listened to the click-clack of keys a moment before I walked forward and lifted the headset off his ears. "Got a minute?"

"Can't pause." He nodded his head up. "Can you put those back on, please?" I set them back on his head and turned toward the door. "I'll be done in five."

"It's okay," I said unsure if he could even hear me.

He came downstairs in what was more like twenty minutes to find me surfing flights on the couch.

"What's up?"

"I'm going back to San Diego. We should have a car here. It was stupid to not drive in the first place."

He nodded. "Want me to get you a charter again?"

"No." I shook my head quickly. "I'll connect. It's fine. I got it figured out."

"Okay," he sighed while he said it, dragging out the word dramatically.

"If you want anything else from the house text me. So long as it can fit in the car."

"I'm sure I'll think of something. When are you leaving?"

"Tomorrow morning."

He eyed me skeptically. I had always been an easy read. I felt like he could tell I was keeping something from him. But he only shrugged like he knew he wasn't going to get anything more from me. "Just... don't be too long."

I felt relief as his gaze left me. But I knew it was already too late. He'd seen my deceit.

PRIVATE PLACES

I had some time to kill before my flight and I decided to take a walk to check out the employee houses before seeing Amy in California. The resident homes in Carson's Pass were all on the same stretch of road, but the employee housing was tucked away down its own street that branched off. It was a cul-de-sac, and it was disorienting to see such a suburban setup in the mountains. I walked down the middle of the street trying to see through the windows, but they all had blinds drawn. There was sawdust in the yards and the tracks of heavy equipment.

It looked deserted. The driveways were all empty. And two of the houses in the cul-de-sac were just wooden frames. The lumber was not blond and fresh but greyed by time. Suddenly, something flashed from behind the trees and I flung my head to see a giant dog bounding toward me. It took me a second to realize it was not coming up to me with kind curiosity. Its snout was wrinkled in an ugly snarl. There was no way I'd be able to get away. I took a panicked step back and yelled, "Hey!" I turned to run but as I did the dog slid to a stop like it hit an invisible wall and began to bark at me furiously.

It was some kind of livestock guardian. Tall and big-headed with a thick coat of white fur. But it obviously wasn't friendly. I started walking back the way I came, and the dog followed me, toeing an invisible line. "Invisible fence," I said aloud, looking at a large collar around its neck.

I started walking to the other side of the cul-de-sac and the dog took off. It was doing a large loop around to meet me on the other side. Strange. The dog was obviously here to defend the homes, but from what?

I looked at the drawn blinds and felt the prickling sensation of someone watching me. It was time to go. I turned quickly before the dog could reach me again and went back home.

I didn't want to be alone with the chauffeur driver, so I had Miranda take me to the airport. I flew from Gypsum to Denver. Denver to San Diego. With layovers it was later than I'd hoped when I landed; 5pm.

Amy had said she'd come to me. And when I texted her while we were taxiing on the runway, she told me she was already at a bar in Pacific Beach. I was a little frustrated. Urgent as this was, after a day of traveling, I wanted to drop off my bag at home and shower.

I Ubered home first but skipped the shower. I put the pictures of the missing girls into a big purse I never used and drove to the address of the bar she'd sent me.

When I stepped from the setting sunlight and into the cool bar, I paused for a moment and looked around. Amy waved at me timidly from a booth. I looked at my feet as I walked over. A dingy dive bar. A booth. I smiled, thinking the whole thing felt like a scene out of a movie. I guess things were written that way for a reason. Where else would you meet for a secretive meeting, the mall? Dark bars have the duality of being both public and private.

I scooched into the booth and pretended not to react when I saw Amy's glazed eyes and smelled her empty glass emitting a reek of Vodka. My face must've given me away though and she immediately apologized.

"I'm sorry. I've been here for a couple hours." She rotated her glass on the table and looked over her shoulder. "You weren't followed?"

"No," I said wide-eyed. The thought never even occurred to me. It was entirely possible I was.

She stared at the door I'd come in from. "Where's your phone?"

I pulled it from my pocket, and she extended her hand. I entertained her paranoia and gave it to her, and she put it under a sweatshirt that her phone was under, too.

She reminded me even more of Claire now. Her messy hair. Her eyes red and wet from alcohol. I felt my stomach shrink and I clutched the purse close to my side.

"We need to be careful. I got a letter. A piece of paper was slipped under my door." Amy fumbled in her back pocket and slapped a piece of paper that looked like it'd gone through the wash on the table. The ink had bled but I could still read it.

Close your eyes to us before we close them for you.

I looked up at her. "A threat?" I felt like an idiot. I just didn't know what else to say. My pulse was practically in my throat.

"Yes, a threat." She snatched the paper back and stuffed it in her pocket.

"Do you think it was Philip?"

"Something to do with him, certainly. Unless the dog groomer that started selling its own locally sourced shampoos wants to close my eyes forever. I'm not working on any real journalism right now except the Philip Pope story. And I've *never* worked on something that anyone would threaten me over. Rationally, at least."

"Have you gone to the police?"

She scrunched her face in confusion. "Are you kidding? They might tip someone off." She looked at the door once again.

She was too paranoid for her own good. I tried to reason with her. "I mean. I don't know." I shifted in my seat and rubbed my blushing cheeks. "It's just... if your life is in danger..."

"Threats like this mean we're looking in the right direction. They're on their heels."

The only person on their heels here felt like Amy but I kept my mouth shut. "Did you see anybody leave the note? Do you have a doorbell camera?"

She leaned forward. "Ever since I posted that article about Paradise of the Palisades and the McCanns, somebody has been watching me. There's this black SUV that sits on my block. No plates. Cops don't bother to come check it out when I call anonymously. The windows are tinted but I can see shadows inside. And no one sits in a parked car for hours unless they're watching someone."

I was bothered she'd kept this from me. I felt manipulated. "Why didn't you tell me you thought someone was watching you before?"

"I'm sorry, but I needed you. This story was dead if I couldn't get someone on the inside at Carson's Pass. I don't want you to think I'm using you." She reached across the table and put her hand on mine, but I yanked it back. "They don't know we're working together. I promise."

"You need to tell me everything. I'm risking my life here," when I said it, I realized for the first time it was true. I needed to get serious. I needed to get smarter.

"Ok, I will. That's all I kept from you. I promise."

"It's a big thing to keep," I said abruptly and slid from the booth. "I'm going to the bathroom."

I walked towards the back of the bar feeling everyone's eyes on me. Once there, I kept playing the part of Hollywood and laved cold water on my cheeks at the sink. Really, I just needed to feel clean. All the stress and traveling made my skin feel like unbrushed teeth.

A real case, just like I always wanted. One that fell into my lap. But truth be told I almost didn't want it. I wouldn't have wanted it if it weren't for finding Claire's pictures among the others. As I dabbed my cheeks dry, I paused and widened my eyes at my idiocy. I never told Amy I lived in Pacific Beach.

LOOK CLOSER

I had to confront her. I would be doing the opposite of what I wanted to do, which was say nothing and excuse myself. I walked back head high, shoes clacking confidently on the tile. I slid back in the booth and set my arms on the table. I pretended to be someone else, someone stronger. I stuck my neck out as I talked. "Amy, how'd you know to come to Pacific Beach? I never told you where I lived in San Diego."

"What?" She looked genuinely, drunkenly, confused.

"When we met the first time, and on the phone. I've only said I'm in San Diego. How'd you know to come to Pacific Beach?"

"It's on your Facebook."

I leaned back. I wish I could've laughed. I'd felt so smart finding the shoebox of missing girls, but all that ego was gone. Amy must've thought I was an idiot.

"Sorry to creep, but you know." She shrugged. "Way of the world these days."

"It's fine. *I'm* sorry. It's just that I felt I couldn't trust you for a minute, with you not telling me things and all."

"Let's put it in the past. I know we're both on edge. We're on to some serious shit. I want you to set up a PO box in Gypsum. We need to be able to communicate. I don't trust them with your mail at Carson's Pass."

"There are encrypted email services we could use."

She shook her head. "I'm not trusting anything digital. These fuckers removed results from Google, for God's sake. If we do this, we do it old-school. Pen and paper. Burn the letters after in the fireplace."

"Ok, I like it."

"Ok. And sorry I've been drinking. I'm just scared, Katie. We're going to be professional about this." She sat up straight. "What can you tell me about Carson's Pass? Anything interesting yet?"

I told her everything, from the photos in the wall to the dog and the incest. We agreed we'd look at the pictures somewhere more private, not in the open at the bar. But the one thing I didn't tell her was my connection to Claire.

When we got outside, it was dark and Amy was stumbling a little. I decided then that I was going to drive us both back to my house for the night. She was fine with it, but when she stopped at her car to get her things out of the trunk, I froze. "Amy." She held her arms akimbo for balance as she stepped up the curb and didn't respond. "Amy, have you searched your car for trackers?"

She paused and scratched her head. "Under the bumpers. I looked."

I'd done what I'd seen in a dozen TV shows, since the written world of crime seemed to be grounded in reality thus far, and I stuck my hands under the wheel wells.

Front, right: Nothing.

Back right: Nothing.

Back left: My hands found a little plastic box.

My heart soared. Fear once again eclipsed by pride. All the amateurism I'd displayed in front of Amy was redeemed. I twisted the box, and it came free from its adhesive patch.

I held it in my palm and stepped to her. "You might want to look closer."

Amy picked it up delicately like it might bite her. Her mouth was slightly agape. "I'm sorry," she said. "I'm so sorry."

But I realized why she had apologized, and my slight smile faded. Of course, she was sorry. Because now they knew she was visiting someone in Pacific Beach. And I'm sure it wouldn't be hard to put together who. I took the tracker and before we drove back, I stopped and threw it in a dumpster.

*

Back at my house, I spread out all the photographs from the box on the kitchen island. I separated the first five photos from the others. "These are the ones I already searched," I said. "Three got results, and all were active missing person cases. I marked the back with check marks and wrote their names." I picked up a photo to hand to Amy, but she was distracted, looking around my home in awe. She realized I was looking at her and she spun her head back to me, embarrassed. "I'm sorry. I don't mean to gawk."

"I grew up poor," I blurted out and blushed. I was hopelessly awkward in the face of wealth.

"I mean, I kinda figured you were wealthy when you mentioned it wouldn't be a problem to get into Carson's Pass. But I guess I forgot. Your Toyota is deceptive."

I shrugged. "Yeah. It's a good car."

"That's restraint. I'd be rotating Range Rovers if I were you."

I didn't know how to respond to that and went to get her a glass of water. Then I filled one for me too, so the gesture of "sober up" was less subtle.

"Do you want to keep these?" I asked and gestured at the photos.

"We're a team now. We each get a say. Do you want to photocopy these for me so we each have a set? Or should I try to figure out how these girls are connected while you keep your eyes peeled looking around Carson's Pass?"

I paused, chewing my lip. But I already knew. I wanted to stick to our original roles, and I knew she was suggesting it, too. She wouldn't have anything else to do if I didn't put her in charge of looking for a connection between the missing girls.

"You do it. I'll go back and keep searching the houses. I haven't searched my friend Miranda's yet or even my upstairs to be honest. There's plenty for me to do there."

"Just be careful. We'll communicate every day. Just a text or two so we know the other is okay. But make sure not to text anything serious."

I entertained her paranoia for now. "Ok. I'll mail you my PO box address as soon as I have it. Can you give me yours?" She gulped nervously as her eyes flickered over the pictures of the missing girls.

"Amy?" I said trying to get her attention.

"There's forty-six of them."

"Yeah."

"How can you possibly traffic that many people without a trace, I mean, is that even possible? Isn't it more likely..." Amy trailed off as her eyes danced over the pictures. "That the simpler answer is they're all dead?"

Amy and I didn't stay up much longer. I was tired from fear. Yet it was a primal, prey-like exhaustion where my mind and body were tired, but my eyes stayed wide awake. I wished I had brought the pistol back with me. Instead, I locked my bedroom door. I still didn't trust Amy 100%. Only after a scalding shower did my eyelids feel like ingots and I slept deeply under thick covers.

In the morning, neither of us ate breakfast. I was rarely hungry when I first woke up and coupled with my anxiety, the last thing I wanted was food. But in the daylight, I was feeling better. I felt my fear begin to evaporate with the shining sun.

I was ready to get back to Carson's Pass. I'd slapped the fear out of myself. Committing to do something difficult and dangerous was admirable. More admirable than anything I've ever done. And to think, somewhere in this I may find that I didn't kill my best friend with my silence. Maybe Claire didn't wander into those woods to take her own life.

I searched my car for trackers, but it was clean. The fact didn't bring me much solace. If Philip was tracking Amy, he would put two and two together after finding out that she had come to Pacific Beach. I drove her back to her car and when I stopped to let her out, she wrapped her arms around my neck and buried her face in my shoulder.

"Thank you," she cried. I was surprised and slowly put my arms around her. "I'm sorry I brought you into this. You don't have to keep going." She leaned away from me. Tears raced from her eyes. "If you don't go back, I won't blame you."

I set an awkward hand on her shoulder "We're going to get justice for those girls. And maybe make something of ourselves in the process."

"Ugh." She wiped her tears and then dried her hands on her thighs. "I'm always quick to cry when I'm hungover." She let out a little laugh. "I'm just not used to this. I've heard journalists talk about what it feels like to really have something. The fear and excitement. Financial freedom finally in sight. It's a thrill that I've been after since high school and now that it's in sight well… be careful what you wish for."

"I'm feeling the same," I said. It felt like there was more she wasn't telling me. Her tears were strange. Guilty.

"I'll try and find a connection with the missing girls. Keep looking around those houses. And please make sure to get out of there if you ever think you're not safe."

"I'll be okay."

Amy set her hand on mine and squeezed. "I mean it. If you think someone's going to hurt you, then get out. Don't wait."

"Of course," I said, and she looked away quickly and stepped out of the car.

*

I stopped and got a coffee and while I sat parked, I plugged Gypsum into my maps. The drive there was more than thirteen hours. 948 miles. It was already almost ten in the morning and I was not a long-haul driver. Time did not fly behind the wheel for me. My mind had the tendency to make four-hour trips feel like an eternity. I'd have to break it up. Six hours today, seven hours tomorrow. Give myself some time to cool down after everything that just happened. I had to decide whether I wanted to even stay in Carson's Pass. The box of pictures stashed in the wall creeped me out to no end. But how could I say no to Amy?

I couldn't flake out. Here I was, rich girl. Hobby journalist. If things got too deep, I could just climb out. Amy had mentioned with glee the possible financial freedom this case could bring for her, but was she just manipulating me?

She was smart. I couldn't help but think she said that to remind me that some people had to worry about bills.

I had plenty of time to think on the interstate as I made my way into the desert. But while I always plotted to do so, I never did much good thinking while driving. My mind just rotated in circles like the rubber below me.

I stopped that evening in some little town in Utah not far from the start of I-70. I found a diner and had pancakes for dinner and watched the traffic woosh and roar past the unwashed windows. I texted Howard telling him I was spending the night in a different town up the freeway a bit. It was a little lie, but it wasn't to deceive him. Sometimes it felt like I was always so easy to be found. In that moment, there was something cozy about the idea of no one in the entire world knowing where I was.

I should've called ahead because by the time I got in all the chain hotels were all booked. I got a room at a crappy motel with a monstrous parking lot behind it for truckers who, for reasons I tried not to think about as I stared at my bed, needed more space than their sleeper cabs supplied.

For a day of travel, I went to bed strangely happy. I think my body was relieved to finally feel hidden. I was tucked away in some transient corner of the country where no one looked at one another twice. And for what would be the last time in a long time, I felt unseen.

CROWN VICTORIA

Don't speed. Don't speed. Don't speed. It was my mantra all morning. Howard had texted when I was still asleep at 3am. He sent a photo of a firetruck and an ambulance. A crowd stood in their coats all hued in red and blue from the whirling emergency lights. Howard's texts only said something serious had happened. Then, at 3:47am he messaged again, saying the *coroner* van was there.

Of course, when I tried to get ahold of him this morning when I woke up, I got radio silence. I told myself it wasn't strange, which was true. Howard was probably up all night and then went to bed at dawn. It could be noon by the time I got ahold of him. I could be home.

Miranda hadn't answered when I called either and I bit my thumb nervously, consciously lifting my leaden foot from the gas pedal every few minutes. I took back everything I had said about the slow drives of my life. This one had a hellish kind of time dilation, like I was some god in a Greek myth, tortured so it seemed like ten minutes was equal to an hour.

My mind jumped to Miranda. She was living alone in Carson's Pass. I couldn't believe I let her come with me in the first place. It was just like me to entangle my friend in something dangerous and then leave a day later. I pounded the bottom of my fist on the wheel angrily.

I got to Gypsum around one in the afternoon and still had no new messages from Howard. I didn't use directions once I got there. The route was simple enough, even though everything looked a tad different since it had snowed while I had been away. I started driving into the mountains. When the roadside bar came into view, Fool's Gold, I remembered that's where I had to turn. I peeled onto the dirt road to Carson's Pass and finally gave it some gas. I passed a cop right away and cringed while hitting the brakes. It was one of those Ford sedans. The kind of cop car I grew up seeing as a kid. A Crown Vic.

He didn't wave. I just saw him eye my California plates and grimace at the gravel road ahead. The side of his cruiser read: Gypsum Police Department. I felt some relief. The cops here probably couldn't be bought by California money. If something happened to someone, they'd want to get to the bottom of it. Philip wouldn't be safe with his wealth and connections.

When I crested the little mountain, the clearing was empty. No cars. No people. Trees rocked in the wind and the clouds flew low and quick overhead like they were fleeing something. An anxious migration. When I got closer to our driveway, I saw another police car sitting near the end of the road by the little grocery store. When I was pulling up out front, Howard opened the front door before I even parked. The wind tossed his hair as he stood in the doorway and I turned off the car and raced to him. "What happened?" I gave him a hug and simultaneously pushed him inside to get out of the wind. "Why didn't you get back to me?"

He shut the door behind us, and the world became suddenly silent. "I didn't want you worried, and I didn't want to lie to you."

"Well, I was pretty fucking worried anyway. You should've called. Miranda hasn't gotten back to me either."

"She's in the guestroom, still sleeping. I invited her over after last night."

"What happened?"

"Do you remember Leah and Ted, the Miller couple?"

They were the two who couldn't keep their hands off each other at the welcome bonfire. "Yeah," I said quickly. "Sure."

Howard rubbed his cheek as if there was something he didn't want to say. "They're dead."

"What?" I said quietly.

"They were found last night. Dead in their house." I walked into the living room slowly and sank onto the ottoman. Howard followed me, worried. "Are you ok? It's not as bad as it sounds."

"It's not as bad as it *sounds*?" I said. "Are you joking?"

"At first, we were all freaking out. The grocery kid, Jacob, found them. We didn't know anything when the circus arrived. It was cops, firetrucks, every first responder in the county. Me and Miranda were both in the crowd watching and we saw them take out *bodies*. No one was telling us anything. Miranda didn't want to go back and sleep at home all alone, so I brought her here. She needed a bit of liquid courage to get to sleep. But anyway, I finally spoke to Philip this morning and the police are saying there's no threat to the community. Which is code for..." Howard made a finger gun and shot me and then himself. "Domestic. Hubby killed her and then himself or something. There's no threat because the threat is dead."

I set my elbows on my knees and bent over. I was tired from driving. Tired from stress, and now a pretty young couple hasn't just disappeared... They're dead. "No," I said firmly. "No, that can't be right. Did you see them together? When I saw them you practically couldn't pry them apart."

Howard looked at me, disappointed, as if I'd said something stupid. "Couples like that always have the most skeletons. The brightest flames burn the hottest and all that. I've been thinking about how sometimes couples move somewhere because they need a fresh start. They think new scenery will change their relationship. Things don't work out and one of them realizes they're stuck with a partner they hate and then boom. Ah, fuck." He started laughing and I frowned.

"What?"

"I hope you don't think I meant we're like that, too."

"No." I shook my head violently. "Of course not. I get what you're saying."

"Right. Our circumstances and why we're here are a little different. Besides, let's face it you'd probably be the one to murder me."

"Howard?" My breath had become ragged and anxious.

"What?"

"I think this might have something to do with why I'm here."

"Their deaths?" He squinted at me and I nodded. "Why do you say that?"

"Because I'm not—" I closed my eyes and breathed. "Did Miranda not tell you last night?"

"Tell me what?" his voice rose in annoyance.

I was actually shocked that Miranda had kept her mouth shut even after people had been murdered. "I'm not investigating Philip for embezzlement. I'm investigating him for human trafficking."

Howard let out a single, sarcastic hiccup. "Seriously?"

"I can show you everything. There's plenty of evidence," my voice sped up as I defended myself. "People have gone missing. Young women, girls. One time a whole family. I found a box of missing person photos in a secret compartment downstairs. I can—"

He held up his hand gently and I stopped. "Why didn't you tell me?" He looked hurt. His brow wrinkled and his eyes softened. My guardedness subsided and my shoulders sank.

"I didn't want you to say no to coming here. I felt like I had to do this. And if you said no and I went anyway, we'd be done."

He looked away from me. "Maybe we should be done."

"What?"

"Divorced. Get it over with."

I felt sick. "Is that what you want?"

He stared at me for a moment and I watched white-hot anger flicker in his eyes. "No!" he shouted, and I flinched. I looked at him cautiously, like an animal that'd been hit. He held out his hands gently. "Sorry," he said quieter. "I'm sorry. It's not what I want. I *want* you to talk to me. I want to trust you. The fucking basics, Katie. And that's manipulative shit, you know that. How were you ok with not even telling me why you wanted to move across the country?"

"I kinda told you." I closed my eyes in shame as soon as I said it.

"You kind of didn't," his voice was harsher now. "You said some journalist was interested in Philip for financial crimes, not human fucking trafficking."

"Keep your voice down."

He suddenly looked around the room. "You think this place could be bugged?"

"No." But my stomach dropped; I had never even considered the house could be bugged. I just didn't want him to wake Miranda with our fighting.

"All these years and you still don't think I can tell when you're lying?"

"I didn't know we'd be in danger here."

"What did you think this was going to be? That you'd play your detective game while I just sat in the dark?"

I paused. Him saying "detective game" was exactly why I kept this from him. Even in a universe where Howard did agree to come to Carson's Pass knowing the full truth he would've been belittling. He never would've believed me. He'd pat my back and act like a parent that was entertaining their child's make-believe.

I looked at my feet. "I wanted to show you that I was capable of something. Show everyone. Surprise! See? Katie doesn't just review what she binge-watches on HBO. Look at me, world. I *did* something with my life."

"I understand where you're coming from. I get it. But right now, our new neighbors are dead. And are you saying you think they were both murdered?"

I didn't respond right away. I just stared at the far wall in thought. It didn't make any sense. Those forty-six girls were missing cases. Even if they were killed, it hadn't happened out in the open like this. The Millers were found. The police were here. Maybe the truth was the obvious answer: A husband was far more likely to kill his wife than some stranger.

"I have no idea," I said. And I really didn't. This time, I wasn't lying. I was missing something.

Howard went upstairs to cool down and shower off. Miranda came out of the guest bedroom a half hour later. I couldn't help but think we'd woken her up with our fighting, but she stayed in bed to be polite.

"Morning," I said, realizing it was well past noon. "Or afternoon I guess."

"Ugh. I hate sleeping this late."

"I think it's ok, considering the circumstances."

Miranda shook her head remembering the night before. "So, are we leaving? I take it Howard told you everything."

"He did, and he learned this morning that the cops think it was a domestic situation."

"What do you mean—like murder-suicide?"

"Yeah."

"Huh." She scrunched her face. "You know, I ran into them at the market a couple days ago and they invited me over for dinner on Friday. Who makes dinner plans right before doing something like that?"

"Well, who asked you to dinner?"

"Oh." Her shoulders sank. "Yeah, the wife," Miranda looked at me quickly. "They think it was the husband that did it, right?"

"I don't know. I'm assuming."

"It's just... *awful.*" Miranda sat on a stool at the kitchen island. "To think that happened next door and I had no idea. I mean, I keep wondering where I was exactly when it happened. What was I doing the second he pulled the trigger?" I caught her staring at a wine bottle by the coffee maker. Her eyes kept glancing back to it.

"Do you want a drink?" I gestured at the bottle. "I'd even join you."

"Ugh," she said in relief. "Please, I need to throw a shade over this ugly world."

I poured two glasses in a kind of silent ritual. Then we sat in silence for a minute, sipping.

"So," Miranda said as she swirled her wine. "Does Howard not want to leave anymore? You should've seen him last night—he was a man on a mission. He was set on getting the hell out of here."

"I think the domestic news settled him down. But didn't you want to leave too?"

"Of course," she lowered her voice and looked towards the stairs. "But your husband was hysterical about it. You know me, I'm not rash. I'm not driving down a mountain pass with all my possessions at four in the morning. Especially when every cop in a one-hundred-mile radius was here last night. You should've seen it. I saw police cars from *Aspen*. They came from all around to take a look. I guess there's probably not a lot of murders around here. I can only imagine their disappointment when they figured out it was already solved."

"Is it though? I mean, you met the Millers. Were they always as lovey as they were when I saw them at that bonfire?"

"Oh, no." Miranda laughed. "I'm already tuned into the gossip machine. The McCarthys live near them. They said before it got cold enough to keep the windows closed it was fireworks from their house every night. *Screaming*. And I mean they're not that close. They were hearing that from a hundred yards away."

"Really?"

"I know this is super insensitive, but I feel validated. Whenever I saw the Millers together it was disgusting. It was like they were a high school couple who just discovered love. I always figured couples who acted like that were fucked up behind closed doors and now I have my proof. Love isn't a fairytale."

We heard Howard on the steps, and both looked over our shoulders as he came into the kitchen. "Hello." He smiled when he saw our wine glasses. "Do you mind if I join you?"

"Please," I pulled out a stool for him and he poured himself a small glass and sighed as he sat.

"We were just discussing lovey-dovey couples," said Miranda. "The perennial honeymooners who deep down really want to kill each other."

"Well, your hypothesis seems to be half-right. Poor girl."

"Who, the Misses? Don't feel bad for her. When Jane McCarthy told me about their fights, she said it was Leah Miller who would yell the loudest. We don't even know who killed who."

"Fair enough. Katie's told me the secret you two have been keeping. I hear you're both breaking the human trafficking case of the century."

His sarcasm made me feel small. And again, I felt less guilt for lying to him about why I was coming here.

"I was just supporting a friend," said Miranda. "I'm not looking into anything."

"But you moved here still knowing all this?"

Miranda threw her hair over her shoulder and crossed her arms. "Someone needs to support your wife."

Howard drummed his fingers on the counter and looked embarrassed. "So, do you think they're still doing a welcome bonfire today?"

"There's new people?" I said, happy to change the subject.

"If they weren't scared off by this. When Philip dropped by to tell me about the Millers deaths being domestic, he also said to be at the garden around four. I guess we're having another welcoming committee. But tell me..." He shook his head annoyed. "You really believe that old architect is a murderer?"

"Yeah." I surprised myself as I suddenly stood. "I have to show you two something."

Downstairs, Howard and Miranda both stood as I bent and unscrewed the faceplate of the outlet. "It's a hidden switch." I turned around to them quickly and saw Howard mouthing something to Miranda. They both straightened up and stared at me. I looked back to the outlet, reached my hand in, and flipped the tiny lever. As the section of the wall dropped open wide, so did their eyelids.

"There was a box in here full of old photos of missing girls."

Howard bent so he could see in and squinted. "Where is it now?"

"It's part of why I went back to San Diego. I had to give it to the woman I'm working with. She's looking for connections between the cases."

"You find a box in the wall, in the basement, full of photos of missing girls and you don't come and show me?"

Miranda looked at us sideways, pleadingly. The kind of look you give when you're about to be plunged awkwardly into the middle of an argument.

I looked at the floor. "I messed up. I'm telling you now."

"Do you believe this?" He pointed at Miranda. Her eyes widened in panic as she realized she was being asked to pick sides.

"Maybe. She told me some messed up stuff connected to Philip."

"Oh, she told *you*. But not her husband. Bravo, Katie. You make me feel great about us."

He flapped his hand dismissively and marched up the stairs. I looked to Miranda to say I was sorry, but I paused because instead of being mortified, it looked like she was trying not to laugh.

I knew Howard was already drumming up the sarcastic comments he'd make about my work. "Playing detective." "The human trafficking case of the century." I wished he realized how small those comments made me feel.

"Whew," Miranda said and whistled.

"Sorry." Howard usually had the self-awareness to never fight with me in front of others. But it was the wine, my lies, and, of course, the dead neighbors. I really couldn't blame him.

Back upstairs, Howard was talking to someone at the front door and Miranda and I went quickly to see who. Philip glanced past Howard's shoulder and gave us a tight-lipped, apologetic nod. "I was just telling your husband that we're all gathering in the garden. The Sheriff will be there to answer questions. And I suppose I have some explaining to do as well. I'm so, so sorry this has happened. It's just awful." Philip spoke like he was reading a script. There was something off about his tone. I crossed my arms and tried not study him so hard that he'd notice.

"It's ok," said Howard.

Philip cleared his throat. "It's not ok. I wish there was something I could've seen in the application process. As you know there's a background check and the Millers were spotless. Typically, there's prior abuse to something like this happening. We weren't so lucky."

I thought I put my finger on what was wrong with his tone, he was annoyed. Angry beneath the surface. This incident would cost him money and maybe the whole project if everyone wanted out of Carson's Pass.

"We'll be there," I said. "When?"

"Now, if you don't mind. I'll meet you all there in just a second. I have a couple more doors to knock on." He turned on his heel and I watched him grasp his hands behind his back as he walked, his knuckles whitening as he squeezed his wrist in rage.

Howard shut the door but stayed facing it. "You're telling me that dweeby architect is a criminal mastermind?"

"I don't know, Howard. But I know I have evidence that suggests something shady is going on here."

Howard stared at me intently before speaking. "If those two were murdered, you don't really want to stay here—do you?"

There was no way I was going to let Howard be right and just leave. I was staying. But Miranda spoke before I could. "Did Philip seem angry or is it just me?"

"It's not just you," I said. "He was pissed."

"Yeah, because this entire project could be over today if people leave. I think we're jumping to conclusions by assuming the Millers were murdered. What's the motive—that they saw something they weren't supposed to? Don't you think that's a situation a human trafficker would account for when creating this place?"

I agreed with her there. "Yeah."

"And what's the term for the most likely answer is usually the right one?"

"Occam's Razor," said Howard.

Miranda stood between us as she talked. "So, a couple who've been heard fighting frequently are found dead. What's the most likely answer here?" Howard and I both said nothing. "I know it's not sexy or exhilarating or a good story, but it probably was just murder-suicide if that's what the police are saying. I mean life's not the movies. You can't just kill two people and make it look like something else. There's blood splatter and bullet trajectories and defensive wounds. There's an entire story in a crime scene and it's hard to make one up."

Howard took his coat from the wall and started worming his arms into it. "Well, the police here don't exactly seem well funded. They're still driving cop cars from fifteen years ago."

"What's money got to do with detective work?" I said.

"I'm just saying that it didn't seem like the pro's were on the case last night."

I was annoyed. It seemed like something an out of touch rich person would say. "Why? Because they weren't in the latest model of Chevy Suburban?"

Howard rolled his eyes and Miranda stuck her arms out. "Guys, please. Let's just go to the meeting. Have the cops answer our questions."

I felt silly then, the way I was flaring my nostrils at my husband ready for war. So petty was my pride that I didn't even want to tell Miranda that she was right. That we should just shut up and not jump to our own conclusions. I sat to lace my boots and soon we were walking to the garden. And I still felt sure there was a murderer in our midst.

WHO KILLED WHO?

We walked into the garden with tight smiles and were greeted with the same. Someone had lit a bonfire, but no one sat. Everyone stood in a circle and made room for us as we approached. "How are you all?" the hippy woman, Jodie, asked us with kind eyes.

"Processing," said Howard, and she nodded solemnly with a squint as if Howard had said something very wise.

"We're processing, too. We moved here for peace. To never have to read about such nasty things in the newspaper, knowing they were happening just down the street. And now…"

"This is the closest I've been to something like this," Miles McCarthy stepped forward. "I mean, when I lived in Brooklyn there was a shooting every now and again, but this? This is a door down." Both the McCarthys were much livelier than they were the first time we met them. Maybe their son was right and they were high when we first met them.

"You're looking at this the wrong way." We all turned. It was the old man that had been sitting by the fire alone the first time I'd been here. He had just gotten to the garden and looked at the fire as he spoke. "You could build a gang-less, crimeless, all Ivy-educated city and still, a husband will kill his wife now and again. That is the way of the world. It is not something you can escape from. That is unless you want to live a hundred miles away from anybody."

Nobody said anything. They kicked their feet and coughed awkwardly, clearing the air. I saw Philip's aide, Jessica, start walking towards the road as she answered a phone call. Movement took my gaze to the woods, where I saw the McCarthy twins talking quietly with one another.

I stared at them intently. Too intently, because when Kenna stared back at me, I watched her eyes widen in fear like she'd been seen. She averted her gaze quickly back to her brother, and when Aidan saw her changed expression his face grew serious, too. But before he looked towards me, I looked back quickly to the bonfire.

Soon we were all staring down the path as Philip walked with the sheriff in front of him. The Sheriff took off his gloves, rubbed his hands together, and started shaking all of our hands. I was a bit confused at the hospitality but remembered he was a politician, and we were new to his county. And rich.

He looked exactly like a rural county sheriff would in my head. Jowly, freshly shaven and maybe a tad overweight. When he'd shaken all of our hands, he put his gloves back on. "I'm so sorry, folks. Wish I could've met you under better circumstances. I'm Sheriff Casey."

Kenna came walking up with her arms crossed. "Who killed who?"

The sheriff tilted his head back and considered Kenna. "Excuse me?"

"I mean, it was the husband, right?"

"Um. Well..." He took off his hat and scratched his head. "Their bodies are still at the coroner's. See, we're waiting on toxicology to make sure there wasn't anything more to this. They both had single fatal gunshot wounds." Kenna stared at him, undaunted, waiting for an answer.

"But at the moment, it appears that the husband shot the wife and then turned the weapon on himself."

I watched another cop emerge from the woods, but he walked slowly and stayed on the perimeter of the garden, like a mysterious funeral guest. He wore a tan windbreaker with his badge shining on his belt. I figured he must be a detective and it's more than germane to mention that he was handsome. I mean one in a thousand men, Hollywood handsome. He had dark eyes, dark hair and sharp dark stubble. He looked like he should be climbing out of the sea in a cologne commercial.

"The whole thing is pretty cut and dry," said the sheriff. "There's nothing to indicate this was anything other than a domestic dispute. It's just one of those tragic calls I get too

108

often." His handcuffs jingled as he hiked up his utility belt uncomfortably. The handsome detective stuffed his hands in his pockets and watched the sheriff skeptically.

"Did he have a record? How the hell was someone like that allowed in here?" said David, the hippie woman's husband. The question seemed directed at both the sheriff and Philip and they looked at each other for a moment before Philip turned to speak.

"He had no record of violence. No record of anything. The same as all of you. I'm sorry, but there wasn't any way of stopping this short of having applicants complete psych evals. And we don't want to invade your privacy." There was some whispering in the small crowd and Philip held his hands out. "Does anyone have questions for the sheriff?"

"Are we safe here?" Howard asked while watching the sheriff closely. It looked like he was gauging his reaction to the question.

"You are. There's no threat. As scary as all this was."

Howard nodded, satisfied. I wanted to ask specifics. How did they know it was the husband? Why didn't anybody hear gunshots? Was it a small caliber weapon? Why did Jacob the grocery kid find them so late—had they placed an order for delivery? But I felt like I couldn't do it here. I was afraid any suspicion would give Philip reason to be onto me. The police said it was a murder-suicide. Cut and dry.

"So," said Philip. "I've been talking with Jessica and have already called some of the investors and it's agreed. If you want to leave, we'll buy your home back from you. We don't have any interest in residents who don't want to be here. It's not going to lend a sense of community to anybody. No need to make up your minds now. Discuss. Sleep on it. The offer stands until this time tomorrow."

Miranda showed a bit of surprise at the offer. I was hoping she would go. It was a mistake to let her come in the first place.

The sheriff took off his gloves for another round of somber smiles and handshakes. Afterward, he started back down the trail alone. I looked for the handsome detective and saw him stare down the sheriff as he walked past. There was something going on between those two.

I was distracted watching them and flinched as Philip clapped his hands to get our attention. He looked at his watch. "Everyone, please stick around. I know these aren't the best of circumstances. But please try to find your smiles. We're still doing our welcoming committee."

I had assumed it had been called off. "You can't be serious," I said and walked to Philip. "You want us to talk to new people and not bring this up?"

"What do you want me to do? Have them stay in a hotel until the shock of all this subsides? Besides, I think *you* specifically may be pleasantly surprised."

I was going to ask why when I was cut off. Two blond bobs of hair came down out of the woods and raced by my elbows shouting, "Hi, Aunt Katie!" I looked up the trail with my mouth hanging open.

And I was still speechless as Beatrice came up to me, beaming.

"Surprise! I hope you didn't think you were going to have all the fun in Colorado without me!"

STUPID, IDIOT

I couldn't have found my smile if I tried. Beatrice outstretched her arms for a hug and the embrace brought me back to reality. I slowly hugged her back.

"Don't be too happy to see me!"

"Beatrice," I spoke bewildered over her shoulder. "What the hell?"

She laughed. "I wanted it to be a surprise. We heard about what happened." She leaned into my ear and whispered. "Just our luck. I bet me and Randy would've got our place a lot cheaper if we waited a week."

"What are you doing here?"

"We're living here! I thought it sounded super cool after you told me, so we applied for one of the affordable homes for funsies and they said they really want families! I told them to keep it a secret from you."

"This is... great! Really." I furrowed my brow, angry at myself. Was I going to pretend to be nice for the rest of my life? I nodded at Randy. He had a big, stupid smile on his face. We were in Colorado, and he was high, of course. I took Beatrice gently by the elbow so we weren't in earshot of others.

"You do know Howard and I aren't going to live here full time. It's more of a winter place, that's the plan."

"I know that!"

"But we're only here a few months out of the year."

"What makes you think we'd need you and Howard to be happy here? It's incredible!" She wheeled around with her arms extended to the sky.

"I mean, it might get lonely." I needed to stop. I was talking like she wasn't already here. Like I could still talk her out of it.

"There's other people, Katie. We didn't move here just because *you* are here, too."

111

I watched Beatrice look past me as Miranda stepped forward and gave her a quick hug. "Oh my god! I can't believe it's you guys!"

"I know. It's a nice surprise, isn't it?" she said to slight me. "San Diego was getting so expensive. The affordable homes here aren't bad. I can work remote, it's just a longer drive to the post office. And Randy got a job groundskeeping!"

"That's awesome! I can't believe you did all this and kept it secret. That had to be such a hard move."

"We made it work. That school district suspended the boys *again* and for nothing. It just felt like it was time to go. Stars aligned. Randy and I have always been doers. Goers. When the universe gives us a sign, we take it."

"Well, I'll say hi to the boys." Miranda looked over her shoulder at me sympathetically as she walked away.

Bea nodded her head at Miranda's back. "*She* was excited."

I was distracted by her mentioning that Randy had gotten a job. She and the boys would be in the houses we were worried about. Then again, Amy and I's theory that they would traffic people from employee housing was only that—a theory. I composed myself. "Beatrice I'm excited too, it's just... first Chicago, and then you moved to San Diego. Can you blame me for being skeptical about why you moved out here?"

"Sorry, I didn't know I needed your permission to move. And I'm not getting into this with you again. Not now, I'm in a good mood. I had been thinking of moving to Chicago before you applied to college there. And everybody was moving to SoCal. You're not that special, Katie. Why can't you be happy? I mean, you get to be by your nephews and your sister. Why is this a bad thing? I honestly thought for once you might be happy with me."

"It's just sudden. I'm sorry," Howard was talking with Randy and I couldn't imagine what about. I pointed at Randy. "And he's onboard with this?" I couldn't picture Randy living more than ten minutes from an abundance of fast-food restaurants and liquor stores.

"Randy *loves* nature." I looked over to see him on his phone, hitting a vape that was half hidden up his sleeve. "You don't know us at all. I pictured a happy reunion. But really, I knew this would happen. Try being happy for other people. Just because I didn't marry filthy rich like you doesn't mean I can't make big life changes."

"That's not what—"

Suddenly we turned as Braxton or Brayden yelled, "Stupid, idiot!" One of the brothers hit the other over the head with a thin stick that cracked in two. They started wrestling in the snow and Bea marched off yelling.

Randy didn't step over to help. While everyone was busy watching the boys, I noticed he was taking the opportunity to flick me off like a middle schooler. He rubbed his middle finger on his oily forehead pretending to scratch an itch. He had always hated me. Probably because of how much Bea complained about me to him when they were alone. He knew my sour reaction to their arrival would launch an hour-long tirade he'd have to listen to. I watched him look into the fire and mouth, "Bitch."

I took a long breath trying to ignore him. Some men love the word bitch and Randy was one of them. It's an insult and a label. "She's a bitch," one man will say, and another will nod. As if that says enough about a woman's entire personality. If a guy's a dick and I call him that it isn't the same. Some will think he's just confident or a lady's man. But bitch isn't open-ended.

Randy's a man-child incapable of handling complex emotions. His masculine ego is so fragile he cringes at the idea of changing a diaper. He's in desperate need of therapy, a bath and personal responsibility. But that's all too complicated for him. His insult wins because that's a mouthful, and I'm just a bitch.

I thought about saying something to him but instead I did what I'd done for thirty-six years, and I say nothing. Quiet again. One day, I think. You'll get yours, Randall Duffy.

Howard took advantage of the commotion to come over to me.

"Fuck."

"Thank you," I said. "I agree."

He laughed and I felt myself smile a little. He got closer and whispered, "You don't think you could tell her about the crimes? About why you're really here?"

"She'd say I was lying and just trying to scare her off. Even if I showed her the evidence she'd probably scoff. Not only that, but I could see her telling Philip to spite me."

"I could talk to Philip..."

"What do you mean?"

"We paid a lot more. I could explain the situation. Clingy, crazy sister, following you across the country for the third time. I could probably kick them out."

I literally recoiled. "We can't do that."

"I bet we can."

I didn't know why Howard was bringing it up. He knew I'd never throw her out like that. "I mean we *can't*. I'm not doing it. I'm not backstabbing my sister like that. She's here." I pointed at the boys. "They're here."

"Ok, if you're sure. But I'm in this too, and I don't want them here. I'd prefer if you were happier and not stressing about her."

"I'm sorry, but no. I can't do that to her."

"I knew you'd say that," he sighed and stared at me until I met his eye. "Just know, Katie, one day you'll learn that blood isn't thicker than water." He walked towards the coffee dispenser and I took the opportunity to slip off. I didn't even say anything to Miranda or look over my shoulder to see if anyone noticed me leave. I walked back down the trail with Howard's words about family echoing in my head.

I had spent my entire life apologizing and sucking up to my sister. A normal woman with a backbone would've burned this bridge years ago. But she was so good at guilting me, and I was even better at giving into it. Now she'd followed me a third time, playing the spoiler. And how could she not when she got off on it? She knew I'd let her. Quiet Katie will cope.

I was so used to Beatrice stealing the show that typically, I'd just take it. Walking home, I felt like I'd made some personal progress. I guess it was a little growth that I left the welcome bonfire instead of sitting and smiling through it.

Halfway back, where the trail crossed the road, the handsome detective stood texting next to his car. It was a newer model Ford, and I figured he wasn't with the county sheriff's office. If he was a homicide detective he'd be from a more populous part of the state. I didn't even think, I just veered towards him. I raised a hand up awkwardly. A waist high wave. "Hi," I said.

He looked up at me and then back to his phone before putting it in his pocket. "Hello." He smiled, showing teeth whiter than snow. "Jack Martin, State PD." He shook my hand and said nothing else. He was waiting for me to tell him why I had come over.

"Homicide?" I asked.

He chuckled and looked at his feet. "Your uh... sensei?" he said speaking of Philip "He wouldn't be very happy if I said so. But yes."

"Oh, you mean our cult leader?" I said teasingly.

"I was just looking for a euphemism."

"That's quite polite of you."

"But can I put that on the record?" He smiled slyly and pulled a pen from behind his ear. He clicked it a few times. "This *is* a cult then?"

"I'm not in it, unfortunately. I just wanted a house in the woods that I could still order a pizza to at 10pm."

"Well, who doesn't want that?"

"So," I sighed to indicate a change of subject. "You're just wrapping up then? Making sure there's nothing you missed?"

He eyed me skeptically and the flirting fell from his voice. "Why do you ask?"

"The sheriff says it's cut and dry. Murder-suicide. Bang, bang. If that's true, I imagine you're just wrapping up is all."

He eyed me for a moment. "Look, I have to be delicate. I don't want to ruffle feathers and contradict or start a panic but there's a few things we need to piece together. The county police are rushing this. The sheriff is especially keen to have this over with and I can't help but think that Philip fella is promising some campaign cash to keep it cut and dry."

My eyes bulged. "So, there was foul play?"

"No, no, no." He held both hands out. "No one's saying that. There are just some parts that need piecing together. Like a motive, for instance. We don't have one. I want to do interviews and the sheriff is saying there's no need for that." He patted the phone in his pocket. "But he'll be getting a call this evening from my superior telling him too bad."

Since learning of the murders, I'd been feeling alone and overwhelmed but now I had someone I could maybe work with. "I'll give an interview," I said.

"Did you know the Millers?"

"Kind of. I met them a couple times," I lied. "But I know some stuff about this place that I think would be worth your time to hear."

He looked me over, maybe he thought I was some true crime junkie trying to interject myself in the case. Or that I had a crush on him. He was probably used to women wanting to get alone with him. But my heart lifted as he nodded.

"Ok, anything helps."

"Right now?" I asked, pointing at the ground.

"No," he said quickly. "No, I can't do now. I have to go back to the scene for a little bit. Are you free this evening?"

"Yeah," I said too eagerly.

"Ok, can you meet me at the bar at the bottom of the road?"

"Fool's Gold?"

"Yeah."

"I can do that."

He opened his car door and got behind the wheel. "Be there at seven."

MOUNTAIN TOPS

I cupped my cheek in my palm as I peed—a portrait of a woman in thought. I didn't tell Howard I was meeting a handsome man at a bar. When I put it that way, I should've felt a lot worse than I did. But this was business and besides, I didn't want to hear some snarky comment about how I was wasting the detective's time with my games.

I stood, flushed and washed my hands. Howard's doubt only filled me with the determination to keep going. I wasn't going to high-tail it out of Carson's Pass after two nights. I was going to finish what I started.

I went to my closet and selected a bookish look. Dark jeans, black sweater. Serious. I went into the den to find Howard at his computer. I told him I was going to Gypsum to open a PO box. It was a half-truth, I would have to do that tomorrow, but I hadn't noticed the slip in my lie until I said it. The problem was that it was 6:45 and the post office would be closed. But Howard just shrugged. "Have fun," he said and looked back to the computer screen. It's possible he knew they were closed and wanted me to drive all the way there only to come back looking like an idiot. He'd smile like a jackass and shake his head at my idiocy.

I was entering the danger zone for any relationship. That moment where you start thinking your partner is thinking ill of you without evidence. I realized he probably just thought I needed space after Bea's sudden arrival. He wasn't going to question me. I bent over and kissed his cheek and the spot my lips hit fell into a dimple as he smiled.

"I love you," I said.

"Be careful on those roads."

"I'll be fine. There's no ice."

"Drive like there is."

I went all the way downstairs and put on my boots before I realized I'd left my phone upstairs. I went back up and picked it up off my nightstand. I decided to be sweet and poke my head back into the den to give Howard a kiss goodbye.

"Hey!" I said as I ducked in through the doorway. Howard wasn't expecting me. He jumped in his seat and then sighed, pissed off. There was a stack of papers in front of him and his phone was laid flat on the desk taking a call. "Let me call you back," he said and hung up.

He calmly moved the papers to the other side of the desk, but I could still see them. There was a name printed on the front sheet, "Ryan Westerberg." It looked like a movie script.

"You pivoting to screenwriting?" I asked, half-joking.

"Ok, you caught me." Howard held up his hands. "I can't just retire this young so I'm working on a little something. My friend, Tom, knows some producers in LA... and I figured well... why not put my creativity to work?" He cringed and reddened as he spoke. Howard liked to keep his cards close to his chest and I could tell it pained him to be caught with this. He probably felt foolish since he, like me, was also taking a shot at something he'd never done before.

Maybe his belittling of my project came from his own insecurities about trying something new. I felt a hundred pounds lighter. My husband wasn't being mean for the sake of it.

"Well," I said, "You don't have to show me yet. But if you want another set of eyes..."

He grinned and nodded. "Ok, ok. I'll let you see it, just give me a bit."

I leaned forward and kissed him on the cheek. This is what our relationship needed. It felt like we were both vulnerable now. Each of us taking new chances in life. "I'll see you in a little bit."

Outside it was freezing and I walked quickly to my car. When I got behind the wheel, the first thing I did was lock all the doors. It was probably just the dark and my overactive imagination, but I felt watched. I was used to the white noise of the city and the silent forest made my hair stand on end.

119

I glanced out the window at the woods as I drove. The mountains were visible under the moonlight. But I couldn't admire their beauty before my stomach dropped. Up on a ridgeline, what might've been miles away, a light sliced the dark. It was the broad, expanding beam of a flashlight. And it bobbed as whoever held it walked. I slowed down to watch it, my mouth opening a little in wonder. My first thought was that it was Jack. Searching the woods with a flashlight was certainly the kind of thing a detective would do. At least in my mind. Then I realized if he was meeting me at seven, he'd have no time to get down from there. Besides, he was dangerously far up the mountain. Pointlessly far. What could possibly be up there?

The light swept so it no longer illuminated the side of the mountain. Whoever held the light was now looking down into Carson's Pass. They were looking toward me. Just as I told myself it must be hunters, hikers, or someone far more comfortable with the woods than I could ever imagine being, the light blinked out and the blackness was intact again. I held onto the steering wheel tight and felt my heartbeat quicken. *Come back*, I asked of the light. *Come back.*

But it didn't. I waited thirty seconds. A minute. Nothing. The idea of someone being out there made my skin crawl under my heavy coat. I started driving again, slowly, with my eyes latched onto the mountain. And I was all but certain someone was staring back.

I wanted to turn around. As I left the clearing of Carson's Pass and started downhill in the woods, I kept picturing spike strips, or a tree felled over the road as a barricade. I should've brought the pistol if just for peace of mind. But none of that happened.

Several minutes later, I let out a breath as I saw the lights of Fool's Gold through the trees. Of course, the anxiety lingered. I had to drive back. And by then it would be even later.

There were a few pickups in the parking lot. The only sedan I saw was the detective's car from earlier and my shoulders sank a little in disappointment. I wished he wasn't here. I wanted to have some sort of answer to the light I'd seen. I wanted Jack to knock on my door the next day saying sorry he missed me, but he had pressing matters to investigate in the woods.

I practically flew from my car once I parked. When I pulled open the back door to the bar that familiar smell wafted out to me—a mingling of beer and light cigarettes smoked decades ago. That dive bar scent that seems the same everywhere, like the identical odor of dumpsters. But there was a mustiness behind it, like the place was molding over.

I tried not to flare my nostrils at the smell while I was regarded by two tired looking men in flannels and stained ball caps. Jack sat squinting at some papers in front of him. When he saw me, he moved them into his briefcase and raised his beer from the bar in greeting.

The bartender turned towards me. Her heavy hips swayed as she walked.

"Hey!" she said as I walked the length of the bar to Jack. "Get you something?"

I hesitated. I wanted to fit in by picking the right drink. "Uh, a beer please."

"Any in particular?" she said, still smiling.

"Uh, Heineken?" I pointed at the tap head.

"Sorry, hun, kegs dry," she tapped the Coors spout. "What about a Banquet? Always cold on tap."

"Sure," I said and sat next to Jack.

"Good choice," he said and nodded down at his beer.

"She picked for me." I looked around. The place was more modern than I'd expected. I had pictured pine paneling and buck mounts but the walls were bare of those things. The lack of taxidermy certainly threw me off. Then again, most the of places you'd hang a deer head were occupied by brand-new flat screens showing different sports.

She set my beer in front of me. It was an awful pour. Mostly foam. When I looked up to her to say thanks she'd already started towards the other end of the bar. I thought her nice greeting was genuine but now I wasn't so sure.

I titled my glass and considered the foam. "I don't think she likes me."

"What makes you think that? We love rich Californians who buy land in Colorado."

"Is it that obvious that's where I'm from?"

He ran his eyes over me and shrugged slyly. "No. I told the bartender I'm a forester. She thinks you're here to discuss replanting logging sites with me. They're very curious about those deaths last night. I wouldn't let on that you live up there."

"Thanks. And I didn't think my outfit screamed California." I looked down at my sweater. "And by the way, you might be surprised. Some of us are nice additions. Or at least nice people."

"Oh yeah? Did you see your house in person before you bought it?" I blushed, defeated and laughed. "I take that as a no."

"We wouldn't have bought it if it were in an actual neighborhood that would drive up prices." I was trying to keep the conversation in jest but felt myself getting defensive.

"Hey, don't worry about it. I kid. It's beautiful here but sometimes pretty boring. It's fun to have an enemy. An us-versus-them. Keeps things interesting."

"I'm not picking sides." I held up my hands innocently. "I'm just here for the views."

"Hmm." He narrowed his eyes at me. "That's what they all say. Next thing you know the local coffeehouse burns down under mysterious circumstances and there's a petition to replace it with a Starbucks."

"Is that so?" I smiled.

"I'm just saying." He tossed his head back to finish the last sip of his beer. It wasn't a professional look. I thought maybe he was one of those guys who always kept his guard down with women, or maybe it was just a reflex from frat days. Regardless, the drinking and the banter felt too casual for a discussion about a possible open murder investigation. I think he sensed it, too. He cleared his throat and pushed his empty glass away. "So, you said you know something that might help me out?"

I wasn't sure if I could tell him everything. When I worked in Chicago, I never dealt with law enforcement as part of my job. I had no idea what the rules were between journalists and cops. If I told him about me and Amy's investigation but not the details, could he demand them from us? After all, we'd be impeding a possible unsolved murder investigation. And, of course, there had to be some odds that he'd give the story to some local journalists he knew and trusted more. The local cops might shut us out entirely. They'd take what we knew, and our story would be over. I pictured Amy yelling at me about how I blew it. I would have to lie a little to Jack. I would play him for what he knows for the sake of our story. I was going to be the bad guy.

WITHOUT A TRACE

I kept what I knew light. "After I moved to Carson's Pass, a journalist reached out to me. She said she's doing a story on Philip Pope and it doesn't cast him in a good light. She thinks he's sketchy."

"Sketchy how?"

"She wouldn't say. She wanted to interview me once every week about what it was like living here. What I saw. That kind of thing."

"What paper was she with?"

"It's some start-up website. I can't remember."

"Can you get me more on this? Like her number?"

"I'll try, but she's secretive. I can tell she thinks it's a big story."

"Is she local?"

"No, she's out by me."

Jack leaned back and tilted his head up like something suddenly made sense. "Her story wouldn't have anything to do with missing persons, would it?"

I frowned. "How do you know that?"

"You won't meet a detective in Colorado who doesn't know everything about the Williams girls."

"The who?"

"Oh." He blinked, surprised. "I take it she didn't tell you then. Don't be mad, she's a journalist. She probably didn't want to scare you off from coming here."

I was beginning to get frustrated. "Tell me what?"

"Carson's Pass is famous, at least locally. Did you know that?" I shook my head. "Well, it used to be a secluded hiking spot. It could be a Saturday, perfect weather, and you wouldn't see anyone else on the trail. Anyway, in 1995, a group of four cousins went hiking in the woods here and they never came back out. Searchers looked for days but found nothing. Not a trace. They gave up eventually, or at least they gave up looking for anybody alive. A few weeks later, other hikers found clothes. There was a pair of pant legs sticking out from a big boulder on the shore of an alpine lake. When search and rescue came and looked closer, they found four full sets of clothes partially hidden in a boulder field. The clothes were confirmed by family to belong to the girls."

The bartender came over to ask Jack if he wanted another beer, but he shook his head vehemently, as if to signal to me he'd never drink more than one beer while discussing business.

"So, there's some logical explanations. Feeling hot and taking off your clothes is a common symptom of hypothermia. It was September, and there were some lows in the forties and rain. It was possible it got cold enough for hypothermia to set in. The problem? Some of the boulders that the clothes were found under weighed close to 400 pounds. Maybe, I mean *maybe* the four of those girls could have moved something that heavy together. But why? Why would you hide your clothes and shoes there? Hypothermia can make you crazy, but it doesn't give you super strength. If anything, it makes you weak. Anyway, that's all there is. The government sold the land eventually. Too many people were hiking off-trail in Carson's Pass to look for the girl's bodies. They'd get lost or hurt themselves. So, the forest service cut trees over the old trails. Whatever maze those girls got lost in was closed forever. That was it."

The bartender had made her way back to within earshot and pointed at me. "No, it wasn't. Tell her why those girls went missing."

Jack's gaze left me, and he looked at her, amused. "You believe those legends?"

"Legends? Tell that to my brother-in-law. He was so afraid he had to move. I don't see my nieces anymore."

"What legends?" I moved my eyes between them as I spoke.

"Legends keep us entertained around here." Jack leaned back, and his bar stool creaked. "After the girls went missing there were reports of cult gatherings at one of the alpine lakes around here. The same one where their clothes were found at. Morrow Lake." I frowned. The name was familiar, and I realized it was on the property of Carson's Pass. One of the hiking trails I'd seen in the pamphlet referenced it. "The rumors always changed as to what the cult did, but it usually involved human sacrifice."

"That lake was used for devil shit," said the bartender, who leaned close to us now.

"Sure," said Jack, suppressing a smirk. "Devil shit. But in reality, it's... what do you call it... a bunch of baloney."

There was some hint of recognition between the two of them while they talked together. It felt like they knew each other. Like they'd had this conversation before. Something seemed off and I made a mental note to be cautious. *Trust no one.* The bartender huffed and I turned to her. "So, what did your brother-in-law see?"

"One of them cousins."

Jack butted in. "Many people have supposedly seen the girls that have gone missing in recent years wandering around the woods. Usually around the big drinking holidays."

"It's not *supposedly*. My in-law saw one of those Williams girls. He saw the oldest, Susan. She was standing naked in his backyard. He said she smiled right at him and walked back into the dark. And he's a perve. I'll tell ya, it must've been one unsettling smile for him not to follow."

"When was that?" asked Jack.

She tilted her head with her mouth open. "2004. Sometime around then. It was a good bit after those girls had been gone, but he said it was her just older. You couldn't convince me that the rich couple who killed themselves at that new cult up the road weren't connected to this. Weirdos, all of them."

Jack pulled out his phone. "Take all the BS surrounding these disappearances with a grain of salt. Those legends just complicate the case. But it's true that those girls didn't just get lost. Someone was out there. I can send you an article the Denver Post did for the twentieth anniversary of the

126

disappearances. You can send it to your journalist friend with some aggressive question marks after it. She should've told you."

I was disappointed. It was hard to believe Amy wouldn't have known about it. But she was desperate for this story. Desperate for the money she hoped would come with it. But she had told me so much already and I still wasn't scared off. Why withhold this?

"That's funny." Jack was frowning at his phone.

I leaned over. "What is it?"

"I can't find it."

"What, the anniversary article?"

I watched his face contort in confusion and then I knew. "No. Anything. I can't find anything on the case." The search results had been scrubbed.

"That's weird," I said and sipped my beer. I wasn't going to tell Jack what Amy had told me about Philip's brother-in-law in the media. I didn't want to let on that I knew more than I did after already lying. Even if Amy had manipulated me, I still felt loyal to her. If I confronted her, I felt like she'd come clean. She felt guilty stringing me along. I could tell that when she hugged me in the car.

I couldn't stick around the bar any longer. A clock on the wall ticked to my anxiety. I needed to text Amy to see if any of those pictures in the box belonged to the Williams girls. While Jack was still scrolling, I started to standup. "I can't guarantee she'll want to talk to you about her story on Philip, but I'll ask my journalist friend, ok?"

"Oh, you're leaving?" He said it with such surprise that I lingered with one butt-cheek on the barstool.

"Well," I said. "I don't have much else for you. But... do you have a partner?" He raised one brow and I blushed. "Not like that! I meant like a police partner."

"Like in the movies?" he continued before I could respond. "I'm based out of Denver. As you can imagine there's not a lot of homicide detectives in this part of the state. But if this case matures to unsolved murder then they would assign another detective or more. But I don't have a partner I always work with."

"I ask because I saw a light in the woods on my way here. It was far up the mountain you face when you're driving out of Carson's Pass."

"Probably hunters."

"In the dark?"

"Sure, they camp."

"It was just weird." I pictured the light sweeping to face me and then turning off.

"This is why I don't like using the word murder. Everyone gets jumpy."

"But do you agree with the sheriff? Can you say there's absolutely no threat?"

He paused and looked over my shoulder, presumably to see that the bartender wasn't paying attention. "If this gets out, I'll know it was you. So, can you keep a secret?" I nodded. "The woman's body was moved. She didn't die where we found her. She was shot in the basement. So, why would her husband go through the trouble of moving a body upstairs if he was just going to shoot himself? And then there's the motive. Nada."

I remembered what Miranda had told me about Jane McCarthy hearing them fight. "There's a couple that lives in Carson's Pass, the McCarthys. They said they heard them fighting."

"I was told. But that's not much to go off. Couples fight. When there's a murder like this there's almost always a long pattern of abusive behavior. He hits her, and she'd been covering up bruises for years. People notice. But I've talked to their families and they're genuinely shocked. They've only seen what other people have told me. In public they're a very affectionate and loving couple. Again, this doesn't prove anything. It's just different. Then there's Leah Miller's complaints..."

"What?"

Jack grimaced like he'd let the last part slip. "She had complained to a friend on the phone about seeing footsteps in the snow that stopped at her backdoor. She was pretty spooked. We saw from phone data that she had called local hotels the night she was killed. I'm telling you this because if you see anything like that, call me."

I was thoroughly afraid. But my expression was confused. Something felt familiar.

"Anyway," said Jack. "This case has just left me with a lot of questions and the county police want me to say it's a wrap."

"Look, I promise I won't go running through the hills screaming bloody murder, but what does your gut say about this case?"

"The dramatic detective in me can't help it." He rotated his empty beer. "It's not cut and dry. I think there's more. That something happened."

"Like what?" I asked.

"Like they caught a glimpse of something they weren't supposed to see."

HEAVY BREATHING

I drove back recklessly fast to the point where I was far more likely to get killed by speeding off the road than I was by someone ambushing me in the woods. But dying in a car accident was a far less scary thought than being murdered by Satanists.

I was going to have to call Amy. This was moving too fast for mail. The idea of sending a letter and waiting half a week for a reply was maddening. Besides, she was being *too* paranoid. I found it hard to believe we couldn't just call each other. I needed to know if the Williams girls' photos were in that box.

The call could wait, however. Amy stressed me out with her paranoia. It was night and I was tired. I'd call when I felt safer in the daylight. When I got inside, I kicked off my shoes and saw a text from Miranda asking if she could come over. The idea of having her stay in the guest room until she went back to San Diego was appealing. The more of us there were under one roof the safer I'd feel. But I knew Miranda wanted to drink, and she'd cajole me to have a cup. And the next thing I know, I'd wake up at four in the morning, dry as the desert, with a high heartbeat and a hangover.

I wanted to tell Miranda what Jack told me, but not over the phone. If I wasn't careful, I could scare her away. I wanted her to stay in Carson's Pass now. The idea of being stuck with my sister and rich strangers was enough to silence my conscience that Miranda might be in danger. I texted her saying she could sleep at our place, but I'd be going to bed. I wasn't a shitty friend. I didn't want her to sleep in her house alone if she didn't want to.

I went upstairs and knocked on the doorframe of the den to get Howard's attention. But to my surprise he wasn't at his computer. He was drinking a steaming mug of tea and staring out the dark windows.

"Hi," I said.

He turned slowly. "I was going to text you... Did you say you were going to the post office?"

"Yeah, and I remembered they were closed halfway down the mountain."

"You've still got city brain."

"Guilty."

"Sorry, I would've said something. It didn't really register."

"It's fine. It's been a long day." I was dying to tell him that a homicide detective thought the Millers were *both* murdered. A professional thought there was something sinister happening here. But I caught myself from saying anything. It would come off as a childish "I told you so." I didn't have to vindicate myself to him. He'd know I was right eventually.

"I'm going to bed. Miranda might come over. I told her she can sleep here anytime if she wants."

"Ok, I'll be up to let her in." He sat in front of the computer and wiggled the mouse to wake it.

I stepped back into the hall. "I'll tell her to text you."

He mumbled a goodnight and snapped on his headphones.

On my way to the bedroom, I looked over the balustrade to the first floor and saw my coat had fallen off its peg. It was sprawled in the middle of the entryway. I sighed and quickly shuffled down the stairs. But as I bent to pick up my coat, I froze. Somewhere, as if the sound came from the walls, came the deep muffle of a man's voice. It wasn't a conversation or a sentence. It was just one word. I didn't move. I stayed bent over feeling my pulse peel my eyelids back. It was my name.

I almost wasn't sure I heard it, and not for any lack of clarity. It just seemed too strange. The more likely answer was that the sound was in my head. It had been a terribly long day. But no. I could recall it too well. The voice was muted and purred, like someone speaking into a pillow.

I pretended like I heard nothing. I picked up my coat calmly and hung it over the hook. Then I walked back and set my ear softly against the wall that the stairs climbed up. My own heartbeat was too loud to hear over. I breathed deeply, silently, and counted to sixty.

When I put my ear back on the wall, my pulse was still present but there was something else. I switched sides of my head and I plugged my other ear with a finger. There was a shuffling sound, so loud I flung my head off the wall. It was like someone moving their foot.

There was the shush of a shoe and the crack of small bits of dirt. I put my ear back, delicately, and beyond the pounding of my heart I heard heavy breathing. I felt my eyes burn with tears of fear and I quickly blinked them away. Was this what happened to Leah Miller?

I examined the wall closely. There didn't look to be a creased line where a trap door could open like the spot in the basement. It was stained pine with no cuts or scars. If there was an entrance it seemed to be somewhere else. I sighed again, giving my best impression of being casual and started up the stairs. I raced back to the den.

"Howard?" I said nervously.

He didn't respond. His big headphones were on but he wasn't playing anything, his computer screen was just the screensaver

"Howard," I said louder and put my hand on his shoulder.

He jumped and took off one headphone. "Fuck! Do you have to be so sneaky?"

"I announced myself."

He reached forward quickly and clicked off the monitor. "What's up?"

"Can you lend your ear, literally? There's this sound coming from under the stairs and I don't know if it's a pipe or what." I didn't want him to roll his eyes at me. I couldn't say it sounded like there was someone in the wall. But if he could reach that conclusion himself...

"Sure," he said and stretched.

"Ok, just press your ear against the wall under the stairs."

I walked back downstairs quickly before Howard could get there. I didn't want him asking me anymore questions about the sound and tipping off anyone if someone was in there. I went into the kitchen and turned on the tap.

When I came back towards the stairs sipping a glass of water, Howard had his ear pressed against the wall, squinting.

"I'm not hearing anything."

I set my glass down and joined him. We stared at each other while our heads were pressed to the wood wall. I didn't hear anything either. I exhaled, both relieved and upset.

"Hey." He looked at me curiously. I knew he could read from my expression that something was wrong. "What did you think you heard?"

I shook my head. "I don't know." The idea of someone being in the wall seemed ridiculous. My eyelids were heavy and I was drunk-tired. That was all. But I bit my lip doubting it was that simple. I had heard *something*.

"Katie, come on."

I stared at my feet. I was more sick of lying than I was of looking like a fool. "It sounded like breathing. Like a person. And—" My eyes widened as I defended myself. "Is it that crazy to think there could be some hidden compartment after what we found in the basement. I mean—"

"Katie." Howard put both his hands on my shoulders. "There's no one in the walls." He said it pityingly and without sarcasm in his tone. "Let's get out of here. We tried it and it didn't work. We can have the place bought back and go."

I shook his hands off my shoulders and stepped back. I couldn't even meet his eye. I was too embarrassed. "No," I said. I could take the sarcasm and the doubt, but it's a special kind of pathetic to be pitied. "I'm staying. I know it's your money. You can sell. I'll stay with Miranda. And if she leaves, I'll even do the unthinkable. I'll live with my sister if that's what it takes."

His face twitched a little. "You'd stay with your sister?" He put his hand on his hips and flared his nostrils. "Let me tell you something about spoiled wives like you..."

"Excuse me?" I said. I wasn't going to take that.

"Oh, sorry." He put his hand on his chest. "Excuse *me*. I said that wrong," he turned his head and mumbled something under his breath. It was hard to hear but not impossible. I heard another hiss of an S after the word spoiled. I just stood there with my mouth open not knowing what to say. He'd called me a slut just once before when we first fought about Ryan. Ever since we'd had sex, I could tell he'd been more bothered than usual. I spoke quieter now, more hurt than mad. "Just don't fall in love. Do you remember just before our break when you said that to me?"

"Oh, shut up. I didn't know that meant you were going to screw someone and let my friends find out before me. And now I've come here for you, and you're such a scared little girl, you think there's someone hiding in the wall. I thought coming here was for our relationship, not for making you famous."

"When have I ever said I want to be famous?" The accusation was so preposterous I snapped to attention. "I just want something to call my own. Some sort of accomplishment. Do you not get that? I can't just do nothing for the rest of my life because my husband struck it big. My whole life I've asked for something to be dropped in my lap and now it's here. I'm not going to turn my nose at it."

Howard looked at me and shook his finger at the floor. "I thought I was that something!"

"Howard, please. The money is great." He narrowed his eyes at me, waiting for the but. "But it's not complaining when I say I still need to do something with my life. And if we're not starting a family..." He widened his eyes in fear and spun his head away. I felt my stomach lurch. He couldn't even *talk* about kids. "So yeah," I went on, speaking even quieter. "I need my own pride. My own success."

"Sorry for giving you the world."

"Can you just give me this? Can you let me try to do this job without all the patronizing?"

"You know what, Katie? Some people are patronized for a reason. Good luck with your goose chase." He started back up the stairs and as I watched him go, I wanted to shout a last word in righteous anger, but all I could do was cry.

DRILL BIT

I couldn't sleep. Howard's bullying played on repeat in my brain. Eventually, I managed to get my mind to wander away, but only to the unpleasant possibility that there could actually be someone in the wall. I didn't care if it was a long day and I was sleep deprived, I heard something. Maybe it wasn't breathing, but something had shifted. A foot. A shoe. Something too big to be a mouse.

Howard came in around midnight and once his breath steadied, I rose from bed. I tip-toed over to the dresser and slid open the bottom drawer as slowly as I could. I took out the gun case and went into the bathroom.

I loaded the silver pistol for the first time and tied my pajamas tight, so it was held in the waistband. I gasped from the cold steel against my skin, then I couldn't help but laugh. It was just a tiny exhale of amusement at the entire situation. I'd been up for nearly a day, met with a detective about what might be a double-homicide and now I was checking to see if someone was watching me from my walls with a gun in my waistband.

But reality hit quick and the smile faded from my face. Maybe this is what Howard meant. That this was more serious than I was taking it. I was never much more than an assistant in Chicago. I was never an *actual* journalist.

Still, I'd found the box and I was about to do something that takes guts. Maybe it was stupid, but I didn't care, I was doing it. I was drilling a hole in my wall. I wasn't that crazy, there was no chance I could sleep another night in the house anyway without seeing if someone was under the stairs.

I turned on every light I passed as I left the bedroom. Miranda's shoes weren't by the door, and I hadn't heard her come in. She must've stayed at her place and I pictured her passed out from wine, still clothed on the couch. Perhaps it was better than staying up all night, afraid.

The only problem with my plan was that the drill I was thinking of was by the other tools in the boiler room and at that moment I had a childlike fear of the dark. When I went down the stairs, I transferred the pistol from my pajamas to my palm. I rounded the corner and went down the next set of stairs to the basement. I paused at the bottom and flicked on the light switch quickly. Nothing moved but little stars raced around the periphery of my vision. I got the drill from the boiler room and double-timed it back up the stairs.

This wasn't my home. In my head, that was still San Diego, but there was something awful about feeling so unsafe in the place you slept. I felt sick. My body was crying for sleep, but my mind was wired and awake.

I'd have to be careful not to wake Howard. I could imagine him packing his bags that night if he found me drilling holes in the wall. I grabbed a couple dish towels and wrapped them around the drill and gave it a test squeeze. It was still somewhat loud. But diffused through the towels, the bedroom door and finally Howard's sleep, it was in no way loud enough to wake him.

I fed a 6-inch bit into the drill and spun its mouth tight. The bit wasn't very wide. I'd have to drill multiple holes next to one another to make one big enough to shine a light in and look through. I set my ear and the drill bit against the wall and pulled the trigger. The drill didn't have enough pressure to bite and the bit ran noisily across the pine panels. I cursed. To give it enough force I'd have to set my heel on the back of it, which meant putting down the pistol. I put the gun back in my pajamas and wiped my forehead with the same wrist that held the drill. "Ok," I said aloud and tried again. This time, with one hand on the back of the drill, the bit took, and it spun out corkscrew shavings of pine as it sank into the panel. It only took a few seconds before it was through all the way.

It didn't take much more than a minute before I had four holes in a tight square. Next, I held the drill at an angle and bored out the space between them. Just like that I had a hole the size of a half-dollar. I set down the drill and took a step to the side. I didn't want to stand in front of the hole. I pictured an eye staring out at me, leveling a gun barrel in the black.

I took a deep breath and turned on my phone's flashlight, then I started a video. I leaned against the wall so my body was far from the hole while I stuck the camera lens in. There was no gunshot. If anyone was in there they'd be completely blinded by the light. I rotated it to get a couple of angles and then brought my phone back to me.

My heart shook my ribs as I played the video back. On the screen was a tiny concrete room. A dusty floor. A drain. But there was nobody inside. That was apparent from the very first frame. It was also obvious that there didn't appear to be a way in. The floor seemed to be solid concrete and the walls were smooth with no signs of being able to open. I put my phone's flashlight on again and looked through the hole myself.

There was nothing remarkable. The existence of the room itself was strange, but it was possible the house had been designed with a half-bath or laundry room in mind that was abandoned. Covered up. I leaned back. The dust on the floor looked disturbed, but there wasn't a thick enough layer of it to show footprints if someone had been in there.

Still, it was empty. There was no one in the walls. I felt a hundred pounds lighter and I couldn't have cared less about breaking a story then. I wanted my bed. Now that the possibility of a threat was largely gone my mind was receiving signals to sleep. But I had to cover the hole or Howard would think I was insane. There was an old oil painting of mountains hanging on the living room wall. I took it off its hanger and then hung it over the hole I'd made. Howard probably wouldn't even notice it was moved.

I bent down and blew the wood shavings away, then I tossed the drill under a couch cushion. I'd deal with everything in depth when I was rested. For now, sleep. But when I reached the top of the stairs there was a sound, and I paused.

I almost didn't want to stop when I heard it. A part of me wanted to keep walking, go to bed, never let it register. It wasn't my name this time. It was that sound that says close but no cigar; two clicks of a tongue against teeth.

I twisted my head to look downstairs. Silence. The clicking could have been anything. After all, there was no one in the wall. This time I was convinced it really all could be in my head. At least that's what I told myself as I opened the bedroom door and instead of putting the pistol back in the dresser, I stuck it in my nightstand.

A WORTHY WIFE

It was almost ten when I got out of bed. I hadn't even woken once to pee, a rarity, but now my bladder was burning. When I'd pissed away the pressure in my gut, I pulled up Amy's contact and dialed her. It took a little coaxing to have the conversation on the phone, but she relented. She admitted mail moved too slow but insisted I set up a PO box in Gypsum anyway. It was a compromise.

She was quiet for a long time after I told her what happened to the Millers. But she suddenly broke her silence with a barrage of questions.

I interrupted her quickly. "I actually met with the detective..." I paused, hoping to gauge Amy's thoughts on the matter from that sentence alone.

"Did you tell him anything about our story?" she asked anxiously.

"No. I just told him that a journalist reached out to me when I moved here. That you were doing a story on Philip Pope and thought he was suspicious."

"That's already too much," Amy said, annoyed. "You told him about me?"

"I mean, no. Nothing other than the fact that you exist and are doing a story. I didn't say your name or anything."

"Fuck, Katie. He could steal this story from us in a heartbeat. Or at least the next thing we know we'll be reading about this in the Washington Post after an FBI raid. We have to keep this close to our chests. We're small fish and this is a big story. If this goes national before we can break it ourselves, we lose."

"I'm sorry. I was never briefed on how to talk with cops."

I heard her curse under her breath. "Look. Just keep the details down. You didn't tell him about the box, did you?"

"No." I shook my head strongly as if she were there. "No, I didn't."

"Good."

I was angry at myself. Here I was, conceding to this girl who if anything had been manipulative toward me. I hated how passive I was. We *had* to involve Jack. To not would make this seem like we were less interested in truth than we were with making sure it was us who discovered it. But perhaps, I was learning, that was part of being a journalist. Still, I had more than one reason to be bothered with Amy than her making me feel like I was abandoning my morals.

"Amy, can I ask you something?"

"Yeah..."

"Why didn't you tell me about the Williams girls?"

"The who?"

"Oh, come on. Amy. Carson's Pass. The missing hiker cousins in '95. Did you think I'd be scared off?"

"I honestly have no idea what you're talking about," her voice got distant and I could tell she was typing at a computer. "Hold on. Did you say 'Williams girls'?"

"Yeah, four girls went hiking back when this place was public land and never came out of the woods." I started to get nervous. I remembered Jack at the bar not being able to find any search results about the girls. It was possible the case was so scrubbed that Amy never caught a trace of it.

"I'm finding like two results. And neither of these sources mentions anything about it being in Carson's Pass. They just say White River National Forest."

"That's probably why they're still up."

"What do you mean?"

"I mean someone bleached it. They removed every article about the case that also mentioned Carson's Pass. It was probably done just before building this development so no one who moved here would make the connection."

"Katie, can you go to the local library and see if they keep newspaper records?"

"Of course."

"You might need to go to Denver. But a story of four missing persons would've made it to the Post. You should be able to find something. And take pictures if you find anything and send them to me, ok?"

"I'll do that. Have you found any connection with the missing girls so far?"

"No, I'm still just working on putting a name to every face."

"Try and find a picture of the Williams girls. Let me know if you find anything and I'll set up a PO box today."

"Ok... And Katie?"

"Yeah?"

"You don't think you're in any danger?"

I paused. "I'm okay. Don't worry about me, I want to be here. Things are moving."

"It's just..." she trailed off. "Never mind. Just please, be safe."

When I was off the phone, I texted Jack. He'd given me his card before I left the bar and I texted saying my journalist friend was paranoid (mostly true) and didn't want to talk to him. I was worried he'd fire back that we were impeding an investigation but after an hour he hadn't responded, and I realized he probably never would. He thought I didn't have anything more to give him.

Downstairs, Howard sat in the living room. He smiled at me over a steaming cup of coffee as I made my way down the steps.

"Sleep well?"

"Very."

He had a smirk on his face.

"What's up?" I asked.

"It's just not that often I get to be the early riser. I think my hair is even less messy than yours."

I didn't have much to say to him if he wasn't going to apologize for the night before. "It was a good night's sleep. I needed it."

"Fresh coffee in the kitchen," said Howard and I groaned in thanks, shuffling my way there. I poured a cup and stood staring into space. With my eyes peeled wide, I could feel the eye gunk crusted in their corners. I still wasn't ready to be awake. I had that thousand-yard stare of being up too early. But it was 10am. My body was just exhausted from stress.

I wasn't sure I was ready to start the hunt right away and begin searching the local libraries. Yesterday was like three days in one. Being fresh and rested was important. Otherwise, it might be easy to miss something. I was always great at giving myself excuses *not* to do what I should be doing. Chores, homework, the next article I had to write. But honestly, I thought I made a good point. I'd make a fire in the fireplace and have a lazy morning. I'll set up a PO box in Gypsum in the afternoon and that would be plenty of work for what should really be a rest day anyway.

My phone buzzed and I raised it to my zombie eyes. Miranda had texted me saying she wasn't going to sell back to Philip. A selfie came after. Her house had a hot tub on its deck, and she sat in it with a glass of wine, a grin, and the mountains behind her. I guess she was doing just fine here. She wasn't a worrier like me.

While I was still blinking away sleep, Howard came into the kitchen and wrapped his arms around me. It was a sweet gesture, but I didn't return it. I was expecting an apology or a solution. Couple's therapy. Something. But just when I thought his hug might be genuine, might be an attempt to apologize for the night before, his tone told me otherwise. He had a motive.

"So... I don't know if you've heard but there's a blizzard warning for tomorrow. Marcus and Lexi, they've been with the company remotely for the last few years."

"I know who Marcus and Lexi are," I said wanting him to get to the point.

"Well, they're having people at their cabin in Aspen. It's the first big snow of the season and they want to hit it when it's fresh. You're invited."

I've learned rich people like to ski. Like, *really* like to ski. I tried to get into it but quickly learned Howard and his friends don't ski for a leisurely afternoon.

To my flat midwestern mind, they're daredevils, lovers of the double-black diamond runs. I don't mess with gravity—it gives me enough trouble on my own two feet. I'd gone to Aspen once, excited to "hit the slopes," only to end up never feeling like more of a child as an adult. After two days of lessons, I ended up inching down a small run on my butt while Howard and his friends and their wives cannoned down cliffs like the stars of some '80s ski flick.

I would not be joining him in Aspen like I hadn't the last half dozen times he's gone. I wish he'd just be honest. Although I was invited it was said with the polite assumption that I wouldn't be coming anyway. I know even *he* didn't want me there. Howard was embarrassed by the fact that I was too clumsy to ski.

"You can go," I said. "How long would you be gone?"

"Oh, a couple days? Marcus and Lexi are there all week, they're having friends come and go."

"That's fine. Sounds fun."

"You can come. Take some time off the case."

"No, I'd just be doing what I would here. Sitting by the fire."

"You don't want to try to ski again?"

"I'm sorry, I wasn't aware you needed my life insurance money," I said with a smile, trying my best not to be a bitch.

"You're not that bad." He took his arms off my shoulders "I was going to drive down first thing tomorrow. It's only ninety minutes."

I realized he'd be taking the car too, and I froze. I didn't want to make a fuss over it. Miranda and Bea both had vehicles if there was an emergency. "Have fun with your friends. It's ok."

"You sure?"

I was furious he would leave me alone. Murders, missing girls, strange compartments. But Howard couldn't comprehend my fear of being alone. It was forty-six missing girls, not forty-six missing men. Men don't realize how creepy it is to be sought after for their bodies by a stronger sex. What the world needs is an invasion of seven-foot-tall aliens who catcall, harass, and lick their lips over the thought of men's asses. I'd like to see men activate the military to defeat what women put up with their whole lives.

I didn't want to act like I needed Howard to stay with me to feel safe. I was stubborn that way. "Miranda will stay over. Go have fun, I mean it. You're retired, remember? I'm the buzzkill that's still trying to work."

"You're not a buzzkill. You're admirable. Even if this doesn't work out the way you want, you impress me." He put his finger under my chin to turn my head to face him like I was some dramatic damsel in a silent film. But I only stared at him with my eyes as bloodshot as a bum's in the morning light. Life is not the movies. "I want you to know that, Katie. You really impress me."

Howard thought that being married to a man with the kind of money he had was a big success on my part. He figured I should be satisfied with my victory in life. But that was ridiculous. I wanted an accomplishment to call my own and we didn't even have kids.

"Thank you, Howard," I said and gently took his finger off my chin. I should let my ego go, I thought, because there were far worse things than not feeling like you're a peer to your partner. After all, we could be the Millers.

STORM CLOUDS

The following morning, Howard and I made breakfast together and I stood in the doorway and waved like a housewife as he drove off to Aspen. I hadn't seen Miranda or my sister since the welcome bonfire and while I was content to let the frustrations with my sister simmer, I was curious what Miranda had been up to. I found it hard to believe she wasn't fazed by everything that had happened.

Then again, she had her own coping mechanism. Miranda called me hungover and wasn't trying to hide it. She wanted to get some fresh air and hike and we agreed to go to Morrow Lake. I was terribly curious after talking with Jack and wasn't going to do it alone. I had looked at the pamphlet that was left on the counter when we moved in and it had a map of all the hiking trails. Morrow Lake even had its very own path that started where the houses ended.

Miranda said she'd be at my place at noon. She wasn't often late, but it was 12:30 when I saw her walking down my driveway. I opened the front door and we briefly embraced.

"How've you been?" I asked.

"I'm not the one that needs asking. How's your sister?" She looked past me as if she might spot Bea.

"I haven't seen her since the bonfire."

"It's that bad, huh?"

"Her following me across the country this time is just... we're not kids anymore. It's ridiculous."

Miranda set her hand on my chest. "If you feel like you're going to make this place known for another murder, let me know. You can come over and vent."

I wheezed out a laugh. "Thanks. It's okay. Just so you know, Howard wants us to be gone in a couple weeks. I don't have to endure much more of her."

"I'm keeping my place."

"Really?"

"I mean, I get the hippie vibe of *community* was kinda killed along with the Millers, but I'm not just going to up and leave. Those others moving makes room for someone better I suppose."

"Wait, who left?"

"That hippie-looking couple, the Larson's. They sold back to Philip. And that old guy. Michael something. I guess his little speech about husbands killing their wives still didn't mean he was comfortable. Have you checked your email?"

While I did manage to get to Gypsum and set up a PO box yesterday, I didn't do much else. I hadn't checked my email in a while. "No."

"He said they took him up on his offer. But good riddance, in a sense. I'm addicted to this place. I honestly forgot silence like this exists. Have you sat outside at all and just... listened?"

"I haven't really had time."

"Well, are you ready?" She motioned towards the door. "We've got time now." Miranda stepped back outside and whirled around like a child while I slipped on my boots. In a second, we were walking down my driveway together in silence.

It was warmer than it had been the last couple of days. I could barely see my breath. I figured the warm air was going to collide with a cold front, creating our storm. We had a few hours before the snow was supposed to start. The lake hike was one and a half miles each way, but I was still nervous—winter weather in the mountains was especially spontaneous. We'd be cutting it close even without an early onset of the storm.

We took the main road and went past the grocery market and into the woods. The trails were well marked, having been re-cleared when the development was built. The walk there was mostly at an incline and the trail was muddy from melting snow. We made little for conversation. Our hike was all slushy steps and heavy breathing.

After what might have been a mile, we paused and caught our breath. We were zigzagging up one of the mountains, and the stretch of trail we stopped on had no trees to block our view down. Below were the homes of Carson's Pass.

"I can see my house from here," said Miranda. She started to laugh but quickly fell into a fit of coughs in that typical tendency of the elderly or heavy smokers. "Ugh, I need to start working out again." She stretched while I squinted out at the rooftops.

One of the homes closest to us had a dark hole where a window should be. I wasn't sure if it was just an illusion of distance, but when I looked at Miranda's house, the only other visible one, I saw the glass reflecting back the day.

"What house is that?" I asked, pointing to the windowless house.

"Which one?"

"The closest one. Down to the left a little."

"That was the Millers."

"Are you sure?" It was hard to tell which house was which. Carson's pass, while flat, was still very wooded, and the houses hid behind lines of pines.

"I'm positive. It's the last one down the road before the groceries. You weren't here but I was right outside while it swarmed with cops."

"It's missing a window."

"Probably shot out."

I shook my head. "I ran into a detective on my walk home from the bonfire. He told me she was shot in the basement."

"Wait, was he that hot guy standing a bit behind the sheriff?"

"Yeah."

"Hmm, so he's a detective, too." Her gaze grew mischievous. "I might have to get into trouble."

"I think he's a little busy."

"With this case?"

I hesitated. "He says he doesn't agree with the sheriff. He wants to know Mr. Miller's motive. I don't know if he's bored or onto something more, but he wants to start an investigation."

"You didn't care to text me this? What the hell, Katie?"

"I was going to tell you."

"I've been in my house alone the last two nights. Are you telling me a detective actually thinks there's a murderer here?"

"No, he didn't say that. He just said he wants a thorough investigation. It might not be an open and shut case of husband kills wife. So far, there's no motive. No history of abuse other than a few arguments overheard. He's a detective, he just needs it to make sense."

Miranda kicked a rock, and it went thudding down into the woods before silently stopping in a snowbank.

"If you want out you can still sell normally. It's good property, I doubt you'll take a big loss."

"I know. You know what, it's fine. I get it."

"Yeah?"

"I didn't mean to overreact."

"Well, there's more I've been meaning to tell you. I just didn't want to do it over the phone." Miranda loved true crime and I figured there was a chance she knew about the missing cousins. "Have you heard of a case involving four missing girls? They went hiking in Colorado in the mid '90s and never came out of the woods. Three cousins and a friend."

She stared at the ground, her eyes searching. "The Williams girls?"

"Yes!"

"There's an awesome podcast on that story."

"I don't know if you'll think this is awesome or not, but this is where it happened."

"Shut up." There was fear in her eyes. "Are you serious?"

"Yeah, Carson's Pass used to be public land. The detective told me all about it."

"That story creeped me the fuck out." She fanned herself. "That was here?" she asked, pointing at the ground.

"The lake we're going to, it's where the detective told me the clothes were found." She looked back towards the houses, her mouth slightly agape. "I'm sorry," I said. "I thought you were into true crime."

"Reading about it sure. And from the comfort of the covers. Fuck." She crossed her arms. "That case was never solved. Is that what you and that journalist are really here for?"

"No. No, she didn't even know about it."

"I don't think I can stay here."

My heart sank. "What? Miranda, come on. It was thirty years ago."

"Yeah, and if the guy that did it was thirty, he'd be sixty now, maybe still alive. I thought this was about sex trafficking, not murder. You think someone kills four girls and never commits another violent crime?"

"Probably not."

She sighed with her hands on her hips. "You know what? Fine. I'll stay. But you tell me everything the second you learn of it from here on out. I've been sipping wine in the hot tub every night, looking out at the mountains and the forest thinking how lovely it all is and this is where the fucking Williams girls go missing? Life is one big joke. Now I'd rather listen to gridlocked traffic than this shit." She gestured at the woods.

"I'm sorry."

She started laughing. "Whatever. Just whatever. I told you about this place to begin with, remember? Don't be sorry. I've got shitty radar. I probably clicked on the ad for this development because the name Carson's Pass sounded familiar. Didn't remember why, though."

"Do you want to keep going?" I pointed ahead down the trail.

"Might as well."

"Can I show you something?" She stared as I unzipped the inside pocket of my parka and flashed her the pistol.

Her jaw dropped and she huffed. "Really, Katie, who even are you?"

ALPINE FINDS

Miranda and I weren't old friends. Our relationship had never been strained, and I couldn't find the words to shake off the tension between us. She'd been a good sport thus far. I didn't think the Williams murders would bother her as much as they did. We walked in silence for the next half hour. We were too exhausted for conversation. The hike was almost vertical and left us a couple thousand feet higher. There the air felt noticeably thinner, colder and harder to hold in our lungs. We paused when the trail flattened out and snaked away into the woods. We were at the top and the lake was close.

"Do you have a map?" asked Miranda.

"No, but the sign suggests this trail takes us right to the lake." I pulled out my phone to see the distance we'd walked since the trailhead. It read 1.7 miles. "It's been more than a mile and a half. It's gotta be close."

"You should have a map," said Miranda, and she started walking ahead before I could respond.

In about a hundred feet, the trail stopped. It didn't peter out or anything. The forest simply swallowed it.

We stood, scanning the ground between the trees. "I'm not walking through there."

"We're not going to," I said and wheeled around. "We must've missed a spur trail."

"A what?"

"Just look for a trail on the right, I'll look on the left." She nodded and we slowly started back the way we'd came.

Although it was on my side, Miranda was the one who noticed it. Beneath a skirt of branches was naked dirt. Soil that was still too tight from being trod over by thousands of steps to take seeds. I parted the pine branches to see in more. There was certainly the scar of an old trail. Miranda stepped ahead of me and started down it without a word.

"What are you doing?"

"This has to be the trail to the lake, right?"

"This is a great way to get lost. We have to be able to find our way back."

"It's not hard to see the trail."

"But just a little snow and it's gone." And as if the world were listening, a few pale flakes started falling from the sky. I turned my hand over and watched them expire on my palm.

Miranda stood on her tiptoes. "There's something through the trees. Just come, quick." She didn't turn back to see if I followed, but of course she knew I would. After just several seconds of dodging branches that rocketed back in her wake, I could see water the same steel color as the sky.

We broke through the tree line maybe a minute later. The lake was larger than I thought at two hundred yards across and perhaps fifty wide. It was bowled and surrounded by boulder fields. We were on the wooded south end, but the opposing banks, north, east, and west were treeless, stone shores that sloped upwards to rocky summits. The rock beach we walked out on had a tiny aluminum fishing boat. It sat upside down with its metal belly to the sky. Presumably its oars were beneath it. All I could think of while still slightly out of breath was how much of a bitch it would've been to get up here.

"It's not very blue. Aren't glacial lakes typically colored like the Caribbean?" asked Miranda.

I turned to look at the lake. "They reflect the sky," I said, but the wind roared too loudly for her to hear me. Without the trees to break it, the wind was an anxious force. It whipped white caps on the water and froze my face.

"We need to leave," I said suddenly.

"We just got here."

"If we're out here and it starts to blizzard, we're dead."

"It's not supposed to even start for *hours*. And the way back is all downhill. You need to relax."

So, this is what stress was for, I thought. It's not for work deadlines or final exams. The purpose of stress was to save my life. And my stress screamed while I watched the black clouds glide closer from the distance, bringing enough snow to bury us.

"It's not just the weather," I said. "Why build that trail all the way up here only to leave the last bit hidden?" Miranda just shrugged. "It's because we're not supposed to be here," I said.

"We're here now. You want to look around?"

I wanted to leave then and not just the lake or the mountain but Carson's Pass altogether. The wind had a clarifying effect on me. When the breeze lifted the little hairs on my neck, something in me screamed that I needed to get out. Go. And now.

But I was supposed to be investigating. Even though I didn't think we'd find much, I had to keep up that persona for Miranda. "Yeah," I said confidently, contradicting my every thought. "Let's look around. But not long. Seriously, mountain storms are no joke."

"Ok, ok. Let's just give it twenty minutes. Then you can cross it off the list."

I nodded and we started to make our way to the east rim. But I wasn't looking at anything apart from the pace of the snowfall. I was stuck in my head, too aware that a broken ankle up here could be a death sentence. I wanted to turn back. The dark sky and the storm made me think the kind of bad thoughts that were typically reserved for nights. My journalist skills were pathetic. I was pathetic. Amateurish. There was something horribly wrong in Carson's Pass and it needed a professional to figure it out. This entire venture on my part was just the vain hobby project of a rich wife. I shut my bad thoughts off and stopped walking. "Miranda, I think we should just turn back," I shouted over the wind. But there was no answer. Miranda wasn't next to me. I turned and saw her standing several steps back. She'd taken her hood down and her hair danced wildly on her head. Between the blowing strands, I could see her eyes staring into the stones in horror.

"What is it?!" I rushed back to her and was met with my answer immediately. Even under the parka I felt my skin flush cold and my eyes filled with tears. I wanted them to disappear, but the more I blinked, the more I understood what I was looking at: a pair of bloody pant legs sticking out from under the boulders.

SNOW BLIND

The rock the pants were under was not 400 pounds like in Jack's story. Miranda moved it with a firm push and started picking up the jeans delicately. "Wait!" I said, and she flinched.

"Jesus, Katie. What?" She looked to me and then behind me. Her eyes scanned the ridges nervously and I followed suit. When we realized we were alone, our gaze met again.

"Isn't that tampering with evidence?"

"This snow is going to stick. If we leave these here, they're gone until spring." She picked up the pants in pinched fingers as if they were something that stank. I overturned the rock and found a pair of women's socks, equally bloodied.

I turned over a few more rocks and under each one was another article of clothing. Shoes, shirts, jackets. Underwear and bracelets. I did so quickly, because it was snowing harder now. Some pieces were filthy, black with dirt and age while others seemed like they could've just been taken out of the wash.

"How old is this stuff?"

"I have no idea..." Miranda's voice trailed off as she looked up the slope of rock towards the ridgeline. "Do you see that?"

"What?!" I yelled and patted for the pistol, expecting to see someone watching us.

"No, it's not a person. That rock. The flat one up there?"

"Who cares about a rock? Let's take some of this stuff and go."

She took a step uphill. "No, Katie, look at it."

I was already walking back. "There's no time. Let's go!" I picked up the newest-looking clothes and turned them over, searching for blood, something with fresh DNA I could give to the detective. The only pieces with obvious blood stains were the pants and socks. I stuffed the socks in my outer pocket and motioned for Miranda to follow me. She looked up the ridge, back to me and finally to the storm clouds, biting her lip.

"Ok." She slapped her arms on her thighs. "Fine."

I was walking carelessly quick and when the wind blew harder it brought down a shower of flakes. We still had a forty-five-minute hike out. I was worried we'd be buried.

"Katie!" I turned around as Miranda yelled. "Wait, please!"

When she got close, instead of continuing to walk, she bent and stared folding the bloody pants. "You need to calm down."

I was embarrassed that she was the one telling me to relax. Typically, I played the mom in our relationship. I waited for her to be done and we walked calmly, together this time, back into the forest and down the trail. It was far louder in the trees than it had been earlier. The pines hissed and rocked. Branches cracked and fell. The world seemed as if it were being torn in two.

Thankfully, we were more sheltered from the wind the further down the mountain we went. It was still violent, but it felt more like a storm than Armageddon.

"We're getting out of here, right?" I said. I was sure Miranda would want to leave Carson's Pass now.

"On our way,"

"No, I mean we're moving, aren't we?"

"You want to move back to San Diego?" There was shock in her tone.

"You're telling me you want to stay? You're carrying a blood-soaked pair of pants that were found in the same way and in the same place that four girls were all but likely murdered. This is not journalism work anymore. This is for the police."

"I guess maybe I am a junkie." She held up the pants, tight in her fist, and looked at the blood. "I want to meet with that detective. I want to give him this stuff together and review the Williams girls' case."

"Are you serious? You just wanted to leave *before* we found this stuff."

"I'm not being bipolar here. I was thinking about it on the hike up after we argued, and now it feels like a sign to stay. We should solve this. Get that detective involved. It might get scary at night, but I can lock my doors and drink a little wine and it's like I'm fearless."

My eyes were wide with disbelief. If Miranda stayed, I would have to. I'd feel like a joke if she stuck around to investigate this while I left. "Forget fear. There's actual danger here, Miranda."

"This is the most interesting thing I've ever been a part of. By far and fucking away. I'm decided. I'm not hightailing it back to where its sunny and safe. Who even cares if I'm murdered? I don't have kids, or a husband." She took her eyes from mine. "I don't have anything back home."

I pictured Howard's pity if I told him I wanted to move. In that moment, I knew I shouldn't make any decisions. The dark day, the bloody clothes, and my fear of the storm had warped my stress into its own hurricane. I thought I might see everything differently in the morning. But I doubted it. I felt stuck.

"Let's just get back, okay?" I said.

When we reached the trailhead there was already an inch or two of snow on the ground. Miranda and I walked back to my house with hunched heads, clutching at our coats, like a scene of Russian serfs. When I slammed my front door shut the artic whistle of the wind died. It was quiet, apart from the glass gently rattling in the panes.

"I'm calling Jack," I said, and I pulled out my phone. When I dialed there was a three-tone shriek and a recorded voice telling me my call could not be completed as dialed. "His phone is dead or something."

"It could be the cell tower," said Miranda. Philip had installed a small cell tower specifically for Carson's Pass. The range wasn't far, but so far, it had worked. I tried calling Howard and received the same message. "I think you're right."

"Should we put these somewhere?" Miranda held out the bloody pants.

"Yeah."

We went to the kitchen and the two of us put the clothes into a trash bag and set it in the corner.

I was thinking of hitchhiking to Gypsum to notify the police, but it was impossible. We had to wait out the storm. "Want to stay for a fire?"

Miranda raised her brow with a smirk. "Hear me out. Hot tub, wine, blizzard. It will change your life."

"I don't know..."

"Seriously, Katie, it's heaven. Watch your stress evaporate." I hesitated. "It's settled. Keep your coat on. Come on. Don't bother taking your boots off. I have a suit you can borrow if you want to use one."

"Are you sure we should be out in this?" I looked at the snow blowing sideways.

"Yeah, let's just stick to the road. If it gets worse, you can stay over." I glanced at the trash bag on the floor as Miranda pulled on my elbow and soon, we were back in the blizzard. This time trudging through snow already up to our shins.

SOAK

My stomach was empty, and my blood was thin from the mountain air and the stress. The first glass of wine might as well have been injected into my veins. I was wine numb with a warmth radiating from my belly while I stood watching Miranda peel back the cover of the hot tub.

She turned on the jets and the steam that rose carried the smell of chlorine in the cold. I breathed deep before getting in, letting my skin prickle and my feet freeze in the snow a bit longer. I had brought my parka outside with us. I rested a little easier knowing the pistol was just a few feet away.

"Oh..." said Miranda as she stood in the water. "My god." She closed her eyes and sunk into a corner and I followed suit. I tilted my head back and shut my eyes, too. It felt like I just took a hit of opium.

"Do you see why I was so upset with you earlier?" said Miranda with her eyes still closed, her feet bobbing in the fountain of a central jet. "This is as close as I've gotten to heaven on earth. Maybe it's because I got sick of sand so hot that it burns my feet, but the beach has nothing on this."

"This is better than like... eighty percent of all the sex I've had."

"You're lucky. I put it at ninety-five."

We both laughed and I rocked in the water, letting myself float. I could feel the alcohol in my veins, roaring out from my heart with the same force as the jets and dulling the world. My fear and stress really did evaporate. They flew off, like the steam that the wind sent flying from the surface of the water.

"If you get too hot, just stand up."

I couldn't picture having the energy to lift myself up. I sank further in so only my ears and face were above the surface. "I'm good."

"I'm just saying, after like ten minutes it gets hot."

"Okay."

I probably would've fallen asleep if it weren't for the tickle of snowflakes pattering onto my face. Miranda looked passed out, her head lolling in the wake of the water, but one of her eyes was a sliver open. "Don't worry, I wake up when my face touches the water."

I began to laugh but stopped when I heard a shrieking sound in the distance. "Did you hear that?"

I looked at Miranda and she kept her head in the water and her eyes closed. A slight smile was pasted on her face. "Hmm?"

I listened, waiting for it to come again. This time when I heard it, I shot out of the water. I was almost certain it was a women's scream.

"That's a person!" I said.

Miranda opened her eyes like she was waking up from a nap. "What is?"

"Listen!" I paused with my mouth open. There was another cry this time, but fainter and more distant. She frowned. "I think it's just wind."

"No. No, you didn't hear the first times."

"This blizzard wind is crazy I can barely hear *you*. If that was someone screaming, they'd have to be like fifty feet away."

I kept listening, but now it was just the wind, howling and whooshing. But those sounds were so much different than the screams I'd heard, it only made me more confident it had been a person.

I was getting cold already and sank back into the water, still listening. A minute passed when suddenly there was a new sound on the wind. Something like a metallic moan. I stood up again and turned around. There was a lull in the storm. The wind was just as powerful, but less snow was falling, and visibility was almost normal. In the distance, I saw the short cell tower of Carson's Pass swaying in the wind. "That's not supposed to have that much give, is it?"

Miranda stood up and came squinting over to me. "Was that sound the cell tower?"

I didn't think it was. The metallic creak wasn't quite the same as the shrill screams. I said nothing and we stood up, staring. Just as I was about to sit back down there was a crash, and a corner of the tower sank lower than the rest of it. "Holy shit," said Miranda.

The tower began to fall slowly, its scream delayed by distance. It had already fallen into the forest for a second before its thud reached us. Suddenly the jets and the lights died. The water hissed as it settled still, and even more stress flooded back into my brain. "What just happened?" asked Miranda, but I thought she had an unconvincing expression of surprise on her face.

I spun towards the house and the windows were all dark. "It took the power out." All the power to Carson's Pass was underground but I figured the little cell tower falling might've messed with the grid.

By the time we got inside the downy hair on my arms was all frosted white. I shivered and toweled myself dry and I was still a little damp as I started to get dressed.

"You should have some more wine," said Miranda. I heard the clink and glug of another glass being poured.

"I'm alright."

"I'm not asking. You stressed me out on that hike. Storms take power out. There's nothing to freak out about."

I Ignored her and bent to the hearth. "We need to get a fire going. It'll get cold quick without the furnace." I was on my knees looking for logs. "Is your firewood outside?"

"I don't have any."

"What? Ok, get dressed we're going back to my place."

"I'm sorry, Katie." She started to drink the glass she'd poured for me. "But I'm going back to the hot tub."

"What?"

She slid open the glass door to the deck and the wind poured in. "I'm trying to be zen. I can't do this shit right now. Stay, really. The spa will still be hot for hours."

"I can't. Do you realize how cold it's going to get in here? Shut the door, please. You're letting all the cold air in. And that sound. Those screams..."

"You're telling me you think that *wasn't* the cell tower?" She huffed and shook her head. I felt like I was talking to Howard and said nothing. But I was still surprised when she shut the door behind her without a goodbye and walked to the hot tub. She was still shaking her head and I stayed behind, watching her. She sat back in the water and closed her eyes in bliss. It was beginning to snow hard again. The mountains had vanished and if I didn't leave soon, I'd be stuck.

I looked at Miranda one last time. We hadn't said it simply because the thought was too uncomfortable to voice, but I knew we both believed there was a murderer here. But she sat with her eyes closed and her ears under the water. She was senseless, easy prey. And she seemed content not to care.

WORSE WEATHER

When I got home, I set the pistol on the rectangle of tile in front of the fireplace as I arranged the logs. I struck a match that hissed and popped and in a second the kindling was crackling. I leaned back and watched the flames grow to a low roar. The smell of chlorine and woodsmoke was a strange combination. I desperately wanted to shower but didn't know if the handgun was waterproof and I wasn't going to make myself any more vulnerable than I felt.

I pulled a heavy leather chair next to the fireplace and turned it to face away from the wall. I sat, set the gun on the armrest and surveyed my position. With my back to the wall, I didn't have a blind spot.

With no internet and no attention span to read, I sat, feeling the alcohol leave my system. I thought about Morrow lake. The clothes under the stones, just like the story Jack had told me. If the Williams girls' clothing had been found decades ago, who did all the other shirts, shoes and pants belong to? There were at least six sets. Maybe more. It was possible that tourists and true crime sightseers who were obsessed with the case might've brought something to leave themselves, but it felt unlikely. I picked my cuticle and pictured a girl being stabbed and stripped naked on the shore of that lonely alpine lake.

Suddenly I heard a low groan. I grasped the pistol firmly and titled an ear to listen. It was coming from out front, and with the sound of a downshift, I deduced I was hearing a diesel engine. I stood and walked to the door.

A snowplow was clearing the driveway, its yellow light whirling above two people in its cab. When it got a little closer, I realized it was my sister with her husband, Randy, behind the wheel. The snowplow rocked to a stop and Beatrice opened her door and climbed down. She turned around and stood on her tiptoes while Randy handed her a baking dish.

I hid the gun in the pocket of my coat that hung on the wall and I opened the door. Randy waved and started driving off.

"Hey!" Beatrice trotted through the snow with her shoulders raised to her ears to fend off the weather. "You don't have to be happy to see me, but I brought a peace offering." She held the foil wrapped dish to me and I took it. "Casserole! Mom's recipe. It's left over from last night. The boys all wanted something familiar after moving somewhere so different. But the snow is like home, isn't it?"

"Yeah. Thanks, Bea." She stepped in and I shut the door. "Is your power out too?"

"Yep!" She stomped the snow off her boots and slid them off with her feet. "That's why I decided to come over. Remember those winter storms back home when we'd have to do our homework by candlelight?"

"I do," I said and smiled.

"Where's Howard?"

"He's in Aspen to ski this mess."

"The first snow of the year and he leaves you all alone?"

"It's just a storm."

"I mean I just think snowstorms are romantic. You know, baby it's cooold outside. Not a great sign of a relationship to skip out on the first big snow."

"Uh-huh."

"Seriously, relationships are about the little things. Snowstorms, nice walks. Diamonds." She flashed the fat engagement ring she'd made Randy take out a three-year payment plan for.

"Bea, please. It's been a super long day already and I don't want to talk about my marriage. I appreciate the food."

"I'll heat some up for you!" She took the dish from my hands and went into the kitchen. We sat by the fire eating the casserole and Beatrice ranted with her mouth full about how the teachers in San Diego never understood her boys. "They just don't get it. Some boys were born to bully a little. It's biological. Like weeding out the weak. And it's not like girls are never to blame. Showing a little toughness is nothing to shame my boys over." I swear she was baiting me for an argument, but I just changed the subject.

"So," I said. "How do you like your house?"

"Ugh, it needs a lot of work honestly. It's not the best setup. The boys are sleeping in bunks."

"What kind of work?"

"Oh... New beds. More bathrooms. Better heating and insulation. Everything. But like you said. Maybe it's just temporary."

"What do you mean? Are you thinking of moving already?"

"No, no. We'd keep this place but just go back to San Diego for a bit."

I knew what she really meant was if *I* moved again, she'd follow. Randy was such a yes man it hurt. I knew he'd follow her back and forth without protest. He'd uproot their kids and his life for a fourth time in the name of his wife's strange vendetta against her sister. He was the bitch, I thought. I wanted a drink but needed a clear head. "So, when's Randy picking you up?"

"The next time he comes by. I told him to go extra slow. He's not used to plowing in elevation. He hasn't been behind a plow since North Dakota. If he dies, I'm going to kill him."

"Would you buy in the same neighborhood if you moved back to San Diego?"

"Oh, we never sold."

"What?"

"We kept the place there. We're going to Airbnb it."

"You can afford that?"

She huffed and crossed her arms. "Yes, princess Katie. We can afford that."

"Come on, Bea. That's not a ridiculous question."

"You never ask, and I know you don't care what the answer would be, but for your information, the business has really taken off the last couple years. We're not even on Etsy anymore we have our website that thrives on word of mouth and you know why?"

"Why?" I said, unenthused. I wondered if she was selling fake crystals again and figured she probably was. I liked the idea of crystals. They gave people something that science and studies couldn't register: hope. Bea liked them for the prices she could charge.

"I sold a bracelet of Fluorite to a sick boy's mom. His name was Cooper. It's a cubic stone. Gemmy and sea green and lavender. It's a beautiful thing of healing."

She shook her hair over her shoulder. "Cooper was unconscious. He was in so much pain from his cancer that he spent the day sedated. His mom didn't believe in gemstones or prayer or the powers of anything other than western medicine. But she bought one, because he was going to die. That's what the doctors said. He was in pediatric hospice, and you know what began to happen after she strapped that band of Fluorite around his wrist?"

"He survived."

"You say that with no wonder in your eyes." Bea leaned forward and looked at me. "He *survived*. That's not a small word. Don't say it like it is."

"I'm sorry." Bea closed her eyes, reveling in my apology. I regretted saying it before the words were even out. It was just so second nature, so *me* to apologize. My sister managed to make me feel bad about doubting her business that sells expensive and likely fake stones to familes often racked with medical debt. But hey, she offers payment plans.

"His mom whispered in his ear all night that the bracelet was going to save him, and when he woke up, he said he heard her words and believed they would, too. My store and that story have been featured in multiple journals of crystalline and mineral medicine."

"I'm glad he lived. Of course, I am."

"Then sound like it."

"I'm not frustrated about a kid surviving cancer. I'm frustrated with you."

"Just for the sake of argument, let's say the stones don't work and that there is no healing power of crystals. What on earth is wrong with giving people hope?"

"You're not giving hope, Bea. You're selling it for a premium. Did you raise prices after this story came out?"

Bea scoffed and angrily parted her hair back again. I saw a flash of sleek silver, a crown in the dial. "Hope can be priceless. Hope saves lives."

I leaned forward while squinting, trying to inspect her watch. "Is that a fucking Rolex?"

She yanked her wrist away from me. "It's none of your business is was it is." She picked up her plate of casserole off her lap and dropped it hard. It clanked on the coffee table. "I'm leaving. You're awful to me, Katie." She marched to the front door.

I stood, alarmed. "Bea! Don't walk out in this weather!"

It seemed she had forgotten it was snowing. She stomped a foot in frustration like a toddler when she saw the snow out the window. When she turned around her face was an ugly scrunch of a dramatic pout.

"I'm sorry," I said. I was only saying it this time to keep her from walking into a blizzard.

"You're so mean." I didn't respond and she walked back to the living room and plopped back in her chair.

She pulled out her phone and ignored me while I tended the fire. Eventually, the silence grew too long for comfort. "Do you have internet?" She shook her head and a few seconds later set her phone down.

"Wanna hear a story?"

"Bea, I don't want to fight."

"Oh, don't worry. It's not about saving some dying kid with cancer. It's a better one." I leaned back and sighed. "The last time I was in Colorado, I was driving to California from Chicago. It was when we were moving there, and I was all alone, driving the van with my business supplies. I was getting gas at some odd hour. 3 am or something. So, I'm at the pumps at a dark gas station in the middle of nowhere, the kind of place where girls get abducted, when suddenly I see a man in a big coat walking over to me." The fire popped so loud I jumped, and an ember banged against the screen guard.

Bea smiled and started talking towards the fire instead of me. "I don't know if it was from being tired or what, but I didn't feel fear. I just stood there, watching him come closer, when he stopped ten feet from me." Bea was speaking in a strange, rehearsed sort of tone I hadn't heard from her before. I crossed my legs and then my arms and glanced over my shoulder out the window nervously.

"I couldn't see his face," Bea went on. "His coat was this big bison skin thing with a hood. He looked like a frontiersman or someone medieval, I don't know. Anyway, I don't say hi. I'm just looking at him when he starts to talk in this..." Bea tilted her chin to her neck and deepened her voice, "Big manly baritone. He says to me, 'I could sense your energy from all the way inside of my car. It's different. You're different.'"

She leaned forward and put a hand on my knee. "I know you'd run away here. You think everybody's an axe murderer, but the world is more beautiful than that. I didn't mention that my van was filled with healing crystals and that's what he was sensing. Not because I thought he'd rob me, but I wanted to take the compliment. I said thank you and then he took his hood down and he was *gorgeous*. I mean, ridiculously handsome— like what are you doing not being fed grapes between modeling shoots, pretty. Maybe I could sense that when he was walking over. Maybe it's why I stayed still. Anyway, now I'm blushing in a windy gas station parking lot. Trucks with their trailers all lit up like Christmas trees are pounding past into the night and I'm in a fever dream about to get fucked by Buffalo Bill."

She laughed but I stayed silent. "He asked me to come with him into the mountains. He said he needed someone like me. That he couldn't continue his purpose, but I could change that. Something of that sort. I don't remember exactly what. It was weird but it resonated with me. I felt that it was true and that I should go with."

She looked away from the fire and back to me. "I know you're thinking he would've cut me up into a million pieces or something. But the funny part is I knew he wouldn't. I've never felt energy from someone like I did from him. I even walked several feet towards him when we'd been talking, like I was in a trance. I would've gone with. Just left the van there and vanished. But I saw the prairie grass sway," she paused and looked irritated. "Or maybe it was wheat. Whatever. But the grass was blond and reminded me of my boys. I thanked him, said maybe in another life and drove off."

"How far was that from here?"

"I have no idea. If I didn't remember the mountains, I wouldn't have even remembered it was Colorado."

"What about the man, what did he look like?"

"This was so long ago, and I was so tired I couldn't recall details like that for all the money in the world."

"Why are you telling me all this? What's the moral, Bea?"

"The moral is I had a shot at another life, but I chose family. All I ever wanted was to be more in touch with the world and the energies we can't see. I knew if I went with him, I'd see more than I ever would otherwise, and I still said *no*."

"Ok," I said. "Is that some shot at me?"

"It's not a shot, it's advice."

"We're both living a thousand miles from Mom and Dad. What do either of us know about family?"

"Were we supposed to just stay in that tiny town? Jesus, Katie. How *dare you* try and pass your bad blood on to me. I'm a good daughter. I'm a good *sister*."

Her story disturbed me. The mention of the very handsome man made me think of Jack. But I was done listening to Bea bicker. "Forget it," I said with a wave of my hand. "Let's talk about anything else."

"Fine," Bea said. "So, who are you voting for next cycle?"

And then thankfully—mercifully—I heard a diesel groan coming down the drive.

ALONE

Randy came inside while Bea was putting her boots on, saying it was possible that power would be restored in the next few hours. Philip had already paid for a snowplow to bring line workers in from Gypsum to try to fix the outage. Obviously, he said, there was no quick fix for the tower. Cell service would be out for a while. I thanked him and gave Bea an awkward hug. The moment they were gone, I took the pistol back out of my coat pocket.

I abused alcohol when I was in college after Claire went missing. But afterwards I had never used alcohol as anything other than an occasional social crutch. But now maybe Miranda was right about its fear-numbing qualities. My clear head wasn't doing me any favors. As the blue dusk matured to black, my head snapped to look at every little sound the house made.

I found a pack of candles in the closet and did the best I could spacing them throughout the living room, kitchen, and stairs, but they only cast light a few feet from their wicks. I'd been thrown back a hundred years into a pitiful pioneer glow.

I grabbed a bottle of wine from the kitchen and set up in front of the fire again. It wasn't long before it was empty. I realized I wasn't happy here. Even if we broke a big story, did I really need validation so bad I was willing to risk my life? But then there was Claire. She hadn't gone missing in Carson's Pass. Her car was found at a trailhead dozens of miles away. Suddenly I felt sure she would've told me if she was going to kill herself. I was like a sister to her. She wouldn't have left me with that guilt. I was getting nostalgic, thinking of all the good times with her, when my eyelids grew heavy and my chin nodded toward my breasts.

*

I woke with an actual gasp. It was like I'd sobered up enough in my sleep to realize how vulnerable I was. I could've at least

171

locked myself in a bedroom. The fire had burned down to coals and most of the candles were out. The room was almost in total darkness. Despite that my heartrate slowed. I had been drunkenly asleep in a chair for god knows how long in the dark and no one had killed me. That was a safe sign.

I still had a bit of a buzz. I felt dry and the world was soft around the edges, still unthreatening. I stood slowly and patted the coffee table until I found the pistol. I figured I might actually be able to sleep in my own bed, of course, that is after looking under it. And in the closet.

I was closing the glass door to the fireplace, calmer than I'd been in days, when I heard two knocks. They were spaced strangely apart and in the quiet dark, I couldn't place where I had heard them at all. My pulse quickened and I whispered a curse. I raised the gun and stepped around the corner to face the front door. Out the windows on either side of it was complete black.

"Hello?!" I said. My finger was already on the trigger, already applying a little pressure. I took it off and brought the gun down. "I'm losing it," I said aloud. "I'm really losing it."

I turned on my phone's flashlight and kept my right hand on the gun as I went up the stairs. I wasn't hearing things. The sound could have come from the space beneath the stairs. But there was no way in hell I was going to look when I was alone in the house. I went upstairs and as I was about to reach my bedroom door, I heard two impatient knocks in the same second. I threw open my bedroom door and slammed it, locking it behind me. I quickly searched the room and its attached bathroom and found nothing out of the ordinary. I dragged a big armchair in front of the locked door for good measure.

But sleep would be hopeless. I sat on the edge of the bed, and spent most the night in that same position, sobering up completely as I stared at the walls.

Four times in the night I thought I heard knocking from somewhere deep in the house and four times I dashed over to put my ear against the door. I kept thinking about the space beneath the stairs. There was probably a way for someone to come and go that I missed. But why was someone knocking? If the answer was that it was intended to drive me crazy, then it was working.

The windows of the master suite looked out to the front drive. Randy hadn't come back after he picked Bea up. From comparing the driveway to the unplowed yard, I figured ten to twelve more inches of snow had fallen since last he'd left. I pulled the blind back wider, letting as much light in as I could, and finally laid down and went to sleep.

*

It was 2pm when I awoke, feeling unrested. I laid in bed for another hour just staring at the ceiling. My hunger spoke far louder than my fear, and it was enough that I unblocked the door and went down to the kitchen. I kept my eyes on the wooden wall under the stairs as I walked by. In the light of day, I thought I might be able to stomach looking through the hole I'd drilled again.

The power was still out, so I settled for cereal, but while I was sitting and chewing with my back to the wall the microwave suddenly beeped, and I heard the furnace whirl to life below me. I spat up a little cereal in surprise.

Even without cell service I could send texts on my laptop and FaceTime Howard if the Wi-Fi was working. I couldn't call Jack, but I could text him again. I felt relieved. I needed to get these clothes off my hands. With the power back on and the daylight, I felt like maybe my mind had exaggerated last night. That perhaps I was being ridiculous. I couldn't figure out why someone would knock anyway. Howard was wrong about a lot, but perhaps I do watch too many scary movies.

In the living room I opened my laptop and called Howard on FaceTime. He answered just as I was about to close my computer. He already had the beginnings of a ski goggle tan around his eyes and his hair was a wild mess from being under a hat.

"Hey!" I recognized where he was—Marcus and Lexi's kitchen. There were several people chatting and drinking behind him.

"Hey," I said. "Can we talk somewhere private—"

"Yeah!" he interrupted me and the picture went dark before his face appeared again in a bathroom. "What's up, how are you? I got an email from Philip saying the power is down and something about the cell tower being out."

"Being out is quite the euphemism. The entire thing collapsed."

"Jesus, are you okay? Do you want me to come back?"

"No," I said it too defensively. "Sorry, it just looks like you're having a good time."

"Well, you caught me at a good time, we were just going to go back out for a couple hours before sunset."

"Alright, I won't keep you. I was just saying hi."

"I see you survived your sister's visit."

I paused. "How'd you know she came over?" The audio and picture lagged. I could hear Howard's voice in robotic chops. "Sorry, you just cut out."

The picture was frozen still but the audio was perfect when he spoke again. "I said she emailed me at like nine this morning. She told me that I should talk you into seeing a therapist, if you can believe that."

"All too well." It was possible the power had been on briefly while I was sleeping this morning. Bea could've emailed him then. It had probably been rolling on and off all day. It seemed like an unlikely coincidence that it was restored in the first ten minutes after I woke up.

"If you're interested," he said sarcastically, "She recommended some guy on Zoom who goes for a thousand bucks an hour."

"Is she seeing him?"

"It sounded like it. I didn't know she could afford that."

"Poor guy is hardly getting paid enough."

I heard Howard's name shouted on the line. "I've got to run but really quick, how do you feel about hosting a little party at our new place?"

"A party?"

"Yeah. The last one we threw was the most fun I've had with you in a long time. It wouldn't be as big this time. Everybody here is super curious to see the new place and most my friends are planning to be in Aspen until the end of the week. It would be like twelve people. Unfortunately, I doubt we could get away with it without inviting Bea."

"When are you thinking?"

"Friday."

"That soon?"

"Again, it wouldn't be very many people. Twelve tops."

"Have you mentioned this idea to your friends yet?"

"Just a little. An inkling of an idea."

That was code for he'd already drunkenly raved to them about the party they should have at his place on Friday. I didn't want to be the buzzkill. "Ok, probably. Just let me think about it."

"Ok, I'll tell them it's tentative."

"No, it's fine." I almost sighed but stopped myself. "Tell them it's a party."

"You're the best, love. I'll be back either late tomorrow or the next day for sure. I've got to ski. Love you."

"Love you, too," I said, and he waved, smiling while the screen went black.

I wasn't going to be the bad guy and deny Howard a party when he was right, the last one did bring out the best in us. Besides, to my frightened mind, what this house needed most was people. I had wanted Miranda to stay over until Howard got back, but now she was upset over nothing. I was pissed that she got mad at me over being anxious and I wasn't about to apologize. I thought maybe she'd wise up and walk over to say she was sorry. It wasn't on me to initiate contact. I shut my laptop and left the gun on the coffee table. I was sick of carrying that thing around—it was a heavy little reminder of my stress.

I was going to have a gun-free rest of the day and relax. I went to messages on my computer and started typing a carefully worded text to Jack. I didn't know what to say without sounding crazy. He seemed very skeptical about the legends but there was hard evidence with the bloody clothing. It was possible the internet connection was strong enough for me to send a picture of them.

I went to the kitchen to get the garbage bag with the clothes. But when I got there, I froze. Idiot, idiot, idiot. I palmed my forehead. The corner I had set it in was empty. I felt more stupid than afraid. I had my hunches, but now it was more of a certainty: It had to be Miranda. She was the only one who knew where I put the bag. Or was she? I realized when we had walked back to my house from the trailhead that Miranda had been carrying the pair of pants in plain view. Pretty much every house had a view of the road. I didn't know which one Philip lived in, but it would be no different.

Regardless, someone must've broken in here and taken the clothes. But it was freezing outside and if a window was broken, I'd feel it.

I went to the back door and looked out the window. A dual set of dimples came up to the house from the tree line. Footsteps.

My heart jumped and I flung my hand to the doorknob, paying no mind to the mug as it fell from my hand and smashed on the tile. The door was locked, thankfully, but that didn't assure me very much. It was just like what Leah Miller had told Jack. A set of footsteps, trailing out of the woods.

Suddenly the furnace groaned in a falling octave as it died, and the digital clocks in the kitchen clicked off. The power was out. And a few seconds later, I was palming that pistol again.

FOOTSTEPS

I searched every floor. I started in the basement, flinging back shower curtains and the doors to little linen closets, but I couldn't find any sign of someone else in the house. Eventually, my eyes settled where they should've started. But I told myself there was no point to look into the space beneath the stairs again since there didn't seem to be any way to get in.

But I had to. I wasn't planning on getting wine numb again in order to nod off for a few unrestful hours. I took the picture off the wall and turned on my phone's flashlight.

I shined the light in and saw that the space was clearly empty. There wasn't enough dust for someone's footprints to show. So, I spent more time looking at the walls, trying to see a crease or something out of the ordinary when I noticed two square blocks on the bottom of one of the stair treads. They were in both corners and were coated in thick black paint. But there was a ridge in the middle of each.

Hinges.

I left the hole and went to the stairs. Each stair board was a little longer than its base, leaving a short lip of an inch or so sticking off each step. My heart fluttered as I reached under the lip of the fourth stair. My fingers found a dime-sized latch on either corner. I bent to look closer and saw they were barely perceptible to the eye, painted the same color as the wood. I pressed them in, and there was a click. The stair board bobbed loose and I opened it to reveal the little room below.

I sat on the steps for several minutes considering. I wasn't going to climb in. I could see the room well enough from above. I took several pictures and then a video and put my phone back in my pocket.

I had no sense of satisfaction like when I'd found the first compartment. Instead, I felt cold fear. The entry of the stair door was very narrow. Long but just a stair tread wide, twelve inches I'd guess. It would take a thin waist, a woman or a skinny man, to fit through.

I needed a plan. Without the clothing, the secret room alone wasn't going to be enough evidence for Amy. I had to get the police involved. I'd text Jack, and for good measure I'd call the sheriff, too. But first, I had to address the thing that was eating me—I had to find where those footsteps came from.

*

I stayed in the meadow for a long time staring at the point where the tracks stopped. And stop they did—it was like someone fell from the sky into the snow and just started walking. The only conclusion I could reach was that whoever had come to the back door had been standing in the meadow, watching me, long enough for the rest of their tracks to be erased by the snow. That's why it looked like they came out of nowhere. The clearing had a slight incline and made for a good vantage point of my house. With binoculars, it would be quite possible to see through our windows.

But they hadn't stayed here. The footprints went to the backdoor. Did they come inside? I wanted to doubt it—to say a definitive *no*. But I couldn't.

It was Leah Miller's words that raised the hairs on my neck. Jack had said she'd talked about a lone set of footsteps that came out of the woods, crossed her yard and stopped at her back door.

I squatted to inspect the prints better. The bottoms of the tracks were filled in with snow and I couldn't see any tread markings, but from the size I determined they had to have been made by a man. I took a few pictures of the prints and started back home.

I could stay in Carson's Pass if the police knew what I knew. I'd feel a lot safer if Philip was under suspicion. He'd wouldn't want to draw attention to himself by having something happen to me. But in the meantime, I was going to do whatever it took to not end up like Leah Miller.

GUN SMOKE

I searched the house all over again when I got home and made sure I was locked in. The plan was to barricade myself in my room again for the night. This time I'd make it cozier, bring all the candles along with food and wine so I wouldn't have to leave until daylight.

I ate cold casserole and worked until dusk arranging my bedroom. The power had stayed out and I hadn't texted anyone. I almost wanted to go to Miranda's or Bea's to spend the night in the company of others, but I was too stubborn.

With the furnace not working the house was losing heat. I kept on my wool sweater and socks. I knew it might be a scratchy night's sleep, but I was going to make it work. When dusk came and the house began to dim, I took one last look around before retreating to my room with a wine glass and a book.

I took the gun from my waistband and set it on my nightstand hoping that was the last time I'd be walking around with it stretching the waistband of my pants. Hopefully Howard would want to get home after not hearing from me for a bit. I was sick of being alone.

I began to read, or at least try to, but as the house contracted in the cold night it popped and groaned and made a million little noises that wouldn't let me focus for longer than a paragraph. I wished the power was back on so I could have some white noise. Without it, I was destined to flinch like this all night until my eyelids finally closed from pure exhaustion.

I eyed a bottle of wine I left on the dresser while arranging the room and clapped my book shut with a sigh. It was easier with the wine. I didn't have to drink the whole thing. I just needed enough to tell my well-reasoned fear to shut up, but not too much to leave me sick and anxious in the morning.

My fear, however, was quite the talker. Two hours later the bottle was gone, and I got under the covers to attempt to sleep.

I listened to the metal plumbing bang for the better part of an hour. The pipes were particularly unhappy with the chill. I was lying there wondering if I had to worry about one bursting when there was a different sound—a sound so clear I shot up in bed, braced my weight on my palms and listened. A door had slammed closed.

I threw the covers off my legs and listened for what must've been a full minute but there was nothing, just my ears ringing in the dark. I took the gun from the nightstand. I was done with this. Done with the fear and the hiding. It may have been a draft closing a door, but ever since I got to Carson's Pass, I'd felt like someone was toying with me. Whoever left those prints knew I'd see them. Whoever made those sounds knew I'd hear them.

I picked up my phone to turn on the flashlight, but the screen wouldn't light up. The last time I looked it was at more than thirty percent. I was about to start wondering if someone could've got to my phone but then my midwestern memory came back to me and I remembered that the cold wasn't kind to battery life.

I picked up the brightest candle and went out into the hall. In my heavy wool socks, my steps were silent. Gun in my fist, booze in my brain, I was going to be the danger. Quiet Katie was dead. To hell with the scared girl barricaded in her bedroom till dawn.

I thumbed the gun's hammer back and one metallic click echoed through the house. The stairs creaked as I went down them, but my steps weren't nervous. They were the confident, malicious movement of a predator.

My brain began to betray my bravado as I looked into the dark. Someone could be watching me from less than ten feet away, I realized. Someone could be aiming a gun at my head this very second. Every hair on my body shot erect. A board in the kitchen creaked, but the noise wasn't the typical moan and groan of old house, it was like the wood had been relieved of weight.

My heart pounded. Every single beat felt as if I were on a roller coaster just starting to descend from its summit. I was going to be sick. Feigning strength, I raised the pistol in one hand and outstretched the candle in front of me with the other.

The living room flickered in weak orange light and the sound of another step came from the kitchen. The moment was too surreal to process. Someone else was in my house. Someone who's watched me from the snow. From the walls.

A shadow appeared in the kitchen doorway.

"Hey!" I shouted and a soft voice started to speak, but in the same second I gasped, and my gun went off.

The muzzle flash lit up the room like a strike of orange lightning and after the roar, I felt like I'd been dropped in the deep end of a pool. I could hardly hear. The world whined and a muted crash of glass came from just ahead of me. But I knew what I shot. I saw it in the muzzle flash.

I stood, frozen, tears beginning to well. My right ear's whine gave out to a pop and I heard a wet gurgle coming from the ground. I walked forward. In the candlelight, I saw her on the floor holding her neck with both hands. I threw myself next to her, "Oh. Oh, no," I said in shock. "Miranda."

She tried to speak but instead blood spilled out of either side of her mouth. "Miranda," I cried. Her grip on her neck wilted and I moved her hands aside, but from how easily her arms flopped onto the floor I knew she was almost gone. I pressed my palms into the wound. Blood, black in the dim candlelight, raced slick and hot over my hands. "No, no, no! Look at me! Miranda, look at me!"

Her eyes rolled over to me, but her gaze grew glassy and then froze altogether. And I leaned back on my knees not quite able to comprehend what I had just done.

CABERNET SAUVIGNON

It took a while to form thoughts and when they finally came, it all it seemed obvious. I'd been tricked and for whatever reason, paid or blackmailed, Miranda had been the one in the walls, in the snow. She was certainly trim enough to fit through the stair door and she was wearing shoes. If she had come over for a visit, she'd be barefoot. Miranda never wore shoes inside. Never.

But all those frantic thoughts were suddenly brought down with doubt as I saw wine, mixing and blooming in the pool of blood. I picked up some of the glass I'd heard break. Dark pieces were stuck to the glue on the back of a label. I whined as I realized Miranda had been holding a bottle of wine.

I read the label, trying to remember if it was one of my bottles, but I didn't recognize it. This bottle was hers. She had brought it here. Which meant she'd just been coming over for drink. Maybe something scared her at her house. Or maybe it was a peace offering after the argument we'd had.

"No," I said aloud. My muffled voice sounded like it came from another world. From a mixture of shock and still not being sober, I hardly remember the next few hours. I didn't leave the house. I didn't go running to call the police. I went upstairs, and at some point, after some amount of alcohol, I crawled under the covers and went back to sleep.

*

When I woke in the light I thought, I *really* thought, it had all been a dream. And then I saw my hands, and the covers. In a state of shock, I had forgotten to wash myself off and dried blood was *everywhere*. Reality had never been so heavy, and my stomach sank and sank until I bolted to the bathroom and vomited bile into the toilet bowl.

I tilted my head back to the ceiling. I had to go to the police. The consequences spun in my head: I'd been drunk and the first thing they'd do was take my blood. Then there was the possibility Miranda had texted to tell me that she was coming over. My phone was still dead and had been for hours. Another wave of nausea rocketed through me and I flung my head back to the toilet bowl. My stomach was already empty, and I dry heaved.

"I killed my best friend." I said it aloud. "Miranda is dead." Saying the words didn't seem to make them any more real. It was selfish, but I couldn't think of anything except the consequences.

Even if I didn't get charged with manslaughter, I'd be looking at a slew of civil suits. Her parents, her siblings. They'd take me and Howard for everything we had. It wasn't about the money. It was how much of a horrible idiot I'd be in everyone's eyes. The horrible idiot I was. I rested my head on the toilet seat and I sobbed.

Maybe it was the alcohol or the shock or that I was just a bad person, but when I went back downstairs, I started cleaning. I rationalized that it was a mess, after all. A crime scene wasn't necessary to preserve when I'd be confessing soon anyway.

I stared at Miranda for a long time. She'd grayed overnight and her eyes were still open and milky with that cataract clouding of the dead. I bent down to her and tried to apologize to a corpse, but before words could form I began to cry instead.

I filled up a cold soapy bucket of water and got to work. I simply turned my brain off. I was cleaning, that was all. I moved Miranda around to scrub the blood beneath her as if she were furniture.

Two buckets later and the floor and walls were clean. The pool of blood had stopped before reaching the rug and there were no large stains. I stood with my hands on my hips and remembered there'd be a bullet somewhere. It had passed through her neck. I found it on the far side of the kitchen, wedged in the wall. The hole was hardly noticeable. The bullet had buried itself so deep that it wasn't visible itself, and the marking it made wasn't shaped like it had been from a gunshot.

But it didn't matter if the evidence was hidden or not. I was going to come clean anyway. Just not right away. Miranda's death wasn't a real thing in my mind. It was too much to take in at once. It wasn't real. Miranda was dead. She was shot by me. I could repeat it over and over again and yet it was too outlandish to really click. That simply wasn't *possible*.

I knew other people would make it real for me. Like when my head would be tucked toward my chest as the police put me in their squad car. The shocked reactions of my sister, Howard, and the neighbors as they gawked at me while Miranda's body was hauled away—that might make me realize exactly what I'd done.

Howard said he'd be home today or tomorrow, but I needed to go back to bed. I couldn't face this hungover and sick. I couldn't face this at all. Suddenly I found myself in the entryway, putting on my boots and coat. I wasn't even thinking while I walked through the house and out the back door.

I stood in the cold and looked both ways. There were no other houses visible from here and the communal use trail that leads to the garden snaked passed the front. Back here, you could only be seen if someone was in the woods or on the mountain.

Before I could even question what I was doing, I was back inside, and Miranda's ankles were in my hands as I dragged her stiff body through the kitchen and out the back door. She was easy to move until I got to the snow, then she sank into it and became twice as heavy. I'd move her ten feet before dropping her heels and catching my breath. Five minutes later I made it to the woods, and there, beside a spruce tree, snot ran from my nose as I tried to cry as quietly as I could. It all became a little more real as I pushed my best friend under the skirt of spruce branches and began to bury her with snow.

BEDRIDDEN

I scoured the kitchen and living room floors, looking for blood or debris that I'd missed but there wasn't enough to bother with. Some blood was stuck between the hardwood boards but that was all. I wasn't about to go at it with a toothpick. I was just buying time; my plan wasn't to completely conceal a crime scene.

I marched back upstairs to my bedroom, this time wineless as I wrapped myself in the blankets. I didn't even know where the gun was. I had no fear for my own my life. Someone could appear in the doorway, Mike Myers mask on, fisting a knife, and all I'd do is roll over and say "make it quick." Maybe I wouldn't say that, but only because I didn't believe I deserved quick.

The muzzle flash. Miranda's eyes. Her hands helplessly grasping her neck as blood leaked between them. It all played back to me as I stared at the ceiling, as clear as if it were projected there. For the next few hours, I cringed and screamed and in one bout of existential panic, I tossed the blankets to the floor and ran out of the room yelling in the hallway and pulling at my roots until my head ached.

I only began to come back to earth when I ran my tongue across the teeth. They were rough with plaque and sour with the taste of stale vomit. I needed to brush them, yet the idea seemed impossible. After death life goes on, this we all know, but with what speed is the shocking part.

I found myself in the bathroom staring soullessly at my reflection as I brushed. It felt like a silly question, but it dictated my every action: What would I want Miranda to be doing if she accidentally killed me?

I knew I wouldn't want her to wallow for the rest of her life. Nor rot bankrupt and imprisoned like I might. But as the shock went away, guilt wore on me less and less. More questions began to dawn on me.

She must've had a key to the house, but I had never given her one. I shook off the thought, realizing I was probably just in denial. I was trying to make her death seem deserved. Howard probably gave her a key. And she had probably come over because something scared her at her own house.

The power came back on and had stayed on for a few hours. It seemed like it was fixed for good. I plugged my phone in and sat next to it until it turned back on. I had service, too. The tower or at least some substitute must already be back up and running.

Howard texted once, Amy had called twice, but Miranda had never messaged the night before. I wanted it not to add up, but it did. The cellphone service probably just came back when the power did. If Miranda wanted to come by, she would've had no way to tell me. At least it would help my court case, I thought dismally.

Amy's calls were likely begging me to go to a local library. I would not be returning them. I was not in a place to put any pieces together. Instead of being smart, I did the only thing I could stomach doing, and I drank myself to sleep.

*

I woke around 9am that morning, shivering yet buried in the blankets. It wasn't until I felt a soreness in my bones that I figured out I had a fever.

I heard the clank of dishes downstairs, but it was a domestic sound, not ominous or stalking. It was the dishwasher being loaded. Howard must be home. My stomach dropped. I pictured that he'd found Miranda. After all, if he went out the back door my footsteps would lead right to her. I panicked at the thought that he knew what I'd done. I pictured a platoon of police cruisers rolling up to Carson's Pass already. I was an idiot. I should've crisscrossed that field to make my steps less obvious. I rose from bed quickly.

"Hello?" I said from the top of the stairs.

"Hey!" Howard poked his head out of the doorway to his den.

The tan from his ski goggles was now comically pronounced. A figure eight of pale flesh sat sideways across his reddened face.

"Sunny in Aspen?" I asked.

"Oh, is it noticeable?" he said sarcastically before he came over and hugged me.

"Jesus, you're warm."

"I'm sick."

"I'm sorry," he said and rubbed my shoulders. "Since when?"

"Since this morning." Out from under the covers it was twice as cold. I shivered in waves, my teeth clattering cartoonishly.

"Damn. Do you need anything?" I shook my head. "Has Miranda been staying here, too?" I shook my head again. "You should really try to get back to sleep. You're making me cold just looking at you."

"Yeah," I said distantly.

He guided me back into the bedroom, and I let him tuck me into bed. When he turned to leave, I reached out and grabbed his wrist.

"What?" he said, alarmed.

"Nothing it's just... Miranda."

"What about her?"

I killed her and hid her body in the snow, I thought. But I couldn't bring myself to say it. I realized I'd rather let her become a missing person than own up to reality. At the least, I wanted a final few days of quiet before I was always under a legal microscope—before the horrible second half of my life began. "We fought," I said instead. "It's nothing. Just stupid."

"It's ok, you've got sick brain." Howard kissed my forehead. "Just get some rest, ok?"

It was hard to see in the dim room, but when Howard looked at me while he gently closed the door, I swore the look on his face was one of suspicion.

SEEN ALIVE

I only managed to sleep a few hours. When I woke it was still light and I realized it was my phone vibrating on the nightstand that had taken me from my nap. I leaned over to look at the screen—it was Amy calling for a third time. I answered and took a deep breath before speaking.

"Katie? Katie, are you there?"

Amy sounded distressed and I sat up straighter in bed. "Yeah, yeah," I said panicked. "Can you hear me?"

"Yes, I can hear you. Has everything been okay there? Are you safe?"

"I'm fine. There was just a storm. Sorry, I didn't have any service. And I haven't been able to leave or get to any libraries."

"That's okay. I've gotten a lot done the last couple days. Is this a good time?"

"Yeah."

"I hadn't been able to make a connection between the individual cases. Forty-six missing girls. You'd think that'd be enough to find plenty of similarities, but seriously, there's no type between them. Race, class, education level, they're all different. But there are some connections between the cases *after* they went missing."

"How's that?"

"These are cold cases, all of them. No leads for years. Yet for seven of these forty-six girls there have been reports of people seeing them alive after they went missing. Can you guess where?"

"Colorado?"

"It gets more specific than that. All seven were reportedly seen in the Rocky Mountains. In state forests and state parks. Always in the woods. It's typically campers or hikers who saw them and made the reports. The stories are a little disturbing and mostly all the same. A girl is seen acting funny on a trail or a road. Three times the girls were naked, twice they were in a dress. The other sightings don't have clothing descriptions, but the point is these girls are not dressed for a hike. And not once has one of the girls ever spoken back. They always wander away into the woods."

It was just like what the bartender had said at Fools Gold. Just like the legends. "How were these girls recognized?" I asked.

"What?"

"You said these sightings are specific to seven of the missing girls. How did anyone make the connection between the strange girl they saw in the woods and a missing persons case?"

Amy was quiet for a second. "Oh! I see what you're asking. Sorry, I should've led with saying that the seven that have been seen are all local, as in they were last seen within a fifty-mile radius of the sightings. Not all the girls were *from* Colorado, but they all went missing in the area. None of the seven were last seen in Kansas, for instance."

"So, the cases had local coverage here?"

"Exactly and there's probably been a lot more sightings, but they're just not reported, or if they are, they aren't always linked to a missing persons case."

"I can't remember her name but one of those Williams cousins was sighted around here. Did you ever find out if their pictures were in that box?"

"No, they weren't. I don't know if that's a good thing or a bad thing. It might suggest that the case is unrelated. I don't know. Most of the sightings of the missing girls happened pretty long ago. The first one was in 2001 and the most recent and the closest sighting to you was a girl seen just outside of Gypsum in 2019."

"The girl, anything remarkable about that one?"

"Similar story to the rest of them. She was actually last seen alive the furthest from Colorado than any of the other girls. She was in Illinois, but I put her closer since her car was found in the Rockies," I heard her hum as she checked her notes, but I already knew. "Her vehicle was found at the Solitude Lake trailhead. She was one of the last girls in that box to go missing. A college junior named Claire Messer."

STAY

I was going to get to the bottom of Carson's Pass before I turned myself in. I said an oath to myself, and religiously or perhaps superstitiously, I made it to Miranda, too. I was going to do the right thing. But first, the mystery had motivated me to get out of bed. I changed the sheets and showered.

Claire. Alive! Amy sent me her source on the sighting. There was an online article in a small paper that was written one county over from Carson's Pass. The article interviewed a woman called Rose Mackler, who filed a police report saying she was walking her property of forty acres when she saw a woman sitting by its only stream. She said she went to tell the woman that she'd wandered onto private property but when she got close the woman stood abruptly and ran off. She recognized the woman as Claire almost right away.

She used to work as a forester and participated in some of the searches for Claire after her car was found. But that was it. One lousy article in a local paper. But I had a lead: Rose Mackler.

Claire wasn't the type to meet some people in the woods that could brainwash her to be a part of some blood cult. If she was still alive, she was drugged or lobotomized. If she was still alive, she wouldn't ever be the same Claire ever again. But this wasn't just about her. It was about the relief I would feel knowing that she didn't cry for help right in front of me only for me to let her kill herself the very next day.

I was feeling far less ill. My fever had broken, and I took a scorching hot shower to get the clammy sweat off my skin. I let my mind wander in the shower to where I hadn't been letting it. I had chalked my doubts surrounding Miranda's death to plain denial. But now, perhaps because I was playing detective once more, I allowed my conscience to voice its concerns.

I had to know if Miranda had a key. If she did it would still be on her person. I was feeling bold and restless from being in bed all day. I found Howard at his computer playing games and told him I was going to take a quick walk to get some fresh air in my lungs. He nodded, wide-eyed the way he does when his attention is elsewhere.

I went out the front door and circled around to the back. Once I reached Miranda, I patted the heap of her clear and emptied her pockets. I found her phone, keys, and some lip balm. I covered the body with snow again and I took her keys to the front door.

I tried them again and again, but either the keys wouldn't fit in the keyhole or they couldn't turn the deadbolt when they did. I took my set of keys out and unlocked the door with one swift click. It clearly wasn't the lock. Then, I suddenly felt immensely stupid. I took her keys to the back door and on the first one I tried, I was turning the lock.

Miranda had a key to the back door. One I didn't give her. I was about to ask Howard about it when I stopped in my tracks. Even if he'd given her a key that wasn't all. Only one set of tracks came to the back door the night I'd shot her. The set of tracks that started in the meadow seemed too big to be Miranda's, but she could've worn larger shoes.

But why would she bother disguising her prints I wondered, just as something caught my eye in the snow. There was a shiny piece of stainless steel drilled into the last stair on the back step. I bent to inspect it. It was a small circular hook with some string clinging to it. It had been cut and the only bit remaining was the knot. I looked up from the hook and realized it was pointed straight at the woods. I knew I was looking at what used to be a string guide. No wonder the footsteps from the meadow were so steady. They were led directly to the backdoor.

My mind ran in circles. I was far from a eureka moment with the information I had now. I needed to know more. Miranda's phone was locked but I could see she'd received several texts from her sister and some more from a contact labeled "BS" I didn't recognize the initials, if that's what those letters were.

But knowing Miranda, I thought it was more likely it meant bullshit. Something she didn't want to put up with.

I tried to unlock the phone using her address and then her birthday, but neither worked. I wasn't going to be able to see what the texts said. It would be getting dark soon, but I wasn't turning in for the night without a plan. Frustrated as I was, it was simple; to know more I needed to explore more. And first thing tomorrow, I was going to Miranda's house.

BREADCRUMBS

In the morning, I told Howard I was going to Miranda's to check on her since we hadn't spoken since our fight. Howard never paid attention to my arguments. He was bored by gossip. At first, I thought that might be a positive personality trait. His indifference made me feel guilty about gossiping. But the older I got, the more I realized he was just missing out because sometimes the weather doesn't cut it. Nor do I want to try to solve the world's problems over a cup of coffee. Nothing hits like some hot gossip.

So, I was surprised when Howard asked what Miranda and I had fought about. I hadn't thought of a lie. It never occurred to me that I'd need to. I stuttered.

"Um, I ah... I went off on her for defending Bea. She tried to say it wasn't all that horrible of her to follow us out here without telling us."

Howard smacked his lips and rolled his eyes. "Oh boy. Your sister doesn't need an ally."

"Tell me about it." I sighed, relieved that his inquiry didn't turn into an interrogation.

He kissed my cheek. "Alright, well dress warm."

When I was walking down the driveway, I frowned realizing I wasn't hit by the usual sting of guilt when I deceived Howard. I had cruelly adapted into someone I desperately didn't want to be.

"And for what?" I said aloud and then answered in my head. *For the chance to break some news story that I had let destroy my life.* But I was so deep in the hole that to succeed only meant to fail less.

The McCarthy family's home was just before Miranda's. I peeked towards the house with the incestuous siblings. While our driveway road curved, theirs was dead straight. The road ran right to their front door. I almost stopped walking and stumbled a step.

On the side of the McCarthys house, I saw Philip smoking a cigarette. He noticed my gaze and he flicked it to his feet and turned his attention to mashing the butt with his heel. I waved slightly, but his head was tucked too far down to see. He didn't want to acknowledge me. I had already passed the house by the time I saw him finally bring his head up.

I'd never seen Philip smoke. But that wasn't what was weird. Why was he outside the McCarthy's?

There could be a rational explanation. I heard the generator groaning behind house, and I figured Philip was tending to a problem with the power. Carson's Pass didn't seem ready to have residents when we had moved in and Philip had his hands full because of it. I didn't think much more of it. I was distracted. Kenna and Aiden were walking towards me down the road, each with a bag of groceries under their arm.

"Hello!" Kenna said cheerfully when we were still an awkward distance apart. I just smiled and delayed for a second until we were closer.

"Hi," I said. The sound of crunching snow stopped as the three of us met. "How have you both been?"

"Oh, alright," said Kenna.

"Bored..." Aiden said. "To be completely honest."

"You two aren't really at the right age for this place. Not much for a social scene here."

"You don't say," said Aiden.

I pointed at their bags. "Have you met Jacob? He works at the market. And there's another girl at that grocery store around your guys' age."

"Yeah, Sydney's cool. But that Jacob dude got fired."

"Oh, wasn't he the one that found the Millers?"

"No," Aiden's voice rose in confusion. "He was fired before then."

"What for?"

"Breaking the rules."

"Like drugs?"

"No, like—" Aiden looked to his sister and something registered on his face as Kenna glared at him. "Oh. Yeah, drugs or whatever. He did something stupid. Nothing you'd have to worry about doing. But hey, we heard you're having a party."

"Who told you that?"

"Our parents. Your husband stopped by to invite them and he said we could come too. By the way, what're your thoughts on underage drinking?"

Kenna hit him in the ribs with her elbow. "We should get going, these are for breakfast." She raised the grocery bag in her arms in emphasis and started walking but I stepped in her path.

"Wait." I pointed over my shoulder with a thumb. "Why is Philip outside your house? Is everything ok?"

"Uh..." Aiden looked at Kenna for permission to speak but she didn't meet his eye.

"We don't know. Our parents sent us out to get groceries when he showed up like we're actual children. Now, if you don't mind..."

I realized I probably looked like a mess. Sick and sleep-deprived. They said nothing and stepped past me. I watched them over my shoulder and when both their heads swiveled back to look at me, I spun to avoid their gaze.

When I got to Miranda's house, I felt relief. Her car was in her garage and her lights were off. It didn't look like she was home. It would be plenty possible to convince anyone who asked where she was that she had gone back to San Diego. I held Miranda's keys tightly in my fist as I walked up to her front door. I resisted the urge to look over each shoulder before unlocking it. Those kids could tell I was acting strange already and if anyone was watching me, I didn't want to seem more suspicious.

The door opened smoothly, and I shut it gently behind me. It was freezing inside. Her furnace must not have restarted on its own when the power came back on. My breath plumed in front of me as if I were outside.

My steps creaked noisily on the floorboards as I made my way to her staircase. It was similar to mine. But when I got down and searched the stairs, I couldn't find the little latch buttons like I had on mine. It wasn't identical. None of the stairs seemed to open. I stood back and surveyed the room. There were a few rectangles of snow on the floor, the kind that falls from shoe treads. I went over and crouched next to them. It was cold inside, but was it cold enough for snow not to melt for days? I looked further across the floor and my question was answered for me. There was a puny puddle with a melting piece of snow sitting in its center.

I shot up erect and spun around the room. Someone had been here this morning. As my pulse quickened, I grew lightheaded. I had left my gun at home. I never wanted to touch it again after what happened with Miranda, but I was beginning to regret leaving it behind. Whoever it was they could still be here. But my mind was focused on Philip, and he was at the McCarthy's. He couldn't have gotten back to Miranda's before I did.

I stepped into the kitchen. The counters were completely clean, and I didn't need to look hard to find a clue. Sitting next to the coffee maker was an orange Post-it-Note. I knew Miranda's handwriting but only because of how sloppy it was. She'd written me a card for my birthday last month that was a strange mix of cursive and print. As far as I could tell the note wasn't written in her handwriting. The words were blocky but easy to read. For whatever reason it didn't seem like it was left as a reminder. No. The message was an order.

It read in strong bolded letters: Bring her to Morrow Lake

FORTY-SEVEN-FEET

I set the Post-it back on the counter gently and went back towards her staircase. I wanted to see if I could find the trash bag of clothes but couldn't bring myself to go upstairs. The upstairs hallway at Miranda's house wasn't visible over a balustrade like it was in mine. The top of the stairs was walled on either side. My heart beat harder as I pictured someone waiting up there for me.

Before I knew what I was doing I turned on my heel and marched right back out the front door. I shook myself off when I got outside. What did Miranda have to do with Morrow Lake? There could be something that we missed. Something that *I* missed. I hadn't had time to think about those clothes we found. The blizzard hit, and then I was alone in my house, and then...

I stopped in my tracks. There wasn't much to put together. I should've done it so much sooner, but I was a shitty detective.

The little fishing boat on the shore, the clothing and the missing girls. There was blood on some of those clothes. Enough blood to suggest that whoever those clothes belonged to might no longer be alive. This rocky, cold soil isn't great for burying bodies, but who would ever search the bottom of an alpine lake?

*

Back home I took my computer to the bedroom. Howard knocked and stuck his head around the door. I panicked for a moment realizing I hadn't rehearsed a lie for Miranda's whereabouts, but he didn't ask about my outing.

"How're you feeling?"

"Better!" I said, nodding my head too quickly. I was like a child, relieved I wasn't asked the question that would get me caught. "I'm thinking of taking a longer hike later."

"Good, that's great. I was partly asking because of that party I asked you about... I know you're still sick but I kinda already told everyone to be there or be square."

I rubbed my forehead. "Oh, what day?"

"I said Friday, remember?"

"Tomorrow?" I said like the idea hurt. "That's fine. I can be scarce, right?"

"So long as you're here. Can you promise me that?"

"Yeah, I'll be here."

"Seriously, no emergency runs to town or anything like that. I haven't seen a lot of you lately. This party is my one request of you. Please?"

"Granted. I promise I'll be here. We're not doing food ourselves?"

"God no. I already talked to the grocery kids, they're going to get everything we need. It's only going to be about sixteen people."

"Sixteen? I thought you said twelve?"

"Sorry. Word got out. Some of my friends back in San Diego really want to see this place. They think we're in a cult."

"Why, are they trying to join one?"

"No, but maybe they'd invest."

"It's looking like a short-term investment."

"What?" His eyes lit up. "You think you'll be done here soon?"

"One way or another."

"Ok, cool. Let's at least throw a bash before we're outta here."

"Sounds like you're on it." I looked back to my computer and felt his eyes on me as he shut the door gently.

I found a state government webpage that detailed the size and depth of Morrow Lake. The max depth was forty-eight feet. If the wind was calm and the water was crystal clear, I'd probably be able to see all the way to the bottom if I was in that boat. Or at least I'd be able to see the blurry outline of any bodies that were down there.

It hadn't been cold enough for the lake to have iced over since I was there last with Miranda. I could hike up, take the boat out and see for myself. If I found what I thought I might I would really be done. I could leave. I looked out the window and saw the tops of the trees rocking ever so slightly in the breeze.

The weather wasn't calm enough for good visibility. There might be moments where I could see down into the water, but it wouldn't be consistently clear. I wasn't going to wait for good weather. I was in the mountains in winter. The day might not come for weeks but luckily, I had a solution. I had packed my gym bag and I went to the closet and pulled it out. I unzipped the side pocket and grabbed a pair of never used swim goggles. I could dunk my head off the side of the boat to see down. It seemed ridiculous but it would work. Forty-eight feet isn't very deep and that's the *max* depth. The average was probably far lower.

The hike up through the snow might prove difficult but I had seen a pair of snowshoes in the garage. They had looked functional, made of metal and black plastic straps. They weren't the ancient wooden ones that hang crucified on cabin walls. I went into the bathroom and took a literal handful of ibuprofen. I let their sugar shells melt on my tongue before I swallowed them. I was still somewhat sick, but I only had to feel good enough to get up there and get back in one piece.

I told myself that I owed it to Amy, to Miranda. But it had begun to dawn on me that things were not at all as they seemed and that maybe the only person I owed this to was myself.

WET SUIT

I left the house like a pack mule. Snowshoes under my arms, my parka's pockets snug with the swim goggles and pistol. I knew I looked strange, but I didn't care anymore. I took the road I would take to go to Miranda's house in order to reach the trailhead.

When I passed the McCarthy's house there was no one out. The door was shut coffin tight and the blinds were drawn, leaving every window dark. I walked faster and when I got close to the grocer's, I noticed that Randy's snowplow was parked where the road ended. There was a gap between the trees where he parked his blow. I remembered what the driver had said about the old road to Carson's Pass that had become a runaway truck ramp. I went over and looked over the snowbank the plow was parked in front of.

Sure enough, I could see all the way to the highway that led to Gypsum. It was about a half mile of mountain away, all downhill. The runaway truck ramp started halfway down but since the whole spot used to be a road there were just a few saplings growing above where the gravel ramp ended. It gave me a perspective of where I was. I didn't realize we were so close to the main highway.

I went back past the little grocery store and to the trailhead. When I reached it, I stood and paused, considering the path. Something wasn't right. The snow had been packed down tight. It looked like it had even been shoveled. It was possible that Philip planned to keep the trails up year-round, but this was the mountains. It could snow 200 inches in a single winter. To keep this trail clear so just one or two residents could hike it wouldn't be worth the effort. It didn't make sense and it made me nervous. But I told myself that was only because it meant I was heading in exactly the right direction.

It was slow going up the mountain, but with my sickness I didn't have much of a choice. I didn't want to rush anyway. I needed my stamina and I needed to be able to hear every rustle in the woods.

Thankfully, it was far easier to see the little connecting trail that led to the lake this time. The branches and brush that had hid it the first time had all been cleared. Blond nubs of naked tree flesh showed where the branches had been sawn. It was all so fresh I could still smell the sap and pulp of fresh cut wood.

Something was wrong. My gut feeling told me to take the pistol out, but I couldn't. I pictured the last time I raised that thing. Regardless of the danger I kept my hands empty and by my sides.

When I got to the lake shore I was shocked by a maze of footprints. It wasn't cleared like the trail had been and the prints pocked the snow in the hundreds. There were different sizes and treads and there was a big sliding track mark that I assumed was from the boat's hull. One set of steps went around the lake the same way Miranda and I had gone when we found the clothes.

The water was rimmed with a little lip of ice. It was perfectly clear, and brittle. Easy to break through. But the surface of the water was rippled and darkened from the wind. There would be no easy view down to the lake bottom. I would have to get my head wet.

The boat was where I'd last seen it, belly up just before the tree line. But I bit my lip as I got closer. There was a gaping black hole in its hull. It'd been cut crudely, probably with the same saws that were used to clear the branches. It was apparent it wouldn't float. I spun around, my eyes dancing in the woods and on the ridgelines.

There was no one there. Just a strong wind that whipped wisps of snow from the peaks. I was not half-assing this and going home. I could swim and survey the bottom. But if I took off my clothes and waded into that cold water, I could get hypothermia in ten minutes. I had every excuse not to do it: I was sick, I'd be vulnerable, the walk back was long and even after throwing the parka back on it was possible that I'd freeze to death.

But before I knew it, I was clearing the snow from a patch of shore and kicking off my boots. My clothes quickly pooled at my feet. I thought about keeping on my t-shirt and underwear but knew wearing them while wet could kill me. Better to keep them dry and use them as towels.

I took the gun and put it under my coat and then put on the swim goggles. I wasted no time walking into the lake.

The sheen of ice gave way, crackling noisily like a bag of chips. I stopped when I was still just shin deep and stood gasping. It was so cold there wasn't even a shock, just steady burning pain. I stared at my feet which were magnified and corpse-white under the water, trying to prepare myself for what might be the most painful thing I had ever done. Inhale, exhale.

If the water shocked me and I took in a lung full of lake it would be over. I steadied my breath and focused on the glacial stones under the surface—black, blue and smooth as sucked candies. I was losing body heat just standing in the freezing wind. I didn't have time to splash myself wet one cupped palm at a time. I grimaced and dove headlong.

Cold. Cold was an understatement. It was fucking, flipping, earth-shatteringly freezing. I didn't realize water could be as cold as the lake was and still not be ice. Ten minutes, I thought. Tops. Any longer and I'd be in serious danger. I took a heaving breath and put my head under. It was a blue world of boulders and sunken barkless trees.

I started swimming and propelled my feet like a motor behind me. The lake was long and if I tried to swim the full 200 yards each way I'd probably die even if I did make it back to my clothes. I'd evaluate a quarter of the way across. If I felt good, I'd go as far as halfway.

It was astounding how well I could see. The water didn't blur all the way to the bottom. I stopped swimming and treaded water. Whether it was my body getting used to the cold or simply shutting down, I didn't know, but I wasn't in as much pain anymore.

I put my head back under and swam slower, so I was able to see. Not more than a minute later I noticed something other than the plain rocky bottom further ahead. Something bright and pale. I surfaced to see how far I was from shore, further than fifty yards already. My adrenaline had begun to flow. It tingled in my stomach and I knew I had to swim faster if I was to get back fast enough to not freeze.

I pounded the water in the direction of the object I saw. My arms were rowing and my feet thunk-thunked behind me. When I reached where I thought I'd be able to better see the pale thing I was gasping for air. I had to tread water while I caught my breath before going back under.

I submerged myself again. I was right on top of the thing. At first, I couldn't quite register what I was looking at, but my subconscious seemed to realize what I saw because I felt something like a lightning bolt bouncing through my body. I began to sink, slowly, as I stared holding my breath in disbelief. There, on the blue lake bottom, was a dead naked woman. Her hair floated gently in a halo around her head. It was exactly what I had expected to find. Only it wasn't that simple.

My disbelief wasn't from being right about the lake, it was from Miranda's dead eyes staring back at me from the depths.

SLIP

I breached the surface in a panic. I bumped my goggles, breaking the seal and they fogged up quick. I ripped them off my head and let them sink. I coughed while trying to calm myself. *Time to get back. Time to get back.*

The lake was longer than it was wide, and I could reach either shore to my left or right in half the distance it would take to swim back. But then I'd be barefoot in the snow and could slip on a stone. Plus, I figured the wind striking my wet body would probably feel even colder than the water did. I began to swim back as calmly as I could. The blood had left my brain, I pictured it pooling around all my organs, my heart, my liver, my lungs, trying hopelessly to warm them against the wall of icy water outside. I tried to forget everything I'd just seen. Screw the story. Screw success.

Survive.

I counted my strokes, my breaths. *One, two, three. One, two, three.* It was just a little ballroom dance back to shore and down the mountain. One stroke, then one step at a time. Literally. *Picture wrapping yourself in the parka. Pace yourself. Breathe. Repeat.*

Suddenly my feet could touch. I was less than twenty yards from my clothes and scrambled out of the icy water. But I was so focused on warmth I forgot to watch my step. My foot landed on the spine of a sharp stone and I lifted it so quickly that I lost my balance and fell banging my knee against a boulder on my way down.

I lay there coming to terms with death. I didn't think I broke anything. The cold seemed to numb the pain in my knee, but I knew I couldn't stand right away. I had to let the waves of dull pain pass through me. I could feel my pulse throb in my leg. Seconds were precious. It was too soon but I tried to stand. My whole leg was lame. It hurt like hell to put weight on it, but I pushed through.

"Fuck. Fuck, Fuck," I said with every limp step I took toward my clothes. I dried myself with my shirt as quickly as I could and threw on the heavy parka. Before getting dressed any further, I tucked my shoulders towards each other and let myself shiver.

It may have been a minute. It may have been much longer, but I felt myself getting warmer. When my shivers stopped, I got dressed the rest of the way. I went through a little checklist to get calm: I could feel my fingers, I could feel my toes. And I didn't have any serious symptoms of hypothermia, no delusion or hot flashes. I wasn't going to just keel over die. But out of the water I felt sicker than before. I was all heavy-headed with sinus pressure.

I stood for a moment looking at the lake. *Who brought her up here? When? For what?* My brain was bloodless from the cold. I couldn't focus on any one question. They all swirled around my head like dollar bills in a cash grab machine, and I couldn't catch a single one.

I would've already been running home if I found those missing girls instead of Miranda. But it was my own hellish mistake staring back up at me. Still, I realized, I hadn't searched the whole lake. There could be more bodies down there. It suggested that Philip, the other residents, or whoever was behind the disappearances used Morrow Lake as a burial spot. But I was done trying to answer questions myself. Not in the state I was in.

I staggered towards the trail, drunk from exhaustion, my neck barely able to support my lead-filled head. I wasn't being careful. I even knew it when I was walking. In just a few steps my boot slipped off a stone and my right foot fell into a wedge between two rocks.

I tried to keep my balance but with the added vertigo from my illness I fell hard on the rocky shore. I groaned and stayed still. This was bad. It was hard to move but I had to.

There was a sharp pain in my ankle. It was so strong I no longer felt my injured knee. It was just a fall, I told myself. I wasn't *that* old. I moved my foot under me to take my weight as I stood but as soon as I pushed off the ground the pain in my ankle exploded. I fell right back down. I sat holding my ankle in both hands like I was doing some kind of runner's stretch. My head rocked back and forth. I wasn't warm enough to stay out here. Even if I hadn't spent seven minutes in the lake, I'd still freeze to death in these elements.

It was little more than a mile back. I could hop or limp, but this was my life and if I had too, I'd crawl. My body was still losing heat under the heavy clothes and I had some time. I had to *move*. I rolled my ankle on its joint and looked at the trees that swayed where the trail started. But something caught my eye. Mounted above a branch and crudely camouflaged was a security camera.

I doubted my eyes for a moment but after staring long enough its features became clear: The black lens, the stem that connected the camera to its base. And there at the top of the tree, an antenna.

Staring into the black lens was horrifying. It felt like someone was staring back. I grabbed a thick stick and snapped off its smaller branches to make a walking stick. I stood and felt for the pistol in my pocket. Every step was a burning shot of pain, but I clenched my teeth and steadily walked on.

TIME GAPS

I made it. I briefly remembered getting home. There was Howard's shocked and concerned face greeting me in the living room. When I got to bed, he brought me a hot drink and hot towels and then everything faded out. I had fever dreams, strange shifting images, like my mind was a kaleidoscope. I saw Bea holding a knife to my throat while Howard laughed. I saw Claire begging them to let me live. Then all of a sudden Randy was in his snowplow trying to run me over.

While the dreams were obviously fantasy, the sounds I head in my sleep seemed real. There was the groan of an engine and then the sharp beeps of a vehicle in reverse. Afterward there was the muffled sound of men talking. The sounds of construction. But it was quiet when I woke. I looked right and left, surprised to see I was alive and in my bed. There was a heating pad burning my back and blankets mounded on top of me. Weak light came from between the blind slats. Dawn or dusk, I was so disoriented I couldn't tell. I was scorching hot and I tossed the covers off but when I tried to stand from bed, I collapsed under my weight immediately.

I yelled in pain, pressing my face against the rug. My ankle was on fire. I reached back to touch it and saw it was now mummied in a beige bandage. Footsteps pounded outside the door and Howard came barreling in.

"Katie! Are you okay?" he bent to me and I sat up quickly as to not look so pathetic sprawled on the floor.

"I'm fine." I put my palms on the floor and pushed off, groaning as I stood and sat back on the bed. "I'm ok, really. I just forgot."

"I almost took you to the hospital," Howard lifted my foot by the heel and squeezed my toes.

"Ow!" It hurt and I almost batted him away but realized maybe this was exactly what our relationship needed. Him worrying about me might make him realize what I really mean to him. "It's ok. I'm not frostbitten."

"They didn't look great earlier. Sorry for making sure you keep your feet."

I wiggled my toes. They were as pink as a newborn. Howard stood and thumbed a sheen of sweat off my hairline. "What were you doing out there? When you got back here your hair was frozen solid. Were you swimming?"

I looked at my nightstand and then around the room. "Where's my phone?"

"It's with your coat downstairs. I left it next to your *gun*." Howard let out a dramatic sigh. "I don't know what you're up to, but this is ridiculous, Katie. You could be dead." He eyed me with anxiety, and I felt my heart lift a little. I was beginning to think he really didn't give a shit about me. But I had more pressing matters.

"I'm sorry. It'll make sense, I love you, Howard. But can you just get me my phone, please?"

Howard patted my thigh and left the room. He came back several minutes later with my phone in one hand and a steaming mug in the other. "Your favorite," he said and set the mug gently on the nightstand. I could pick up the medicinal scent of alcohol and tea rising from the steam. "Half honey, half whiskey. There's some tea in there somewhere," Howard said. "Get back to sleep. I'll talk to Philip about selling this place."

"No, Howard we need to leave now."

He gave me another disappointed paternal sigh. "I'm not going to fight with you right now. We have a *party* here tomorrow. People have made plans. The next day, first thing, fine we can leave. But I'm staying here unless you want to tell me exactly what's going on."

I licked my lips and opened my mouth, but as I pictured Miranda's body floating along the bottom of the lake, I said nothing.

"Look, I'm not trying to be an asshole but think about it, I'm not dragging you crippled and sick out of here and to some

209

hotel. Your ankle's probably just sprained. After a good night's sleep, you'll probably be able to put some weight on it." He walked to the door and before he shut it, he turned back to me. "Rest."

As soon as the door clicked shut, I opened my phone and stared at Jack's contact. Maybe I couldn't say what I'd done aloud, but I could let someone find out. I'd tell the police there was a body in Morrow Lake and when I was finally confronted, I'd fold. Maybe the missing girls would be found down there, too. Dozens of found skeletons would make Miranda's death a footnote. I wouldn't feel like as much of a fool.

My thumb hovered above the call button on the screen and my heart accelerated. These would be the last moments before my life became a long line of lawyers and courtrooms for who knows how long. I drank my boozy tea to garner some courage for the call.

Only when the mug was empty did I put the phone to my ear, but I was immediately met with an electronic voice telling me the number I had dialed was not in service. I checked my signal, but it was strong.

Then I remembered how Jack had never responded to my text. It was possible I entered his number wrong, but I had no clue where I'd left his card.

I looked up the non-emergency number for the Colorado State Police. I answered a series of prerecorded questions by dialing different numbers. It took punching in half a dozen numbers before the line began to ring to connect me with someone.

A woman answered, "Hello, State PD."

"Hi there," I paused. Talking made me feel winded. "I'm hoping you could connect me with a detective. His name his uh—" I frowned. I suddenly couldn't remember his name. The booze was heavy and burning in my stomach. The drink didn't seem that strong. "Jack!" I said. "Jack... Reid. He's in homicide."

"Um. Just a moment." She didn't put me on hold, I heard a muffled whispering. "I'm sorry but, there's no Jack Reid in homicide."

"Are you sure?"

"I'm positive. We don't have any Jacks. Do you have reason to believe someone may have been impersonating an officer?"

"No. I just must have the wrong name. Thank you," I said quickly and hung up.

I chewed on the thought for a minute, widening my eyes to stay awake. Jack had said he was based out of Denver but maybe he meant a suburb. It didn't feel likely. Something told me he wasn't a cop. Either he was just some whacko interjecting himself into the case or... Suddenly I remembered Bea's story about the handsome stranger offering her a life in the mountains. Could it have been him?

But if he was involved with these missing girls, why did he tell me all that stuff at the bar? It was careless. Stupid. But he probably didn't think it mattered, because I was the next girl to go.

I was sitting up in bed, racking it over in my head. Suddenly I realized I'd been nodding off. I wanted desperately to stay awake. But from the cold shock or maybe the drink, my head fell towards my shoulder and I drifted off to sleep.

LUCID DREAMING

The world was dark and freezing cold. But it was neither of those things that woke me. It took me a second to realize what I was feeling. A pair of puckered lips were pressed into mine. Someone was kissing me. I squirmed and they pulled back with a smack. When they brought their face away from mine, I could see.

Two torches flickered in the wind. They illuminated stones, snow and stagnant water: The shore of Morrow Lake.

"Wake up, Katie," said the lips that had pulled away from mine. Their hair was blown across their face like a mask of long black grass. They parted it over their shoulder and smiled. It was a girl, Kenna. I moved my mouth to speak but only moaned. "Shh." She put her finger to my lips. "Don't speak," she whispered. "Just watch." She smiled again. Her white teeth flashed in the night.

Kenna turned from me and stepped towards the torches and two men stepped from the shadows in ski masks. This has to be a dream, I thought. My mind was somewhere between awake and asleep. I felt like I was high, if anything.

Kenna let her coat slide off before she tilted her head back and stretched her arms high above her head as if she were going to pluck the stars from the sky. One of the men grabbed her sweater and worked it up her torso while the other snapped the fly of her jeans open and tore them off. They took off her black bra and flung it to the lake where it fell like a dead bat.

Even with my blurry vision, I could see her smooth skin become rippled with goosebumps. It was horribly cold.

Both the men held one of her hands to steady her while she stepped out of her underwear herself. Then with Kenna between them, and the torches in their free hands, they began walking uphill.

I realized I was on my knees. I wriggled and tried to speak, but I couldn't form words. I felt pressure under my armpits, and I looked down and to see small, gloved fingers resting above my left breast. Someone was holding me up so I could see. I tossed my head back to try to see who it was, but I took a blunt hit to my spine. It was probably their knee and it knocked the wind out of me. I coughed and as I caught my breath, I saw Kenna under the torch light up the ridge. She was stopped and not all that far from me, but with my haggard eyes I could only see a naked blur.

I bit my tongue, trying to focus on the pain, trying to see if this was real. The pain was muted, like I'd been drugged. Then I ran my tongue across the inside of my mouth and felt the ridges in my molars, the sharp undersides of my canines and I knew this was no dream.

"Katie!" Kenna shouted. "To die is an honor, do you know that?" The men were each running something gently across her skin. It wasn't until I saw a silver flicker in the torchlight that I realized what I was looking at: knives.

Kenna sat on something and as I tried to scream, she waved to me with her fingers like a pageant queen. Suddenly, a ruffling of fabric roared as it rubbed against my ears. Someone was covering my head with something soft. And like the lid of a casket being closed the world blackened, and the lack of any light lulled my drugged brain back to sleep.

BLOODSTONE

When I woke up again, I did not sleepily greet the day. My eyes shot wide open and I stared unblinking at the ceiling for several seconds. I was back in my bed. I sprang up in the sheets and looked around. It was just as it had been. Heating pad, empty mug of whiskey and tea.

I stared at the empty mug with tears welling in my eyes. I thought my drink must've been spiked. I lifted it and smelled the inside. Boozy and honey sweet. Nothing chemical or out of the ordinary. But I'd heard that many date-rape drugs were flavorless.

I tossed the mug back on the nightstand. The scene at the lake shore was real. I was certain it was. There was a path leading up to a stone. I remembered when Miranda and I had been at the lake just before the blizzard. She'd pointed out a rock that she thought looked funny and wanted to check it out so bad. And those footsteps I'd seen there in the snow when I went in the lake, they went right to where we'd found the clothes. To that stone Miranda saw.

I was a shitty detective.

I grabbed my phone off the nightstand. 11:27 in the morning. I got up from bed and raced to the closet to get dressed. It wasn't until I saw the bandage while I was trying to pull a pant leg over it that I realized the pain in my ankle was gone. It was numb altogether.

I frowned and unraveled the bandage round and round until my pale skin was exposed. I prodded the area with my fingers. Numb. In multiple spots there were dimples the size of pen tips. Needle marks, I realized. Someone had injected me with a steroid so I could walk. But last night, I was too drugged to move on my own. If I was actually at the lake, I would've needed to be carried there. I finished dressing and practically jogged downstairs.

"Howard!" I said weaving around the furniture. There was some commotion in the kitchen. I went in and saw the redheaded girl from the grocers who hadn't looked me in the eye. There was also a young man in his twenties I didn't recognize. Probably the replacement for the kid that was fired. They were taking cases of wine and beer off a dolly.

"Hello!" they said cheerfully but didn't stop working.

"What is this?"

"Uh." The girl stood straight and looked at her coworker with concern, but he didn't stop unloading the dolly. She fumbled for something in her pocket. "Delivery order." She handed me a receipt for $1200 in booze. "Hope we didn't spoil a surprise party or something, but Howard said to bring it in."

It felt weird to hear them say my husband's name so casually. It was like they knew him. "Where is Howard?"

"We haven't seen him. He said he'd leave the back door unlocked."

"Ok," I flashed an anxious smile. "Thank you."

I went to the window to see if Howard had taken the car, but it was still in the driveway.

I couldn't find my pistol in any obvious place, but I didn't look much harder. I wasn't as scared as I thought I'd be. If anything, I was confident. They'd had every opportunity to kill me, yet I'd been left alive. But for what?

I went to the front door and suited up. Boots, coat, hat, gloves and I was gone. I wasn't looking for Howard and I wasn't going to the police. I was going to see the vivid scene of my dream.

The trail to Morrow Lake seemed to be packed tight with more prints than the last time I walked it. And when I got to the lake shore, I saw hundreds of footsteps in the deep snow. There was a path that was heavily trafficked going toward where Miranda and I had found the clothes. I followed it, walking slower, skeptically. I knew what I was about to find. And then it stopped me in my tracks: Kenna's thick sweater piled up like a python. I turned around and the rest of Kenna's clothes were

215

where they'd fallen in my dream. A pair of ripped jeans, her underwear lay on a rock. And sunken in the clear water was a black bra.

I started walking uphill. I could see the stone that Miranda had mentioned. I was so afraid when we were at the lake shore together during the blizzard that I hadn't looked closely. But it was hard to miss. A big boulder had been sawn in two, so it was flat like an altar. The top half of the boulder that had been cut was rolled off and fell down the ridge. It humped atop the other stones like a whale's back.

I stopped, putting the puzzle pieces together in my head. Miranda had been the one to find the hidden trail that came here. She'd picked the direction we went around the lake. She'd found the clothes. She'd been showing me everything, and she *knew*. Why?

I slowed as I approached the sawn boulder. Blood had run off the altar in so many drops that hundreds of brown stripes stained the stone. I checked my service: no bars. I looked over my shoulder and started taking pictures. The blood was still wet, and it pooled in the divots where the rock was chipped and pocked. I snapped one more picture and stared down the slope.

It was all true. So, how was I taken from my bed without Howard noticing? Could he have been one of the two masked men that held Kenna? But I couldn't picture him caught up in a cult. Video-gaming, easily embarrassed Howard. He had anger in him. Rage, sure. But violence wasn't who he was. Was it?

But out of all the questions, only one stayed at the forefront of my mind. Someone had wanted me to find all this—the stone, the clothes, the blood. Why?

MANILA

I kept my phone in my hand as I walked back, checking my service every minute. I was going to call 911 the second I had bars. I would wait at the trailhead for the police to come and let my life unravel along with this whole story. But something was bugging me.

I couldn't figure it out. Why would they kill Kenna just to let me call the police? They were either so delusional they thought I'd want to join their blood cult, or they were baiting me. Then there was the fact that Jack said he didn't trust the sheriff, but Jack wasn't even a cop. He was probably the one holding me up by my shoulders when I was at the lakeshore. A branch snapped somewhere in the woods and I spun my head so fast to look that I tweaked my neck. A red squirrel chattered angrily at me and I rubbed my nape.

I had to think. There was something I was missing but nothing came through my brain fog. No epiphany or explanation. I cursed and kicked the snow. Why would they bait me? It still didn't feel like the best idea to call the police, but it was all I could do.

I almost expected to see those masked men waiting for me at the trailhead but there was no one. But as I started walking on the road suddenly my phone buzzed and pinged as it received a handful of texts at once. I stared at the screen. They were all from Amy. I was confused. Based on the urgency of her texts it was as if she'd been trying to get ahold of me for days. They were anxious messages in all caps.

"WHERE ARE YOU?? CALL ME BACK!
PO BOX NOW! Emergency. DON'T CALL. TEXT ONLY."
I texted her back right away:
"Are we danger? Going to PO box ASAP."
She responded immediately:
"I'm ok. Where have you been? PO box explains everything"

217

I texted her quickly that I was ok and going to the PO box now. However, I kept staring at my phone. I had service and knew I should call the police. Yet, my thumb was frozen. I was dying to find out what was in that PO box. If I called the police, the gig was up. I'd be in handcuffs after I admitted to accidentally killing and hiding Miranda's body. Then it hit me. There might not be any evidence that Miranda's body was moved to the lake by someone else. The police might think it was me. They'd think I was lying. I might end up as the only one under investigation. I had to make sure Amy could back me up. I could only hope that the smoking gun of all this evidence was in the PO box.

Carson's Pass was eerily quiet as I walked the rest of the way home. There was no wind, and the pine needles and their endless rustling were finally silenced.

I stared at the McCarthy's house as I passed it. Their cars were in the driveway, but the ground floor windows were dark as they always were. Maybe it was just like the Millers. Maybe the whole family was dead. I remembered Kenna was jubilant on the lake shore. She'd been smiling. She'd been *kissing* me. "To die is an honor," she had said. She'd known about the sacrificial stone since she'd moved to Carson's Pass. I shuddered, remembering seeing the twins kiss that first night. I wondered whether those two men in the masks who stripped her naked were her brother and father.

At home, the kitchen had been stocked with more booze and food, but the grocers were gone. Howard was still nowhere to be found and when I called him it went straight to voicemail. I searched the basement and all the bedrooms. Nothing.

I stood with my hands on my hips chewing my lip in the living room. I had to go to Gypsum, I thought. But where the hell was my husband? Wasn't he having a party? I narrowed my eyes at the floor. On the hardwood, half hidden under an end table, was a dollop of gray stone. I bent down and picked at it with my nail. It was concrete. Dried concrete. I stood lest I get distracted any longer. The mystery of Howard and the damn concrete could wait. I needed to get to that PO box.

*

I did my best not to speed. I spent the entire drive there debating how to get the police involved. I was being outsmarted already. It was too easy. I had a feeling if I came back with cops looking for Miranda's body and the bloody altar both would somehow be gone.

I had to play this right. It all depended on what Amy had for me. Perhaps combined with what I knew this could pin them dead to rights. But I couldn't even begin to guess what she'd mailed me. I parked in front of the post office. I caught myself walking too fast. I slowed, breathed and opened the door.

A middle-aged woman looked up from a book and widened her eyes at me. "Going to the PO box room?" she asked.

"Yeah." I stopped walking. She motioned to a basket on the counter with a lamented notecard hanging from the handle that read, "deposit phones."

"There's someone else in there, we don't allow phones back there. We had an incident the other day with a man taking indecent pho-tos."

"You're kidding?" I didn't want to give this woman my phone, but this was a government building, after all, and I didn't think I'd get my way. She had that rough-skinned rural look that said she wasn't a bullshitter.

She didn't respond. She just stared me down and pushed the basket closer.

I shook my head, pissed off, and tossed my phone in the basket. I wouldn't be more than a minute. I went briskly into the room with the PO boxes.

All the boxes looked the same and I'd forgotten which was mine. Luckily there was a lanyard on the key I'd been given with the number scribbled in sharpie: 112.

219

It took me a second to find it. I went to put the key in the lock, but it didn't fit. I brought the key to my eye to inspect it. There was a tiny bump of what looked like dried pine sap on the end. I had to scrape it away with my fingernail. When it was off, I tried it again and swung open the little metal door. Stuffed inside was a large manila envelope. I snatched it and didn't even close the box behind me. I didn't say a goodbye to the woman on my way out. I just grabbed my phone and tried not to run.

Back in the car, I sat behind the wheel and pulled out the envelope. I flipped it over. In big black letters it read:

DO NOT OPEN UNTIL HOME!

I stared at it and sighed. I reckoned the reasons why Amy thought it was better for me to open it at home. Was it so shocking I shouldn't be driving? Was it not safe to look anywhere except where I knew I was alone?

I ran my finger against the envelope flap. Amy was just being paranoid. I couldn't think of any reason why opening it here was different than at home. I tore the top off and stuck my hand in. I felt slick, lamented paper and pulled out a handful of pictures.

I gasped and dropped them in my lap. I cupped my mouth in my palm and stared down at the photographs. It was an interior shot. A rope was slung over a door and at the end, in high definition, a woman hung at the end of it, her russet hair covering her face. Amy.

I was seeing stars. I pulled out my phone and dialed her number, but it rang only once before I was greeted by three high beeps and the prerecorded apologies of the operator, "We're sorry, you have reached a number that has been disconnected or is no longer in service..." I slowly brought the phone down from my ear.

Close your eyes, I thought. *Before we close them for you.*

The photo had been taken in the dark. Amy's body was illuminated with the cool white light of a camera flash. I flipped through the other pictures, heart pounding, brow sweating.

They were all essentially the same as the first photo, only taken at different distances.

I put them back in the envelope and tossed it into the passenger seat. I needed to call the police in California, but there wasn't much point of sending the police for a welfare check if she was already dead. Besides, I realized, I didn't even know where she lived.

I stared out the windshield and jumped as my phone began to ring. I looked at the screen. It was Howard.

I brought the phone to my ear in a fumbling panic.

"Howard?! Are you okay? Where are you?"

"I'm okay," he said reassuringly. I heard laughter and chatter in the background. "I rented a shuttle to get the Aspen crowd here and went with it to pick them up."

"What do you mean? How'd you leave? I have the car."

"Your sister was going to town and I rode with her. I didn't want you to wake up alone there with no way to leave. I know you've been on edge. But look, I'm calling because I just got an email."

"Yeah?"

"I take it you haven't seen it? It's from Philip." I put Howard on speaker and went to my email. He kept talking as I scrolled. "He says the police are coming to Carson's Pass tonight to question the residents. It's ridiculously filled with typos. I think it was written in a drunk rage or something. He advises us to not answer any questions without legal counsel."

I thumbed my way to my email. Philip's message was sent a half hour ago. It was just as Howard had said, a few angry sentences riddled with typos.

"Are you still having a party?"

"*We're* having a party, Katie. And yes, we're twenty minutes out."

I pictured being arrested in front of an entire party. "Howard, I really think you should just turn the shuttle around. Please, send everyone back to Aspen."

The background noise grew quieter and I pictured him shielding his phone with one hand. "I'm going to pretend you didn't say that."

"You don't get. I haven't been telling you everything—"

"Hey, hey, hey," Howard interrupted me. "Just give it a night. Okay? One fucking night. I don't want to hear about what this place has done to you. Take a breather. You made a promise about this party." *People are dead*, I thought. *Miranda is dead.* But I said nothing at all. "Are you home?"

"No. No, I'm in Gypsum just working something out. I'll be home a little later."

He said nothing for a moment. "Please, just make sure you make it."

"I'll be there. I promise."

"Alright."

"Bye," I said and leaned my head against the seat back.

The police and a bus full of people were on their way to Caron's Pass. That made me feel safe about going back at least. I started the car and pulled off from the curb. Then again, I didn't even trust Howard enough to be sure he wasn't the one who drugged me.

The thought occurred to me that the police weren't even there about the Millers' deaths. Maybe they were coming there for Miranda. No one had heard from her in days and it was possible her sister filed a missing persons report. I could just drive. I had a whole continent I could disappear into. But that idea made me think of something.

I sped past the turn that took me to Carson's Pass and I slowed the car all the way to a stop on the shoulder. I punched in the hazards and got out. The wind was picking up. The brief silence I'd heard at the end of my hike was gone and the wind rumbled like thunder in my ears.

I walked around the car and stuck my hands under the wheel wells until my hands found a bump. I pulled hard on the little rectangle and it came loose. I pulled my hand out and held in my palm the same kind of black box I had plucked from Amy's car.

I got back in my car and sat down hard in the driver's seat. Someone was tracking me, and I was determined to figure out who. I didn't care if I was falling into a trap. I cranked the wheel as far as it would go and accelerated into a U-turn.

ACCUSATIONS

Sure enough, there was a shuttle bus in our driveway. I parked behind it and stayed in the car for a moment. The day had already darkened to dusk while I drove back, and I could see people past the windows talking mutely. I used to dress up for Howard's friends. The thought of walking into a party as messy as I was would've been a nightmare to the old me. But I didn't have it in me to care anymore.

I picked up the envelope and got out of the car. My ankle was stiffer and starting to hurt again. But I still wasn't limping. I opened the front door and paused before taking my coat and boots off. There were twenty people. More. Not twelve or sixteen. It was more like two dozen. A few people noticed me and nodded awkwardly. Others looked away. Howard was soon parting the crowd and came over to me, smiling.

"Howard, what the fuck?"

He scrunched his face and sucked air through his teeth. "Sorry, sorry. Before you say anything, I didn't know there'd be this many people. Some of Marcus's and Lexi's friends decided to join them last second in Aspen and they tagged along here. Then of course, I invited everybody in Carson's Pass. Then my brother called and said he was in Denver. Everything just snowballed."

I recognized some of his old coworkers from Newton Tech. People I knew he didn't even like. "Have the police been by already?" I raised the envelope. I wanted to get the pictures to them immediately.

"No." Howard shook his head

"Will they come here?"

"Philip said they wanted to interview everyone, so they'll have to. The whole neighborhood is here. Look, are you sure you can't just forget about this shit for a few hours?"

224

"Aren't you curious what the police want to talk to us about?"

"They just want to hear about the Millers' relationship," he lowered his voice. "Can you settle down, please? My friends are here. You should go freshen up. How about some makeup? And what's in that envelope?"

I had been worried about Howard since the moment I woke up to an empty house. But the feeling evaporated. I wasn't even happy to see him. I surveyed the crowd and shook my head. Even Philip was here with his aide, Jessica. My ankle was throbbing, and I stepped past Howard towards the stairs. "I need to sit down for a minute." Seeing nearly two dozen people in the house was strange. It made everything seem normal. Something this place had yet to feel since moving here.

"Katie!" Bea waved to me.

"Be right back down," I said and smiled tightly at my feet as I shuffled upstairs. I shut the bedroom door behind me, and I tossed the envelope on the dresser. I didn't have time to rest and think before I heard footsteps pounding up the stairs. There was a knock on the door, and it opened at the same time. It was Bea.

"I need to talk to you," she said and motioned for me to follow into the hall. A part of me just wanted to close the door again, but of course I relented and followed my sister. She walked to Howard's den and stood there nervously with her arms crossed.

"What is it?" I asked.

She yanked me forward and shut the door behind me and then moved so she stood in front of it. "We need to talk about your behavior?"

"My behavior? That's what you want to talk to me about? Bea, I'm in the middle of something..." I moved to get past her, but she took a quick step to block my way like a high school bully.

"It's time for a talking to. Your husband is rich, successful and kind. He throws a party to show off this place to his friends

225

and you come in looking like *this*?" She hissed looking me up and down like a diva. "I mean..." She pinched my coat. "It's not cute to still wear clothes from Target when you're rich. It's condescending. You're not better than anyone, Katie."

She was being unusually cruel. I pulled my shoulder back to get her hand off me. "I'm not going to—" But apparently Bea wasn't done.

"And don't get me started on that fucking Toyota you drive. You have to fit the part, sis. You don't deserve any of the money you have. I've held back watching you for so long, but I'm so done. I thought you'd get your shit together and realize what you have after Howard sold, but I guess not." She clapped her hands in rhythm to each word: "Stop. Looking. Like. A poor. Bitch."

I don't know if it was the stress or not, but I broke character. I let my hand fly from my side towards her cheek, but she was quicker than me. She grabbed my wrist in flight and stared into my eyes as my face wrinkled in pain. "I'm through pretending I haven't always been the better sister." She beamed at me. "My uterus has always reflected it. And one day my bank account will, too."

Suddenly a voice grew loud enough to separate itself from the general clamor downstairs. It was Howard and it sounded like he was on the stairs. "Don't worry, don't worry, those kids didn't forget to drop off the liquor. I *found* it!"

Bea tossed my wrist from her hand, flung open the door and slammed it behind her. I backed up and sunk into Howard's gaming chair. I had to blink away tears. I was so sick of everything, and in that moment, it felt like every decision I ever made must've been a mistake. Because after all, they brought me here. I rolled my sore ankle on its joint. Clockwise. Counterclockwise. A minute later I heard a knock downstairs. Someone opened the front door and the white noise of small talk ceased. I still had no idea what I was going to say but from the quiet I knew it was the police.

CONCRETE

I was half expecting to see Jack, but if I was to accuse him, I needed to not make a scene. I'd be smart. I'd ask for his badge or a card. Surely there'd be some question I could ask that would expose him as phony, but when I looked over the balustrades Jack was nowhere in sight.

It was the sheriff who stepped in from the cold. He was flanked by Philip and a deputy I didn't recognize. "I guess it makes it easier if you're all in one place," said the sheriff. "Is there a room we can use to conduct interviews?"

Howard looked over his shoulder as I came down the stairs. "Sure, the basement is all yours. Can you tell me how long this will take?"

"Oh, not long. We should be gone in a jiff, depending on what you folks have to tell us. We don't mean to interrupt your evening, but we got a funny call this afternoon and thought we better stop by and make sure everything's ok." The sheriff sighed. He obviously thought he had better things to do. "Would anyone volunteer to go first?"

Howard turned to face everyone. "They only want to talk to like the six of us that live here. Don't worry." The crowd chuckled. "Katie?" Howard gestured to me and I nodded.

"Sure," I said while my stomach filled with dread. "I'll show you downstairs." Philip stayed upstairs while the sheriff and deputy followed me to the basement. I stopped at the bar and pulled out a stool but none of us sat. "So..." I pulled on my fingers and tried to steady my erratic breaths. "What was the call you got about?"

"I'm afraid we can't say much about that." The sheriff took out a little notebook and flipped the front page back. "We're just wondering if you've seen anything strange here. Anything at all that stood out and didn't feel right. If not, that's fine. We don't want you to think too hard. Just tell us whatever comes to mind naturally."

"Um... I'm..." I was staring at the carpet like a guilty kid. When I looked up at them, they both frowned back.

"Ma'am, have you perhaps had a bit to drink already?"

"No!" I shook my head. "I've just been sick all week."

"Ah, sorry to hear that. We're really just here out of formality. If you got nothing to tell us go ahead and bring down the next person. We can get on with getting out of your hair."

I closed my eyes and shook my head. "Do you remember the detective that was here the last time you were? It was the day after the Millers were found."

"Uh..."

"He's young, with stubble. Pretty good-looking guy. He said his name was Jack. His card said Jack Reid."

"The name's not familiar," the sheriff looked to the deputy and he shrugged.

"Never heard of him."

"Well then someone was here impersonating a police officer that day. He said he was a detective from Denver and when I called the department there, they'd never heard of him."

"Do you have this card still?"

"No, I um... I don't know what I did with it."

The sheriff and deputy looked at each other as if I wasn't there. "Why were you calling the department about this man in the first place?"

I started to speak but paused. From their sideways gazes I could tell that these two men were more interested in me than what I had to say. "Because something is seriously wrong here. And forget what happened to the Millers. I'm not even talking about that." I started walking towards the wall and I bent to the outlet. The faceplate was still off, and I stuck my hand in the socket.

"This is just one—" but I stopped mid-sentence. The little latch that opened the trap door was gone. I patted around frantically but it was no use. I stood up quickly and pointed. "Do you see this outline on the wall here?"

"Um." They both lowered their heads to see and squinted. "Not really," said the sheriff.

I knocked on the wall. "There's a trap door here. Hear how it's hollow?" I knocked on the wall next to it for comparison but the difference in sound was slight.

"Like some sort of secret compartment?"

"Exactly."

"Well, when it opened was there anything in there?" asked the deputy.

"Photos of missing girls."

They titled their heads back in interest. "Could we see some of these photos?"

"I'm sorry, I don't have them."

They looked at each other again with tight lips as if to say, "Of course she doesn't."

I wanted to scream that yes, I could read their incredulous body language. "Come on." I stormed up the stairs. "I have to show you something." They were slow to follow me, probably busy exchanging another round of skeptical smirks. My heart raced. The latch to open the trap door was gone, but how? I never looked into how it worked. I assumed it wasn't something that could be easily taken apart.

The dialogue dampened when I appeared upstairs. Heads turned to watch me. I knew I had a crazed, searching look on my face, but I didn't care. I got to the stairs and bent to the stair board that had the two latch buttons under it. They were there, the same painted color. Hardly noticeable. I pressed them but nothing happened. The stair tread didn't fling up. The buttons weren't evidence enough. They just looked like painted screws. When I turned around, I saw the sheriff and deputy making their way to me cautiously. It took me a moment to notice the room was silent. Everyone was staring at me with confused frowns.

I caught my breath. I was woozy again and covered in a cold sweat. I knew there was a better way to go about this. Better words to prove myself right, but I couldn't find them. "There's a trap door here." I pointed at the stair tread. "There's a hidden room beneath these stairs." I was met with blank expressions and lots of blinking. I saw Philip standing in the middle of the crowd and pointed at him. "Would you like to say anything about that, Philip?"

Philip recoiled; he looked more offended than afraid. "There's no such thing," he huffed. "I designed these homes. I should know."

I smiled. I thought I had him. Just because he somehow locked the stair door didn't mean I couldn't prove it. "You're telling me there's nothing under these stairs? That there's no empty room with hinges on one of the stair boards?"

"Um, yes."

I moved the picture from the wall and my shoulders sunk as I saw that the little hole I'd drilled had been covered with plaster. Of course, it was. But they were underestimating me. A wood-paneled wall wasn't going to stop me. "Just—" I held my hands out and backed up. "Stay here!"

I dashed downstairs but the drill was gone. All the tools were. There was nothing but a hammer sitting like an invitation in the middle of the workbench. I grabbed it and went back up and was beginning to limp from my swollen ankle.

The murmuring stopped again as I appeared. It was like I was crossing a stage, the crowd chatter dying as I walked to the microphone. Philip held his shoulders in a defensive shrug while he talked to the two cops. The confusion on everyone's faces morphed to fear as I passed them with the hammer.

"Um, Katie?" said Bea. "Whatever you're about to do, don't."

I realized I had to say something before I revealed that Philip was lying. I looked too insane. I tried to laugh to lighten the mood but grimaced as a little lightning bolt of pain shot from my ankle. "It'll make sense in a second. Don't worry, I know how this looks now. But there's a room here." I tapped the wall with the hammer. I went up to the plastered hole. "I drilled a hole here. Do you see this?" I tapped the dot of plaster repeatedly with my pointer finger. "See?!" Everyone squinted. Of course, from further than five feet you couldn't see it at all. It was painted the same color as the wood wall. I was being ridiculous.

I chuckled and took a calming breath. "You know, it doesn't matter. Someone covered it up. Someone thought that would be enough to get me to say, "Oh no, guess I'll give up." But guess what?" I flipped the hammer in my hand, so the claws were facing the wall and brought it down hard. There were gasps and the sheriff looked at Howard before taking a nervous step forward.

The claws were stuck and I twisted the hammer, snapping some of the wood. It broke free and I swung again. Then again. Someone shouted for me to stop, which prompted the crowd to erupt into an angry chorus of "stops!"

"What the fuck are you doing?" said one of Howard's ski friends, Allie or Ellie. I brought the hammer down to my waist and someone snatched it from me. But I didn't even care to see who. I was too busy staring in disbelief. The wall was broken enough to reveal the room. But it wasn't there. What I saw instead was grey, chipped concrete.

"No, this is wrong," I turned to face the crowd. "I'm not crazy. Wait!" I pulled out my phone and went to my camera roll. But I knew even without scrolling that the video I took when I first drilled a hole in the wall was gone. Because right away I noticed that the pictures of the bloody altar weren't there. But that was only hours ago, and I had my phone on me at all times except... the post office. "They took my phone at the post office... You paid her!" I shook an accusing finger at Philip, but I quickly stopped. No one would believe me. "Hold on!" I ran the few steps to my coat and snatched the little black tracking device out of the pocket. I held it out to Philip and then to the sheriff. "I found this under my car."

The sheriff nodded at me as if to say, "May I?" and I nodded back. He took it and rotated it in his big fingers. He tapped it and then peeled the adhesive away. Underneath there was a divot in the plastic like on the back of a remote. He slid it off with a thumb. He looked inside and then poured the box into his palm. Out came a few square fishing sinkers.

"It's just a container," he offered it back to me.

"What?" I snatched it back and looked in. There were no wires or anything, just the lead sinkers to give it weight. "But you're not hearing me. I found it under my car. It was stuck there."

"Ok. Ok." He held his arms out cautiously like he was talking to a crazy person. "I am hearing you. It's just not a tracking device of any kind is all."

I realized what a fool I'd been. I hadn't looked at Amy's tracker twice before tossing in the trash. Could that have been a fake too? Why?

I stared hopelessly at the faces before me. Disgust, pity, amusement. And then, dead center of the living room, I saw Kenna staring back at me over a drink.

"Kenna," I said, almost whispering. "Kenna, you're alive."

Everyone turned to her. "I'm sorry." She looked left and right as if I might be talking to someone else. "What?"

"I saw you last night, at the lake. And this morning... this morning the blood was still wet."

"Umm..." Kenna moved her eyes back and forth.

"Don't you tell me otherwise. I found your clothes this morning. I wasn't dreaming. I was drugged," my voice was rising. "And I remember!"

"Remember what?"

"Leave the girl alone, freak," said Howard's friend Marcus.

"Shut up," I fired back. "She knows exactly what I'm talking about."

"I have no clue what you're talking about." Kenna turned her head to the side, and I swear it was to hide a smirk.

"I don't know why you're messing with me. But maybe it's because I saw you fuck your brother."

"Woah! Woah!" The crowd erupted at me again. Their many voices became a single shout. Kenna blanched and her mouth hung open.

"Is that who's blood is on that stone? Your own brother?!" It was hard to be heard above the jeering and I began to shout. "I thought it was only supposed to be girls." I looked at the cops. "They're killing people here! Forty-six missing girls! There's an altar at the lake and it's covered in blood! You don't get it. There have been legends. And sightings! They're kidnapping girls! You—you don't get it. It's all blood cult. It's some kind of sex trafficking. Or Satanists! It's all there. I've seen it. It's all there..."

By the time I was done yelling I was breathless, and the room was silent. A few people shook their heads. Others covered their eyes or looked away with secondhand embarrassment. Howard simply stared at the floor but the closer I looked the more my forehead furrowed. Because on his down-titled face, I swore I saw a smile.

I had to save myself from this. I wasn't crazy. I wasn't an idiot. Suddenly, I remembered the photos of Amy. I didn't say anything this time. I walked towards the stairs and the room receded like a tide as everyone took a simultaneous step back. A wide berth for the crazy bitch.

The pictures would be gone. Surely. That's probably why they were sent. Someone was making a fool of me. They probably hoped I'd rant about the pictures of my murdered journalist friend only for them to be gone. But in the bedroom the envelope was just where I'd left it on the dresser and picking it up, I could tell it was still full.

I stopped halfway down the steps. I had height over the crowd. I stood over the two dozen sets of repulsed and pitying eyes that all turned back to me. I was confident then. "I'm not crazy." I stuck my hand in the envelope. My fingers found the slick, lamented photographs. "You want to know what's really going on here?" I took out the pictures and gasped. I tried to stuff them back in, but I moved too quickly. The pictures were too slippery and some of them shot from my fingers.

They weren't the same pictures of Amy. Of course not. I watched them sailing through the air, wavering to the floor. My cheeks flared red while the crowd parted to let the photos fall around their feet. Scoffs. Laughter. A mortification I hadn't felt since middle-school.

I stared at the picture that was still in my hand. The one I held was a little classy; my forearm covered both breasts and my crossed legs left something to the imagination. But the others on the floor... They were full-frontal nudes. I wasn't even in lingerie. My face was in frame, legs spread. Fingers spreading parts of me further.

My eyes settled on one where I sucked my thumb, staring doe-eyed into the lens. And just like that, the crowd began to turn and murmur amongst themselves. The decent thing to do was ignore me because the show was over, and my humiliation was complete.

PITY

I sat on the stairs while the party made an exodus to the kitchen for fresh drinks and gossip. Heads rolled over shoulders to catch one last glimpse at the star. Your host, Katie.

When the room had emptied, Howard remained where he'd been standing. I was expecting disgust. Fury. But all his facial features were at attention in triumph. Raised brow. Bright smile. A burning glisten of victory in his gaze. He was alight with my humiliation. He was the only person in the world who had those pictures. The only person who knew my phone's passcode. "Howard," I said shakily. I stood and started walking towards him, but Bea was blocking my path at the bottom of the stairs.

"Come on." She walked toward me and snatched my hand as she passed, practically dragging me up the stairs with her. "Ow, ow!" I said as my ankle twisted and burned, but she didn't slow down. She tossed me into the bedroom and shut the door.

"We're trying to help you."

I wanted to scream. To hit her. I knew she had something to do with swapping the pictures. She had led me out of the bedroom the second I got home. "That's bullshit." I stepped to her angrily and she grabbed the doorknob.

"Don't you fucking think about it," she pointed at me firmly like I was a dog. "I just heard the cops whispering about admitting you. Do you know what that means?" I watched her with my fists balled. "It means if you don't stay in this fucking room the rest of the night like I say, I'll say you're having suicidal thoughts. Then you can spend the next seventy-two hours in a piss-soaked jail cell with no bed sheets."

I couldn't bring myself to respond. "Don't hurt yourself, Katie." Bea stepped into hall and then shrugged with a smile, "Or do." She closed the door with a gentle click as if to signal to others that she'd been just as tender with me as how she was with the door.

I sat on the edge of the bed. A child in a time-out. Downstairs, two dozen adults discussed my behavior. I couldn't blame them. How do you change the subject from *that*? I couldn't go downstairs again. But I wanted to face Howard. Was he really so happy that I had failed? He never believed in what I was doing here and now he was thrilled at my humiliation. Our relationship wasn't mendable. It was shattered. And a thought was breaking in my brain that I couldn't ignore: Did my husband hate me?

I *was* having suicidal thoughts. I wanted to curl up in the bathtub and let the water run over me until it covered my face and just stay there. I should've known I'd make a shit journalist.

I flinched at an explosion of laughter downstairs. There was literal hooting and hollering. Someone had told a joke, and a good one from the sounds of it. It was hard to imagine it wasn't about me.

I thought I'd be stronger. Madder. More motivated to vindicate myself. But instead, I sat and cried, throwing myself a little pity party in my head. I was reduced to a joke. A paranoid, useless wife. I felt smaller than I had in my entire life. This adventure I'd gone on to prove my chops had done the very opposite. Defeated, I opened the dresser and uncorked a bottle of wine I'd stashed when I still was barricading myself in the bedroom. There was an aftershock of laughter. Someone tacking some bit onto the tail of the joke. And in a futile attempt to forget where I was, I tilted the bottles bottom to the ceiling and I closed my eyes.

3...2...1

I woke up with the same drugged feeling I did after I'd been taken to the lake shore. I was in bed on my back, watching my breath plume white above me. The power must've failed again and the furnace along with it. The sky seemed afternoon bright but before I could wonder how late I'd slept I felt a tightness in both arms. Something pulled on my shoulders and my wrist burned.

I flung my head around to look at the source of pain and saw that wrapped around my wrist and leading to the bedframe was a tangle of nylon rope. I twisted my head the other way to see my right wrist was wrapped the same.

My ankles were pressed together too, but I had movement in my knees, and I kicked the blankets to the floor but immediately realized my mistake. In nothing but a thin t-shirt and my underwear the cold swept down on me. I cursed and tilted my chin to my chest to get a better view of my bound feet.

I tugged and tried to bring my hands towards me, but the bindings didn't budge. I let my head fall back hard onto the pillow and breathed. My heart rate was picking up speed. I didn't drink that much. Certainly not enough to be bound and not notice. I remembered taking off my clothes and getting into bed. I felt a dull pain in my shoulder, like from a shot. I must've been drugged, injected with something. For a panicked moment, I pulled at both restraints with all my weight, tossing and turning but I only pulled the knots tighter.

Breathe, I thought. I turned and inspected the rope. It was tight, but whoever had tied it had made a mistake: While my wrists were tied my fingers were free. The rope on my right hand coiled all the way around my palm and I could reach it with my fingers and pick at it.

I rolled the rope with my fingers like I was strumming a guitar. After a minute, I could tell it was getting looser. Three minutes and I could dig my middle finger in between the loops. After that it wasn't long before the rope slacked and in a single movement, I flipped my wrist back and pulled my hand free. I didn't revel in my victory. I quickly got to work on the next one with my free hand. It was tied poorly. I could tell whoever had restrained me didn't have much experience.

Next, I bent to my feet and realized the rope there was already so loose I probably could've kicked myself out of it. I pulled the knot loose and seconds later I was walking across the bedroom to the window. I pinched my forefinger and thumb together and split two blind slats apart. The driveway was empty.

I went back to the bed and rifled through the blankets. My phone was gone. It wasn't on my nightstand where I'd left it and it wouldn't magically be in the bathroom. It had been stolen or smashed. No one was going to tie me up and leave my phone inches away. I had to get out of here and there was no one to call for help.

I dressed quickly and went into the hall. From the top of the stairs, I could see the front door propped wide open. I walked down slowly, looking over my shoulder into the living room. There was no sign of a party the night before. No empty glasses or disturbed furniture. The throw pillows were puffed, and the hardwood shined like it'd been scrubbed. It was maybe cleaner than it was before people arrived last night.

I crept to the coat hangers and put on my parka. There was an underlying anxiety that left my eyes and ears perked, alert. It was the kind of panic that prey must feel. I knew whoever had tied me up would be back. And soon.

I thought about Howard's reaction to my humiliation. Pity was the appropriate response. Maybe anger. But how could anyone who loved me smile at that? But it wasn't the time to go over it in my head until it made sense. I had to get the hell out of Carson's Pass.

I put on my boots but stopped in the open doorframe. I was too dehydrated for my own good. I didn't have time, but I

238

needed water, or I could be in trouble. I dashed to the kitchen and gulped down a large glass so fast that the water ran down both sides of my chin. I gasped when I was done and set it in the sink. I could see a slight shadow of my reflection in the glass. I was a mess. Rumpled clothes, ruffled hair. My brain pulsing like a bell in my hungover head. I may have been thoroughly humiliated, but I wasn't dead.

I needed to rethink things. I'd been one step behind. Tossed around and toyed with like a mouse caught by a cat. All I had to do to succeed was get one step ahead. And untied from my bed when they thought I was trapped there was exactly the advantage I needed. I took a knife with me from the kitchen and walked through the cold house and out the front door.

LIGHTS, CAMERA

The snowbanks on either side of the road were high enough to hide behind. If I heard anyone coming, I could leap to the other side and be hidden. I was going to the McCarthy's house. I would get the story, even if I had to do it at knifepoint.

When I reached the point where the road met our driveway, I noticed the hum of the McCarthy's generator was missing from the air. The road was quiet, and I looked both ways down it. There was no movement apart from the pine branches shaking in the breeze. I watched them sick with anxiety. They looked like hundreds of arms waving in warning.

I walked steadily until the house appeared. The windows dark as they always were, the driveway was empty. Surely, the doors would be locked but I'd break a window if I had to. I started walking again, only slower. The scrunch and squeak of snow underfoot was painfully loud. Suddenly, just before I reached the driveway, I saw the garage door start to open.

I panicked and leapt to the other side of the snowbank. When I had the courage to peek back over, the garage was fully open. I sat waiting and suddenly heard an engine rev and a black car spat out. Its LED headlights were blinding even in the day but as it went racing down the drive I managed to see Bea behind the wheel. I ducked when she passed.

She didn't even bother to close the garage door. I watched her as she drove back the way I'd walked. I felt a little spike of fear as I watched her turn down my driveway. Had she been the one that tied me up? But there was no time to think. I jumped back into the road and dashed down the driveway and into the open garage.

Right away, I paused before continuing to the door. The garage was a massive thing, attached and with three parking spaces. But one of the spots wasn't being used. Instead of slush and road salt on the epoxy floor, there was a large clean rug with a couch on it. I walked closer. There was a flatscreen on a TV stand. An Xbox with a stack of games below it. And littering the rugs were little toy cars and army men. I was looking at a kid's playroom. For some reason my beat-up brain thought of the McCarthy twins, but obviously I wasn't looking at a teenage hangout spot. There was another car in the garage, a black BMW sedan.

I went to peek inside when I heard a rumbling on the wind. It was distant but growing louder quickly. Someone else was coming and the diesel groan didn't suggest it was my sister back already.

There were several wheeled clothing racks, and I dove behind one. Immediately, I realized my mistake. The sound of the engine slowed as it got closer. They were coming *here*, I realized. Tendrils of anxiety crept down my back as air brakes hissed and broke wind. I squinted through the clothes. It wasn't Randy and his snowplow. It was a full-size moving truck, already beginning to back up to the open garage door.

I looked over my shoulder. I still had time to reach the attached door to the house unseen, but I was frozen. I needed to relax. This may be my ticket to safety. If the McCarthys were moving, it didn't mean the movers were working for them. They could drive me to Gypsum. I waited anxiously while the truck chirped in reverse. The beeping stopped, the engine died, and both the passenger and driver doors popped open and then shut at the same time.

I saw the boots of two men, but my heart sunk as I saw their faces. It was Randy and Philip. They walked to where they met at the back of the truck and stopped.

"Are you fucking sure?" Randy stuck his hands in his pockets and spat.

"Don't talk to me like that," said Philip.

Randy shrugged. "I'm just talking."

"Yes, I'm sure. Everything that came here did so on that truck. You can even break shit to make it fit this time. It's all going to the dump, anyway. Start in the garage, make your way inside. We'll be back to help you in a few hours."

Randy sighed, and Philip started walking directly towards me. I brought my face away from the clothes and held my breath as his steps got closer. But they suddenly stopped, and I heard a car door open and slam and an engine start. Salt crunched under the tires as it pulled past the moving truck and down the drive.

Randy stayed still and sighed again. I parted some of the clothes to watch him. "God." His words muffled as he stuck a cigarette in his mouth. "Damnit." He lit it and started walking outside, blowing smoke with his head tilted to the sky.

I took the opportunity to get to the attached door. I leapt over to it, but my heart stopped as I put my hand on the handle. It was locked. I looked over my shoulder in a panic. Randy had turned towards me, but I was in luck. His head was still tilted skyward like a pouting teenager.

In a crouching position I dashed past the rack of clothes. I had to get to the other side of the truck before Randy got back inside the garage. I was halfway there when I stepped noisily in a puddle of slush. My first thought was to freeze but I didn't have time. I took leaping steps as quietly as I could and began to run around the house.

I ran all the way to the back, passing the generator and another side door and I leaned against the wood siding. Silence, and then a huge metal rattle. He was opening the back of the truck. I didn't think he'd seen me, and I didn't even make new footsteps in the snow. I had walked the worn path that led from the garage to the generator.

I caught my breath for a moment and considered the situation. All the windows on the ground floor were covered with their heavy shades. It was a gamble to go in, but I felt like all my answers were inside this house. I wasn't going to start walking toward the highway just yet.

I went to the back door and tried the handle. Locked. I slapped my hand against my forehead and rubbed my brow. I couldn't just break a window anymore, not with Randy around the corner. I sighed and surveyed the deck. There were ashtrays stuffed with cigarette butts and empty beer bottles on the railing. It looked like the back deck of a rock band's pad. Not a scene from a family home.

I started looking for places a spare key might be. I flipped over the welcome mat but to no luck. A snow shovel and a bag of salt by the back door caught my eye. But there was something off about them. They were both placed perfectly, like props. I walked over to the bag. It was open but no salt had been taken out. I put my hand in and my fingers quickly found a piece of freezing metal. A key. I stepped back over to the door and stuck it in. It turned smoothly and I felt the deadbolt click into the wall.

Success! My heart hammered. But when I opened the door I didn't step inside. I couldn't believe my eyes. I wasn't looking at granite countertops and rich wood paneling like in my own house. The walls were bare plywood and painters' tarps covered parts of the floor. A tangle of power strips and extension cords were piled high next to a few space heaters.

I stepped inside and closed the door gently behind me. I could see my breath, but the sight was far less strange than seeing it in a furnished home. The inside of the McCarthy's house was simply unfinished. I felt like I was in a construction site. It reeked of fresh carpentry and paint.

In the kitchen was another power strip. Two microwaves and several hotplates were all that occupied the counter. And pushed in front of where the curtain covered the windows were two black refrigerators.

I walked over and opened them. The dark interiors were filled with Tupperware, soda and browning produce. Some of the containers had names written on them with sharpie. Names I didn't recognize.

Evan
Mckayla
Ryan

I frowned and closed the fridge. There were no cabinets in the kitchen or even framing for them. Instead, big metal shelves with wheels were packed full of food. It was all mostly premade stuff. Canned goods and mac and cheese.

I walked towards the living room. The plywood subfloor was covered in an eclectic collection of rugs. Southwestern style, woven wool and Persian rugs all tossed haphazardly over one another. In the few spots where there weren't rugs covering the floor, white splotches of plaster and paint stained the plywood. There were two sets of bunkbeds in the living room. Between them was a couch and a TV. I was walking slowly in a daze, like I'd found myself in an alien art museum. Only the obvious came to mind: This was not just the McCarthy's house.

But who *was* living here? I wondered. It was a big place, but surely not big enough for all those missing girls. I felt like Claire might be behind any door, but it was a foolish feeling. The more I looked around the more I realized this wasn't a prison of any sort. There were decks of cards on the floor and door locks that could be opened from the inside.

I started up the stairs. They were unfinished and the boards were still covered in some sawdust from being cut to size. At the top of the steps there was a sheet of printer paper on the wall with large black words:

"Only the "McCarthys" can keep their blinds open!!! Failure in   this = FIRED!"

I squinted and went bedroom to bedroom. They had identical contents: a set of bunkbeds, two reading chairs and two space heaters. Some of the beds were made while others had the sheets strewn messily like someone left in a hurry.

I went back into the hall. The three bedrooms were doorless but one room at the end of the hall was shut behind a fresh wooden door. It was unpainted, with a hole where the handle would be. I walked to it and pushed it open with my foot. This room was different. Instead of bunkbeds there was a single and neatly made air mattress on the floor. Pressed against the wall was a folding table with a closed laptop in its center. It looked like someone was using it as a desk.

I went to the computer quickly and flung it open. An empty text box prompted me for a password. I cursed and looked around. There was a pen cup on the table stuffed with pencils and a few stray papers. I started leafing through them. They were invoices. Bills for contractors. The first bill on the stack was for *ten thousand* dollars paid to a concrete company. The memo line read only: emergency services.

I paused as I put it together. Of course, it explained the room under the stairs being full of concrete. The truck and the sounds of construction I had heard in my drugged dream. It was a cement mixer filling the wall. I flipped through the papers and saw what looked like before and after photos of the houses in Carson's Pass. The before pictures made my jaw drop; the houses were moldy, unfished shells. There was a short paragraph below the photos.

Structures have been abandoned since 2009. Client requested the exteriors be resided and painted to appear new for conceptual purposes. A rush premium of 100% was applied to the bill as well as another 10% for hazard pay. The wooden frames of the eight structures showed signs of rot and were unsafe for siding. Project completed September 3rd 2021.

I tossed the papers on the floor. All the houses that were guarded by the dog were just rotted shells. There was nothing inside. Carson's Pass used to be an abandoned housing development. I noticed a short plastic filing cabinet by the bed. I rushed over and pulled out the drawers.

Inside were more paper documents. Paystubs. Building permit records and more invoices for all sorts of projects. I didn't have time to sit cross-legged and put the pieces together. I needed to find the laptop password and leave. I dumped the drawers on the floor and kicked through their contents. Shining back at me from under the papers was the glossy cover of a black notebook.

I threw the drawstring off the cover and opened it. The first few pages were just phone numbers and email addresses. Something bothered me about it, and it took my foggy head a moment to realize why—it was all written in Howard's handwriting. I flipped the pages so fast that the paper snapped loudly. It was used as an accounting book. There were numbers and orders and lists for materials. Plywood. Bunkbeds. Food.

I let the pages race past my thumb and there on one of the last pages was a list of numbers intertwined with uppercase and lowercase letters. Passwords, I realized. Bingo. I went over to the desk and started trying them. I typed slowly with a sole pointer finger. The first one worked. I was in.

The desktop was a mess. There were hundreds of folders and dozens of open tabs. A folder named "Kenna McCarthy" caught my eye, but there were at least a dozen other folders labeled with people's names and jobs.

Mary Wynn (Bartender)

Charlie Farlow (Grocery boy 1)

Ryan Kelce (Aidan McCarthy)

Casey Torben (Sheriff Casey)

I double-clicked on Kenna's folder and opened the first file. It was a professional headshot. Kenna smiled wide at the camera, her white teeth bright against the backdrop of her black hair. I closed it and clicked on the next file. This one was labeled, "Sample 1."

A video player opened, and I clicked the pizza slice to play it. It was a clip from a TV show. Some shitty streaming services' sitcom with C-list actors and recycled plots.

Two men in their late-twenties were sitting on a couch and the laugh-track was trying it's best to make their normal conversation seem like a racket. I moved the cursor to close out of it when the camera angle switched, an apartment door opened, and in came another male character, with Kenna at his side. She was younger by a year or so, and her hair was cut different, but it was unmistakably her.

"Geez, cousin. It's called a stop sign, not a suggestion sign." Kenna stormed to the couch with her arms crossed and plopped down. I froze. The laugh track roared.

I stared past the video at the other folders on the screen, squinting with my mouth open in disbelief. Kenna kept talking and the laugh track kept roaring. I couldn't even hear what she was saying. My mind was elsewhere. Kenna was an actress. What did that mean? There was another roar, this time from the inside of my head, as the truth rushed into my brain like an avalanche.

ACTION

The gears turned quickly. Jack and his Hollywood looks. The kissing twins. The Crown Victoria's I saw. They weren't real cop cars. Of course, they weren't. That car model has been replaced for a decade. I tried to think of the last time I'd seen one used as an actual police car—2014?

They were actors. All of them. The families. The employees. The police.

I thought about Jacob, the grocery store kid. He'd said he was an actor when I asked what he did in California and he blushed at his little slip up. It got him fired, I realized. Because he wasn't lying.

But why hire these people?

Further into the folder I found more. Kenna's name was Marcy Fletcher. She was 5'4 and born in Long Island, NY, 2002. Her role in the sitcom was for a single episode and her film credits were weak. Her roles never had actual names, just descriptions of who she played; "Bank teller 2, girl who cuts in line and Slater's cousin." She was an actress desperate for work. For money. And the others would be the same.

I frantically clicked on the other folders and read the actor profiles. Leah Miller was Catherine Dantzler. Detective Jack was Ryan Westerberg. I remembered that name, it was on Howard's script. His "movie" script. I felt like an idiot. *Was he in on this too?* But I didn't have time to dwell on the thought, my heart sank when I saw another folder on the screen, tucked away in the corner.

Amy (Journalist)

I didn't even open it. I just looked at it, depressed. Every time I had talked to her, she'd seemed genuinely guilty. She told me every chance she got how badly she needed the story. She probably *was* desperate, only it wasn't the story that was going to save her, but the money that someone was paying her to lie to me.

I thought about the kind of money it would take to hire all those people. The outfits, the fake police cars. The houses. It would've cost *millions*. I froze and pictured Howard's smile at the party. His triumph. But things had been good between us. There had to be something else. Something with Philip. The questions bounced around my brain. But the answers never came. Instead, I realized that if everything I'd discovered was faked, then there was no mystery to Claire's death.

I'd been tricked. I didn't realize how uplifted my heart had been from the idea that she hadn't killed herself and at that moment the clouds came back. I started breathing, fast, angry breaths. I went to open a folder labeled, "real roles," when a door banged open downstairs. It was so loud that I flinched and flung my hands from the keyboard like it was a hot stove. I accidentally knocked the pencil cup over and it started rolling toward the edge of the table.

I gasped. By the time I reached out it was already falling. I shot out my hand to catch it but instead of grasping it, I hit it with a clumsy, open palm. The cup had even more velocity now and banged down on the plywood floor. The cup itself stopped quickly but the pens and pencils clicked and clacked as they rolled into each other and the walls for several painful seconds.

I didn't hear anything right away. I thought maybe Randy had just opened the door to grab something and was already out of earshot in the garage when I made my racket. My heart thumped and I closed my eyes as I heard Randy shout, "Hello!" I didn't reply and footsteps started coming towards the stairs.

There was no other way downstairs. If I wanted to get away, I needed to jump. I snatched the laptop and went to the window. A fall from two stories into the snow wouldn't be that dangerous but with my bum ankle I was certain it would leave me crippled. I undid the latch and threw open the window. Randy had heard it and he was clomping noisily up the stairs now.

The big metal roof of the moving truck was just below me. Not even ten feet down. Before I could hesitate, I put my legs through the window and pushed off the inside of the sill with my free hand.

I fell in slow motion, grimacing the whole way down to get ready for the pain. I landed with a metal crash and the pain that rifled up from my ankle was like a bullet. I didn't have time to think about it. I shouted in pain but immediately started to stand.

"Katie!" I turned around to see Randy staring out the window. "You're hurt. Don't move, okay?"

He shot out both hands briefly and turned on a heel to run back downstairs. I was lucky he was one of those "tough guys" who couldn't be bothered to even jump ten feet. But I only had seconds before he'd be back down. I limped towards the front of the truck and scooted down the windshield. I flipped onto my stomach once I was on the hood and lowered myself gently to the ground.

I looked down the road. There was nowhere to run and with the snow that would easily show my steps, there was nowhere to hide. I opened the door to the moving truck and locked the doors behind me. I panted in the driver's seat. Then my eyes lit up and I couldn't believe my luck. There was a set of keys in the cupholder. I fumbled them in my hand and stuck them in the ignition. The truck roared and I threw it in drive. I was turning out of the driveway onto the road when Randy hopped up onto the running board. He was standing on the truck, just outside my driver's side window.

"Katie!" he yelled, catching his breath. "Just stop the truck! I don't know what you're running for?!"

I knew he wouldn't have jumped onto a moving vehicle if that were really the case. He smiled a fake creepy smile and I looked back to the road, pressing the gas pedal to the floor. Randy suddenly punched the window and I jumped in my seat and swerved.

The window didn't even crack and the punch obviously hurt him. Randy flapped his hand loosely in pain but quickly formed another fist. He widened one eye more than the other with an idiot's look of concentration and holding onto the neck of the mirror for support with his other hand, he swung at the window again.

The glass exploded into my lap. I leaned to my right, expecting him to grab me, but the second punch must've hurt more than the first. His mouth was open in a soundless scream and he stared at his knuckles.

This was my chance. I kept the pressure on the accelerator and pulled the little pin up to unlock the door. By the time he realized what I was doing he was still only holding onto the truck with one hand. I opened the door and then kicked it into him. He slipped off the running board, but the mirror somehow held his weight. I saw both his hands wrapped around it. His boots thunked and scraped beneath him against the road. I shut the door again but with the window broken I could hear him yelling, "We're gonna kill you. You fucking bitch! You *stupid* fucking bitch!"

I leaned out the window and watched him kick at the road. "Hey, Randy?!" He looked at me but didn't respond. I could see his knuckles whiten and watched his face flex as he tried to pull himself back up. "What's the matter? Can't do a pull up, little bitch?" he flared his nostrils in noxious anger and I genuinely smiled as I spun the wheel hard left and right. When I centered the truck again Randy was holding on by just his fingers. I slammed on the brakes and watched him fly out ahead of the truck, skipping across the road like a stone.

The brake pedal hiccupped and fought as the truck came to a stop on the icy road. I watched as Randy tumbled over himself the last few yards and came to a stop on his stomach. He was still conscious. And then he set his hands on the road to push himself up, but suddenly, he stopped and looked down. My eyes followed his.

Something was jutting out under his pant leg near his shin and when he started to scream, I knew what it was. Bone. I hit the gas to drown out the sound and I didn't look as I swerved to pass him. I started down the mountain towards the highway and as my heart rate settled, I felt a yell creep up my throat and I let it explode. I screamed a series of warrior's cries while I beat the wheel with a stupid smile on my face. My entire torso was alight with something that lifted my heart, and it took me a minute to realize what it was.

Pride.

FOOL'S GOLD

I brought the truck to a slow stop where the road to Carson's Pass met the highway. To my right was the old bar. Its beer signs were all dark and the only car in the parking lot was the black car I had seen Philip take from the McCarthy's house. Or whoever's fucking house that was.

I put on my left blinker to go to Gypsum but kept staring at the black car. I could come back with the cops. The actual police. I had the laptop and whatever other evidence Randy had loaded in the back of the moving van. But they'd all be gone by then. Howard, Philip, Bea, and Randy with his broken leg. The houses would be torched, and everyone responsible would be nowhere to be found.

I opened the glove box and pulled out a bright orange box cutter. I thumbed the blade forward and then retracted it back. I sighed. It wasn't enough. I tossed the box cutter into the passenger seat, but instead of hitting the leather with a soft thump, it banged against something metal.

There were a few sheets of stapled paper on the passenger seat and something kept them from lying flat. I brushed the paper to the floor, revealing a little revolver. I picked it up gently as if it might bite. I didn't know how to open it, but I could see the bullets in their cylinders from the outside.

I shut off the truck and left it in the middle of the dirt road just before the highway. I didn't want to make any more noise pulling into the parking lot. I tucked the gun into my sleeve and walked towards the door to the bar. It was unlocked and I threw it open with my left hand and kept my right on the gun, aiming. Philip was sitting at the bar with his back to me. A bottle of bourbon sat next to him on the bar top.

"Oh, don't be mad, Randy. I just said I was busy. I didn't say doing what."

I frowned and watched Philip down the rest of a drink and exhale with a hiss through his teeth.

I aimed the gun at his back and stepped in slowly. "It's not Randy."

Philip turned over his shoulder quickly. But when he saw me and then the gun his face was a mask of amusement. "Believe it or not, I'd rather see you anyway."

"I broke his leg. So, you don't have much of a choice."

"Oh, please. I don't want anyone thinking that Randall Duffy is a business associate or even a bodyguard of mine. He's a coworker. That's all." I flinched as Philip stood with his heels on the base of the stool and reached over to the other side of the bar. He sat back down a placed another glass on the bar. "You want a drink?"

"I want to know what the fuck's going on."

"I don't believe those two things should be mutually exclusive." He began filling both glasses with glugging pours of whiskey. "My work here is done. I got my check." He burped, and I realized he was already slightly drunk. "It just cost my self-respect, my conscience and..." he looked around the room and slapped his hand on his thigh. "No, that's it."

I walked a little closer with the gun still raised. "Who tied me up?"

Philip cringed and held out a hand like I was telling him spoilers. "Ah, ah, ah. I don't know anything about that. In fact, maybe we shouldn't talk. I'd like to have plausible deniability."

I clicked the hammer of the revolver back in response. "Alright, alright. No need for that, really. I'm not a child-abducting murderer. I can tell you what I do know. But I've been kept in the dark on more than you might think."

"Speak."

"What do you know right now?" Philip asked.

"I know everybody living in your little commune is an actor."

"It's not *mine*. Oh dear." He tsked his teeth. "You *do* know nothing."

"It doesn't matter what you tell me. I have your laptop."

Philip tilted his head at me curiously and chuckled. "My computer. I use it time to time, but I own nothing here. Everything—the clothes, the cars, the electronics. It's all paid for. It was part of the contract."

"Contract?" I asked, but I suddenly understood. Everything began to come together like tectonic plates forming a continent; a Pangea of *oh fuck*. My mouth slacked.

"Who paid for all this?" I knew but I needed to hear him say it.

"That lunatic of a husband of yours."

My insides grew watery. I couldn't ask why, the question trembled at my lips. I remembered his hot rage when his friends found out about me and Ryan. Howard had been humiliated. But he'd never calmed down. He'd been acting, too. Pretending not to hate me. While he hired actors, writers and graphic designers. While he faked newspaper articles and bought fake blood.

The photos of missing girls were real, but they were just planted. Howard had nothing to do with it. Just like Amanda Bryan. She was a real missing person, but they just used the case to fit into their little fake reality. The fake cases—Rachal McMann, the Williams girls, the ones no one could find online. I realized nothing had been scrubbed from the internet.

There was nothing to scrub to begin with.

I stepped closer. "And the missing girls. The houses with holes in the walls. Paradise of the Palisades. It's bullshit, all of it. Isn't it? This whole thing was a game to trick me..."

"You are correct." He took another sip of his drink. "But *I'm* not an actor. I am an architect. Just one who's had better days."

I remembered seeing the article online about Philip's bankruptcy. That one was real. A feeling began to brew in my stomach. It wasn't pity. A lot of effort and money had gone into making me look like a fool. I no longer cared that I fell for it. No, I was *pissed*. Teeth grindingly mad.

Why wouldn't Howard just divorce me like a normal person? He'd used Claire, my worst mistake to manipulate me to keep searching to stay until... My shoulders sank.

Until I had humiliated myself in front of all his friends. His friends weren't actors. Nor was his brother. They weren't paid. They didn't know about any of this. And that party... making me look like a psycho lunatic was Howard's entire goal. Revenge.

My skin became cold and prickly. I realized it wasn't just vengeance, but business. Dozens of witnesses had seen me delusional and drunk. If I were to be found the next day dead, it would be assumed it was a suicide. Afterall, if Howard killed me my death would be a lot cheaper than divorce. And by a magnitude of tens of millions of dollars. Howard would still come out ahead even after all the money he put into this. I kept the gun pointed at Philip but had to reach out and grasp a table with my free hand to steady myself.

"Your husband is... ambitious. You twist your ankle and within eight hours he'd bribed an athletic trainer at UC Boulder for Toradol. But with all that money it's almost cheating. I thought for sure the woman at the post office would say no or even tell the police about him wanting her to take your phone. But when you offer someone what they make in a year for a few minutes of work, it's too easy. He told her that he thought you were cheating on him and needed evidence. She was almost happy to help. Of course, he had to cover your key in gunk to slow you down..."

I was angry, still pointing the gun at Philip. "It sounds like he just got lucky to me. What if that didn't work? What if I showed those pictures of a bloody altar and the room beneath the stairs to everyone at the party?"

Philip shook his head like there was something obvious I didn't understand. "There were a lot of 'what if's' throughout this whole thing. Your husband always had a backup plan. If you didn't leave your phone at the post office, he was going to have the fake police pull you over for suspicion of drunk driving.

You'd be let go, of course. But only after they took your phone and deleted the pictures."

I realized I'd been more like two steps behind. "Did he tell you why he did this?"

"Did what? Why he spent millions of dollars to have us all play make-believe for you?" Philip shook his head. "There were rumors at the clubhouse that you were a cheater. A horrible woman. But all those actors just wanted to believe you deserved to get strung along."

"The clubhouse?" I cringed. It made the whole thing sound like a game. And I suppose that's what it was. "Is that what you called the McCarthys?"

"It saved money and time to put everyone under one roof. The only houses he paid to have finished were the ones you'd step foot in. And he seemed to know you wouldn't want to go see your sister."

My knuckles had turned white. I was strangling the gun as if it were Howard's throat. "Where is he?"

"He's in Gypsum, seeing off his friends and paying the actors after. He should be back any minute."

I let the gun fall to my side and Philip raised an eyebrow. "I'm sorry," he said, licking his lips. "I was waiting for you to quit pointing that thing at me to say that. It's a lot less genuine to say sorry when there's a gun in your face."

"What did he pay you?"

"One-point-two."

I nodded. "And Miranda—she was paid, too?"

"Oh yes. A million or so. Same with your sister. The actors, of course, were paid a paltrier sum."

"I shot Miranda. Was that part of the plan?" I said it sadly but really, I was relieved. Weight was lifting off my shoulders with everything I discovered. Miranda was never my friend. I remembered how she got close to me around the time Howard and I had a falling out. But I had to give her credit; she'd been phenomenal at being a fake friend.

"Woah. No." Philip waved his hand. "Stop. Stop it. I don't want to hear anything about that. Your husband asked me to help move her or something. That's all I know. I don't know what laws I broke. I don't know what laws *you* broke. I'm not culpable. Nor did I participate." He took an angry swig of whiskey. "My only advice to you is *run*. I know perhaps you don't want to take advice from the morally decrepit, but if you said you were tied up, I imagine they have worse plans for you."

I turned from him to the door. I started breathing deep, heavy breaths. My rage was coming to a boil. My own husband manipulated me with the death of my best friend. My husband who I tried to love till death did us part. If he's coming back from Gypsum, he can come and get me.

I stormed towards the door and swung it open but as I stepped out of the dark bar and into the light, I heard a grunt and saw my sister's face scrunched in exertion. All I had time to do was gasp before the sun was blocked out by a snow shovel, and with a painful thwack, the world went black.

BETRAYAL

I was still conscious, but my eyes stung, blinded by my blood. I dropped to my knees and held an arm above my head to shield myself from another blow. "Bea!" I shouted. Blood dripped from my mouth as I spoke and slurred my speech. "Please!"

"Shut up!" Bea said and brought the snow shovel down again. It cracked into the crown of my head and the world spun. I heard the snow shovel bang against the ground as she dropped it and felt her grab me under my armpits. I was tossed into the back of a car and then hit in the head again for good measure.

The snow shovel was plastic. It wasn't hard enough for a knockout blow, but I was as good as out. We were going back up the mountain towards Carson's Pass. I could tell because Bea was taking the turns with sharp whips of the wheel and I vomited a mix of water and bile onto the car's floor.

She said something but the second I tried to process what she had said I forgot. My ears were ringing and again I dry heaved with my face pressed against the leather. I must've dropped the gun. I don't remember doing so, but it wasn't in my fist and there was no way I had time to put it in my pocket before Bea hit me. I wondered if Bea had it.

My head stopped spinning around the time we reached the clearing of Carson's Pass. I hadn't thought that my sister had it in her to bludgeon me viciously. But then again, I couldn't picture anything she wouldn't do for a million dollars. There was a mumbling sound in my head, and it took me a second to realize Bea had been talking to me.

"$30,000 each and what's that kind of money to you? Nothing. Do you remember that phone call, Katie? The boys were in trouble and I needed your help. I told myself that if you coughed up the money for the twins to get a better education then I wouldn't do this. I'd say no to Howard and his money and this plan. But you never did. You never would. When it came to helping my boys it was a cold, hard no."

She slammed the brakes and I had to brace myself against the seat to keep from falling to the floor. "I told you you'd get everything you deserve and now we're here, bitch." Bea got out of the driver's seat and slammed the door. I was trying to pick myself back up when the passenger door opened. I looked up and Bea grabbed a fistful of my hair at the roots and yanked me out of the back seat. I slid, screaming in pain to the concrete.

"You think you can fuck with my husband? You're lucky Howard has a quick death planned out for you. I might petition to have it changed."

"Bea, I'll double what he's paying you. I have access to our money. Please, I won't tell anyone what's happened here. Let's just go." I wiped the blood off my face with the back of my hand. "You're still my sister."

"Oh, sweetie. You're too much of a goody two-shoes for me to ever trust your word on something like that." She kicked me in the stomach, and I lurched into the fetal position. Bea turned towards someone. "I got her, Randy!" I realized she was in front of our house. "We just have to wait for Howard to get back and we're out of here."

"Give her another for me!"

Bea kicked my hands that were clasped over my stomach and I spat and gasped against the cold driveway.

"Watch her for me." Randy was sitting only a few feet away on the steps. In his other hand was a liquor bottle. I doubted he could do anything to stop me after the fracture I gave him. But the world was still spinning too fast for me to stand.

I rolled over so I was on my back and stared at the sky. It was already evening. I watched the clouds pass low overhead. I couldn't run. I was certain I'd stumble and fall over if I even stood. Bea wasn't long anyway. She came back out holding the nylon ropes that I had freed myself with earlier and violently held my wrists together at my stomach.

"Congrats on getting untied the first time. But no one's leaving you alone now," she started wrapping my hands tightly. I knew before she was done tying my wrists together that even if I was left alone, I wouldn't be able to free myself.

Bea was good at this. Howard must've tied me up the first time. I remember he had once tied me to the bed in a similar way, my arms and legs akimbo for his access. We were laughing because the knots weren't that strong, and when I pulled against them the rope uncoiled limply. Flaccidly. He hadn't gotten much better.

I pictured Howard in the den, looking over his shoulder and pausing his video game before opening a YouTube video on how to bind someone's wrists.

"Come on." Bea pulled me up by the collar of my coat. "Inside we go." She held me like a dog by the scruff of the neck. I was limping on my ankle badly now and she kept pulling me behind her. Randy carefully stood on one leg and leaned against the wall as we passed. He made a fist and I flinched away thinking he was going to punch me.

"Stop," Bea said to him and patted his chest with her free hand. "You'll hurt yourself. She's getting hers. Don't worry."

"I want to be here to hear her scream."

"*You're* going to the hospital. That's the deal. Howard will be back in ten minutes. Come inside."

It all felt much more real when I heard my husband's name coming out of my sister's mouth. She'd known him better than I had these last two months. Even Randy did. Ever since Howard came to these two with his offer of cash and his plan of humiliation, they'd known the man I loved better than I suppose I ever had. I spat a bloody spittle on the steps and pulled my wrists against the bindings, but they didn't budge.

Bea stopped in the little foyer. "Take um off," she gestured to my feet and I stepped on my heels and pulled my feet out of the boots.

"Bea, please."

261

"If you *Bea please* me one more time, I'm duct-taping your mouth shut. Shut up." She pulled me into the living room and swept my legs out from under me in front of the fireplace. I tried to put my tied arms out to break my fall, but it was all too sudden. I couldn't even land on the bear skin rug and my already concussed head slammed against the hardwood. I didn't even try to lift myself into a more dignified position. I stayed flat on my face with my breath fogging the floor.

BURN

Bea bent down and crossed my ankles. Then she began binding my legs together with another length of rope. "I can't imagine having the world like you did and throwing it all away."

"I didn't throw anything away," I said with my mouth muffled by the floor.

"I'm not even talking about you and Ryan. That's the funny thing. Howard did admit to me you were on a break or something. If that's the case, you didn't even *really* cheat on him. I just meant that you wasted everything you were given. You know what I could've done with the money you had? Ha!" Bea shook her head. "Look at me, I'm already using past tense with you. But really, do you know the life and things I could've bought for my boys?"

Maybe I was hysterical from being beaten senseless or the fact that there was just nothing else I could do, but either way I started laughing. It was a cackling, snorty laugh. I was laughing so hard it became hard to breathe for a moment. "Remember," I paused trying to catch a big enough breath to speak. "Remember the Lexus?"

Bea's eyes stormed over. "You think you're so special and humble because you still shop at Aldi. I won't have to tell you again to have some fucking class."

"Oh." I caught my breath for a moment. "Your boys were still wearing crotchless pants when you'd pick them up from school in that thing."

"Funny, and now we'll be millionaires when we pick them up from the babysitters in Gypsum tonight. Besides, at least I have the boys. Look at your life, Katie. What are you leaving behind?"

I recovered from my laughing fit with a sigh. "Just a few nights ago I was tossing and turning at night. I had this urge that

I needed to do something more with my life. But now I'm content just knowing I'm not you."

She finished tying my feet with a violent tug and let them fall. A length of rope stuck out from where it wrapped around my ankles. She picked it up and began to tie it around a circle hook in the brick by the fireplace that opened the flue. She tugged on it to make sure it wouldn't budge and began to knot. "You tell yourself your little lies while Randy and I are living our best lives in the Bahamas."

I wondered how fast Bea and Randy would go through the money. It wouldn't even take them a year, I figured. The thought gave me some solace. They'd probably be even broker then before. More money meant bigger debts. Soon Bea would be hounding Howard for more, maybe even with the threat of blackmail.

Bea tugged at all the knots. My hands, my feet and then the one that connected to the hook in the wall. Satisfied, she stood.

"What are you going to tell Mom and Dad?" Bea looked down at me disdainfully. "You're killing me, right? So, what are you going to tell them?"

"The same conclusion the police will reach. You've been having paranoid delusions and drinking more. A room full of witnesses can attest to that. It's simple, your mental health just slipped after you cheated on your husband and unfortunately you had Dad's gun at the wrong time."

Hearing the plan made me squirm. I'd been stupid and fuzzy-brained. I needed to be begging for my life, but I couldn't bring myself to it. I tried to scare her. "You're not going to get away with this. You think the police are just going to believe everyone left Carson's Pass on the same day?"

"What?" Bea squinted and gradually began to smile a toothless grinch-like grin. "Are you really that slow?" She paused, looking at me, but I didn't respond. "There is no Carson's Pass. Everything you read about this place was made for your eyes only. The website is gone. The actors are gone. Gone with their paychecks and NDAs. Trust me they're not ratting anytime soon. They won't even know what's happened to you. There's nothing for anyone to find."

As silly as it sounds, I couldn't bring myself to beg Bea for my life. I pictured myself ugly crying—hiccupping sobs and snot running out of both nostrils. I was too proud for that. Looking at her now, I realized how much she'd always resented me. If anything, my begging might have brought her pleasure.

It had grown dark in the living room and a pair of headlights swept through the window casting Bea's shadow long and monstrous on the wall behind her. There was another sound further off. I realized it was the heavy groan of the moving truck. She turned and went out the door leaving it open.

There was a nervous pit in my stomach. I was about to see Howard. My husband, who at the same time had become a stranger. Was he going to shoot me? Would it hurt? They were outside talking for a while and I could hear some of what they said. There were three men's voices. Philip, Howard and Randy. Howard was doing most the talking.

"They wouldn't be interested and on top of that they'd need a warrant," I heard him say. "We burn this house after she's shot. This will look textbook, don't worry about it. It's not like if they found a house full of bunkbeds, they'd jump to some criminal conclusion," Philip said something inaudible and Howard continued. "Just take the hard evidence. Computers and papers. Go, now."

Howard kept talking but I couldn't hear whatever it was as the moving truck started again and rumbled back down the driveway.

I heard footsteps on the stone stairs followed by Bea's voice. "Don't worry, it's all external. When she burns it won't show. It's not like I cracked her skull."

When they both came into the living room they stopped and stared. I wanted to stare back at them with accusing eyes but bloodied and hogtied on the floor I looked away like the wounded animal I felt I was.

"You really did a number on her."

"I went easy," Bea said defensively. "Did you see what she did to Randy?"

With an effort I brought my chin up to look at them.

Howard wore a navy suit under a thick wool overcoat. He stuffed his hands in his pockets and looked me over like I was an ex he hadn't seen in a while.

He turned towards Bea. "Could we have a minute?" Bea shrugged indifferently and went back outside closing the door behind her. When Howard came closer my heart thumped in my throat. He squatted and tilted his head at me curiously. "Three times." He held three fingers in front of my face. "Three fucking times I had to lure you to that lake before you found that goddamn altar. You even found where we dumped Miranda before you saw what I wanted you to see."

"Why?" I said, trying my best to hide my growing rage.

"Well, maybe I'm ridiculous. But the party wouldn't have been the same had you not said all that nonsense about human sacrifice. Man," he ran a hand over his face. "That was incredible."

I looked into his eyes expecting to see something different— an evil I'd missed before. And while he looked just the same, I still felt like I was staring at a stranger.

Bea yelled something at Randy, her voice muffled by the glass. "I know." He looked over his shoulder. "It wasn't fun working with your sister. Trust me." He smirked and hiccupped with a little laugh. "It might've been the hardest part of this whole thing, honestly."

"She's going to mess this up for you," I said. "She'll blow through the money by Monday. Please," I said but looked away as I said it. "You'll get caught."

"Oh, Katie." He stroked my cheek with a thumb, and I recoiled from his touch. "You think I'm just going to move back to San Diego after all this?" he scoffed. "I have a plane waiting on the runway in Gypsum. And you're right, it's your sister we're talking about. But by the time she's broke she won't even have enough money to hire a PI to find me in order to blackmail me."

My eyes searched the floor for something to say. Something to persuade him against this. "Howard. Please. You won. You embarrassed me in front of everyone. You don't have to jump to murder. We can get a divorce. I won't—"

He grabbed my chin. "So, you could fucking humiliate me all over again? Take half my money and make a fool of me twice?" He bit his lip and shook his head venomously. "My original plan was simpler than divorce." He made a finger gun and pointed it at me. "Boom." He turned it under his chin. "Boom. The Millers were a fantasy of mine. I thought it was fun to put them in the script. A little easter egg of my true feelings."

He grasped my chin tighter and my lips scrunched together.

"I even bought a shotgun two months ago. I wanted it to be messy. And then while I was sitting outside our bedroom while you slept, feeding those big bullets into the shotgun, I realized I was being horribly unoriginal. A man murders his wife every day in America. I had money. I had options. Why not be more creative? Why not keep my money, be rid of you, and restore my pride in the process?"

"You're pathetic," I said, and Howard moved his hand from my chin and quickly slapped my face.

"I'm pathetic? You fell for every crumb I left for you. It was all from TV shows and movies. From shit we watched *together*. Trackers under wheel wells. Footsteps to the back door... Sure, you needed a little nudging in the right direction sometimes, but... come on. The party, the stairs. The hammer. I can't stop picturing how crazy you looked. Miranda thought it was stupid to go under the stairs to make noises to mess with you but I knew it would pay off. You swinging that hammer into nothing but concrete..." He clenched his fists and tilted his head to the ceiling. "*God*, that was gold. And just like that, everyone realized my wife was insane because that's the only kind of woman who cheats on *me*."

I spat out bloody phlegm. "Congratulations, it only took several million dollars."

"Come on." He said in a baby talk voice and gestured around the living room. "Can't you appreciate this? I'm a genius. I was terrified when I found Miranda's body out back. I thought the whole thing was fucked. But I realized you weren't going to go to police, and it turns out all you did was save me 750k. If you ever cared to tune into the town gossip you would've known Miranda had dried up her trust fund years ago. She's been living on credit card debt."

Howard looked around the room. "Did you kill her in here? I am curious how it happened. Did you know it was her when you fired, or did you take a shot in the dark?" I was done entertaining him. I kept my mouth shut. "Tell me, was she carrying a bottle of wine? We agreed whenever she was coming in or out of the house, she'd carry one. That way if you caught her creeping in, she could say she came for a late-night drink." He waited for me to speak but I just breathed heavily through my nose like an angry bull. "Ironic, isn't it? You've now killed *two* of your closest friends."

He was talking about Claire, but I wouldn't explode. I wouldn't give him the satisfaction. He had used my guilt over Claire to keep my interest here, to keep me around until he could humiliate me. I started shaking my head, slowly. I was infuriated. I made up my mind and I wasn't going to beg for my life.

I spat out my words with hate. "You're really going to kill me over your ego? I sleep with someone while we're on a break and you buy a circus to try to get your pride back. Tell me, Howard, did you do this because I fucked someone else or because your friends found out?"

"You couldn't begin to understand." He stood from his squat and snarled down at me. "You made me look like a cuckold," he said matter-of-factly as if it explained everything. I saw Howard for what he was then. For what he had always been. An insecure man, who let the perception of others dictate his thoughts of himself. It was so absurd that I couldn't help it, I started to laugh. Howard kicked me in the gut but as soon as I caught my breath again, I kept on cackling.

"Bitch," he hissed. I could tell I'd ruined his fantasy. He wanted me blowing snot bubbles and begging for my life till my voice went horse.

"Beatrice! Randy!" Howard yelled over his shoulder and the front door opened. Howard held out a hand. "Give me her pistol." Randy clung to the wall as he hobbled in on one foot. "Randy!" Howard shouted at him and beckoned with his fingers. "The gun."

Randy's face went white and his mouth opened in a stupid little O. "I thought you had it."

"What do you mean? I told you to bring it from the clubhouse." Randy didn't respond. "We had a whole conversation..."

"I remember now."

Howard raised his brow. "So, where is it?"

Randy had already thoroughly numbed himself to his injury with whiskey. His eyes were glassy and mostly closed. "I just meant I remember the conversation. I don't know where I put it."

Howard took a breath to calm himself. "After we drugged her the first time, I gave you her gun. I didn't want her to be able to find it anywhere in my house. You remember me saying that?" Randy nodded quick and dumb like a court jester pleading for his life. "You said you would hide it in the clubhouse. So, dumbass, where's the gun?"

Bea butted in. "His bone is sticking out of his fucking leg! Go easy."

"It's somewhere in the clubhouse," said Randy.

"We can just use this one." Bea took the revolver I'd found in the moving truck out of her coat pocket.

"Hey," Randy limped towards her. "That's mine."

"Jesus. How stupid are you people?" Bea glared at Howard and I saw her knuckles whiten as she gripped the gun. "This is supposed to look like a suicide. We have to use her gun. That revolver you have is not even the same caliber. You know what, forget it. Let's just burn the bitch. The fire will destroy the rope. We can just leave her tied."

My eyelids peeled back in fear.

Howard shrugged at me. "What? It's what they used to do to sluts like you. Bea, light a candle and take it to the kitchen, put it on the table and set it under the curtains. I'll take Randy to the hospital. I want you to be the last one to see her alive. It's always suspicious if it's the husband who does."

"You want me to start the fire, like now?" Bea pointed at her chest shyly.

"Yes, don't get too sentimental."

"Don't worry about it," said Bea. I could tell she was angry at Howard. She looked down at me with guilt in her eyes and I realized I had a chance. She was family. Would she let this happen to me?

I was starting to panic. I tugged at my feet in the restraints. "Please, Bea, Randy. Don't let him do this. Please." The idea of burning to death broke the dam, and the hot, snotty tears I was determined to not to shed were pouring now. "You'll all get caught."

"There's nothing to get caught doing. The last person to ever see you alive was your own sister and she describes you as delusional. Suicidal. Right, Bea?"

"Yeah." Bea licked her lips nervously. "Suicidal."

Howard turned to leave. "It's a story that happens a few times every single day in this state. Alcohol, suicide. No one's raising a fuss over your death, Katie."

"Please!" I shook against the restraints. It made me sick to give Howard the satisfaction, but panic had taken over me. "Please!"

Bea went into the kitchen and I heard the grind of a lighter's wheel turning, she stepped back into the living room backwards. In the dark house, I could see the shadows of orange flames already flickering from the kitchen. Curtains light up quick, I realized.

Howard took the lighter from Bea and tossed it on the floor. Then he took my phone from his pocket and tossed it on the couch. "Wait outside until the house is ashes and then call the fire department. It will take them a half hour or more to get here anyway. Philip won't be long, make sure he's left with the moving truck before you call."

Bea looked me over once more. I didn't say anything. I hoped my eyes could do more than my words and I looked pleadingly into hers. But she just bit her lip and went outside.

Howard came over to me quickly and pulled at my bound feet and then my hands. He was looking nervously towards the kitchen. The fire already roared and crackled. A billow of smoke blew into the living room and began to spread across the ceiling. "Try to get a deep breath of that," he pointed at the smoke. "That way you won't have to *burn*."

He stood and walked quickly to the door. "No, no, no," I said, panicky. I rocked back and forth on the floor. "No, you don't have to kill me! You're all fucking sick!" But then the door slammed, and the sound of the fire grew even louder.

The flames were already licking out of the kitchen doorway like it was the mouth of the devil. Some hungry growth, coming to consume me. I kicked my bound feet at the hook and bit at the rope around my wrists, but it was no use. There wasn't any slack.

There was no way out. The only thing I could think to do was roll over on my stomach to try and preserve the rope as best I could. That way when I was found, foul play could be suspected. But the floor was wood too. The whole house would burn. There wouldn't be anything left. I'd probably be nothing but bones and there wouldn't even be blood to test to see if I had been drugged.

I could feel the heat already. "Bea!" I shouted. "Bea, please! Please! You're still my sister!" I tugged hopelessly at the restraints. She certainly heard me, but my cries were lost on her. I saw her outside, staring at the flames in awe.

The fire crossed the walls and became a full-blown inferno. It was so hot in the room—I would burn to death before the fire even reached me so I could burn off my restraints. But then I had an idea. My wrists were bound but I could still move my arms and grasp things with my fingers. The bear skin rug in front of the fireplace was just within reach and I got hold of one corner and dragged it closer to the flames. It caught fire quick and once it was roaring steadily, I pulled it back toward me.

There was no way around it. This was going to hurt like hell. But not as bad as burning to death. With the smell of burning bear hair singing my nostrils I plunged my hands into the flames that reached up from the burning rug.

White. Hot. Searing pain. Hurt like hell was an understatement. I saw stars and my ears began to ring. The sound of the fire deafened as I screamed one horrific note of agony. The ropes weren't burning fast. They were a quarter inch thick and took their time to shrivel and blacken.

I fought the urge to pull my hands away. The smell of burning hair was replaced by a familiar scent, something like cooking meat. I could see the skin on my hands bursting and curling away. Flesh was dripping down into the fire. I kept screaming and kept my hands flexed against rope. Suddenly the ropes gave, and my hands burst from the bindings. The pain wasn't as bad as I thought until I realized the burns were third-degree. I'd burned the nerve endings away.

My fingers were useless. They wouldn't bend. I couldn't get them to do what I wanted. But I needed to untie the knot attached to the flue handle to be free. "Move or die," I told my fingers. Something came crashing down in the kitchen. A wood support beam. Then another and another. Sparks shot out from the doorway. The fire was just feet away now. "Move! Or die!" My fingers curled finally, and I put them at the base of the knot and started prying at it. Bea hadn't expected me to be able to reach the knot when she'd tied it and I was able to easily undo it.

I kicked the ropes off and ran for the door and it opened just before I reached it. Bea must've been watching from the window. Before I had time to speak, she raised the revolver and fired.

I wasn't lucky enough for her to miss. It was like getting hit with hammer. The bullet tunneled into my shoulder like a hot metal hornet. I screamed and she fired again. She must've missed the second time. I didn't feel anything. I was only a few feet away and lunged towards her. Another shot rang out and I felt a bullet graze my ribs like a blade.

I knocked the gun from her hand and grabbed the back of her coat. In one fluid motion, I swung her behind me and she went tumbling inside towards the fire. She disappeared into the flames but quickly burst back up, screaming. Her hair was alight, and she flew past me, her head a ball of flame.

I bent and scooped up the revolver, then followed her outside. I thought she'd already be in a snowbank dousing the flames, but she rolled around on the hard snowpack of the driveway. She couldn't see well enough to find the snowbank, I realized.

"Katie!" Her hair had burned off completely already and the flames were creeping down her coat. "Katie, please put me out!" She wasn't that badly burned. She would live. I thought this was where I would be the bigger person. Where I would pat out the stray flames and save her life. But I just watched her toss and turn.

"Katie!?" She cried. "I'm your sister!"

I realized I wasn't going to do any of that, and I raised the gun. As demented as he was, Howard was right—blood wasn't always thicker than water.

"Fuck you, Bea," I said, and I fired the revolver until it clicked, empty.

273

RUN

I tossed the gun on the ground. Something in the house shifted and I turned and watched the second-floor crash down to the first. A million sparks shot toward the sky. I was so far from triumphant. Howard had still won. If anything, he'd say I just saved him another million dollars by shooting her. In less than an hour he'd get on the private plane and be off to some faraway country with no extradition.

My left arm that had been shot was useless. I couldn't raise it. But with my right I took Bea's phone from her pocket. If I could reach the police I could have him stopped on the runway. But there was no service, and I let it fall back on to her.

I realized the option I did have. Howard had left not even ten minutes ago. He and Randy still wouldn't be on the highway. Before I finished formulating my plan, I was running.

Shot, burned, concussed. I pounded in my bare feet down the frosted drive. I didn't even feel my bad ankle anymore. From the adrenaline or the other injuries, I was able to propel myself into a sprint. I was in another world. My body was so shocked that when I told it to run it entered into a prey-like drive to survive.

Instead of running towards Fool's Gold and the highway, I went towards the other end of Carson's Pass near the grocers. In the clubhouse, I saw a flashlight shining inside the room I had leapt from. Philip was still gathering files and electronics. I ran the rest of the way to the moving truck, but the door was locked. "Fuck!" I hissed.

Philip wasn't one to haphazardly toss the keys in the cupholder like Randy. I was sure he had them on him. I thought about running back to get the gun. Then I'd bluff that it was loaded. No. No time. It would be hard to catch Howard in the moving truck anyway, I realized.

Then I remembered there was another place Randy might toss his keys—the snowplow he drove that sat at the end of the runaway truck ramp. Then I wouldn't have to chase them. The ramp went right down to the highway and if Howard was going to Gypsum, he had to pass it. I could beat him there.

But even if I could find the keys my plan might not work. What if there was too much snow for the plow to move downhill? What if the trees that had been planted to deter using the ramp to get to Carson's Pass were too big to get through?

I started running again, my bare feet burning on the cold ground. Please be unlocked. Please be unlocked. I was only one hundred yards from the plow. Howard would be on the highway passing the point where the ramp met it any second now. My lungs hurt more than anything as I sucked the freezing thin air into them. I tilted my head back and bounded the last few yards. I didn't even slow myself. I just crashed into the driver's side door of the plow and then flung it open. Unlocked. The snowplow was ancient and there was no bulb that lit up when I opened the door. I patted around blindly for a set of keys. Nothing.

I pulled the sunshade down and then opened the glove box. I could feel objects but not textures. My hands were too burned, and the pain was starting to register. I reached in further and the bullet in my shoulder felt like a saw blade as my body ran out of adrenaline. But if I let the pain in, I'd be incapacitated. I tossed musty manuals and folders out of the glovebox and then I heard the unmistakable jingle.

Keys.

I saw a silver flash of metal and then fumbled them into the ignition. The engine turned over slowly but surely, like an old work horse that was reluctant yet reliable.

But when I turned the headlights on my heart sank. There was a snowbank in the way of the hill that led to the runaway ramp. I could clear it with the plow but that would take time I didn't have. I threw the gear shift into reverse and rocketed back twenty feet. Then with a jerk, I put it in drive and slammed the gas. I wasn't going to move the snowbank. I was going to blast right through it.

I held the wheel tight, bracing for impact. When the plow blade hit the snow, I shot forward, and my ribs hit the wheel. The collision sent a nauseating wave of pain through my shoulder, but I didn't have time to react. The truck had broken through to the other side of the snowbank, and I was in free fall. It was like the edge of a cliff. Of course, a runaway truck ramp would be built on a steep slope, but I didn't realize how much of a sheer drop it was. For a second or two the front wheels were suspended in mid-air before they hammered back down on the ground.

The snow was thick, but gravity was on my side. At the steep angle nothing was stopping the plow. The saplings were swallowed under the hood. I could hear them crack and bang underneath the frame. I heard something hiss and pop and then engine lights lit up the dash. I hit the brakes, but they didn't respond. It was too steep. I'd found myself behind the wheel of a runaway truck.

With every shake and jostle a sharp pain shot out from my bullet wound. I tried to grab the source of the pain but as I moved my hand, I saw my melted skin had stuck to the wheel. The sight made me sick. I stared out the windshield as I noticed the ride had become smoother. I had gotten to the gravel part of the runaway ramp. The section that had been plowed in case it still had to be used. I pumped the brakes again, but my efforts were futile.

Two hundred yards ahead was the highway, but the road didn't sit flat in the bottom of a valley. The highway ran along the side of the mountain. I would rocket past the two lanes and then keep falling down into another steep gorge. But the next gorge wouldn't be cleared. There'd be pine trees as big around as Volkswagens.

I'd made a mistake. I was picking up more speed. I had just seconds before I'd reach the road. But then I saw lights. Headlights were wrapping around the bend going towards

Gypsum. They would be crossing in front of me as if they were on the top line of a T-intersection. I noticed that the headlights were blindingly bright. They were LEDs. It was Howard. It had to be. The timing from when he left was right.

I quickly turned off the headlights so I couldn't be seen and in a flash through the trees, I saw a black car coming around the bend. I didn't have time to hesitate. I could yank the wheel and try to flip the plow, so I wouldn't break through the guardrail and barrel to my death or…

There was no time to think. The headlights coming towards me were getting brighter. The highway was twenty yards away. I prayed my timing was right and pressed all of my weight into the gas.

The world became a blur of tunnel vision as I accelerated. I opened my mouth and screamed a battle cry. When it was too late for him to avoid me, I turned on the headlights. It was just a flash, less than a single second. But in that frame, Howard's car appeared in front of the hood. I saw him turn to look at the truck with a panicky flick of the head and I knew he saw it all. This giant beast roaring out of the black with his screaming wife behind the wheel. His expression morphed to horror and there was noise like an explosion as we collided.

The truck shot through the guardrail, with Howard's car spearheaded on the hood. Suddenly, there was no sound but a gentle jiggling of glass. I thought I was dead. But then I realized I was airborne. The pines closed in quick. And just as the cold air blasted through the shattered windshield, the truck stopped like it hit a brick wall, and my head met the wheel.

TBI

"Now you understand that it might seem like they're normal at times or that they're coherent, but after sustaining injuries like this there's really no way to tell for sure. *Particularly* when the patient is nonverbal."

I was sitting upright in a hospital bed, bandaged to a cartoonish degree. Hands wrapped; head wrapped. Ribs wrapped. Shoulder in a sling *and* wrapped. My legs were free at least, I didn't need a wheelchair. A doctor with a thin mustache and bulging bug eyes tapped his pen on his thigh as he talked.

"When people get brain damage like this, it's best they have family to take care of them. Even with what you could afford, assisted living care would be mediocre, at best. To be blunt, the system's a bit cruel to the cognitively impaired."

The doctor cleared his throat with his fist in front of his mouth. "We used the letter board this evening and he could spell with blinks." He sighed. "And your husband is adamant he doesn't want to be taken into your care. If you're willing to be an attentive caregiver once you recover, I'm willing to ignore his request for now. I believe your husband currently lacks decision-making capacity."

The doctor continued. "He did blink 'yes' in request for receiving blink-to-talk software. Maybe you've heard of it before. It's the Stephen Hawking setup. I'm hesitant because when we used the letter board, he was belligerent. When people suffer a brain injury like your husband did, their whole personality can change. And it may be a bit... taxing if he's vocal. Even with the letter board he was trying to call you names. You are the surrogate through durable power of attorney. So ultimately, when it comes to his care the choice is yours."

Howard was paralyzed from the neck down and I was to be his caregiver. It was all too strange. "Can I think about it?"

"Of course!" The doctor uncrossed his legs and buttoned his white coat, embarrassed. "Of course, I'm sorry. There's no need for an immediate decision. Especially considering your own circumstances. We're going to keep him under observation for a couple more weeks. Minimum."

"Thank you."

He smiled tightly and left the room, closing the door gently. It was nighttime. The bustle of the hospital had died down to a sleepy pace. It had been a dark day in Denver. The clouds never cleared and as night fell, they stuck around, glowing orange from the city lights.

It was my first day without an EKG. No IV. No tubes twisting from my arms. I could finally walk to the vending machine for Pop-Tarts and not send the nurse with a dollar.

I rose from bed and stood, feeling the cold floor on my feet.

It'd been three days since the events of Carson's Pass. Howard had just woken up from an induced coma for brain swelling and I'd already had two surgeries and was still waiting to do skin grafts.

The doctors had all repeated the same old cliché: *We were lucky to be alive.* Maybe I was. I would resume a normal functioning life one day while Howard... Well, Howard was *unlucky* to be alive. It was unlikely he'd walk or even talk again. He was essentially a brain trapped in a box.

Randy, meanwhile, had been pinned against a pine and died at the scene of the accident. As soon as I was conscious and talking my life became a whirlwind of cops. They were intensely curious about the bullet in my shoulder and the whereabouts of my sister. I said I didn't remember much, just that there was a fire, and I'd breathed in a lot of smoke, burned myself, and was trying to get to the hospital. The police were suspicious but when they came back for questioning, I'd already disappeared, the way the wealthy will, behind a wall of attorneys.

I didn't press them when they mentioned my sister was missing. I knew right away that Philip must've found her and tossed her and the pistol in the back of the moving truck. I was content telling no one about that anyway. It would be too much for my family.

My mom and dad were in town, doting over their wounded daughter and orphaned grandsons. I felt bad for the boys, but my parents were still plenty young and would make for better parents than Bea and Randy ever were. They were already talking formal adoption.

I didn't think I was ever going to tell the truth about Carson's Pass. I certainly had the money to hire a private investigator to find all the actors and maybe even Philip depending on how far he ran. But it felt vindictive. They were poor desperate people, led on by my husband. They didn't know there was a plan to kill me.

No, I was done. It felt like I won. There was just one more thing on my mind.

HUMILIATED

I put my feet into my slippers and opened the door silently. I couldn't tie my gown with my bandaged hands, and I smirked as I felt the cold air on my bare ass, sticking out from the curtain.

There was a lone nurse at the nurse's station, picking at her cuticle. I let the door close before turning the handle back so it latched silently, then I walked without a sound down the hall to my right. I shuffled in my slippers and when I got to room 838, I opened the door just as slowly as I had closed mine.

The room was noisy. Lots of beeping and heavy breathing, and in a bed in the middle of the room lay Howard. He peered at me from behind his bandages as I came in. His heart rate began to pick up on his EKG and I froze. If it went too high a nurse would be alerted. "It's just me, Howard. But I guess that's probably why you're so nervous." The machine's beeping steadied as Howard relaxed. "You know why I'm here?"

I ran my mittened hand up his arm and pried his pillow out from under him. He fell back hard without the support. He looked at me hopefully. Of course, he wanted me to kill him and put him out of his misery. I held it out in front of me, took a deep breath and started lowering it over his face. He closed his eyes peacefully, but then I fluffed it, smiled and put the pillow back under his head.

"Oh, Howard," I said sarcastically. "You're such a fighter." I knew from the pleading look in his eyes that he just wanted to die. "The doctor just came by." I sighed and sat slowly in a chair next to the bed. "I know you want a blink-to-talk device but maybe it's best for everyone involved in your care if you remain nonverbal. Afterall, the decision is up to me."

I paused as the beeping grew quicker again. "I know you're afraid of being humiliated. But I want you to know there's nothing wrong with shitting in a bag and being fed liquid the rest of your life. With your money I can afford a nurse, it's no problem." Howard was looking at me with a combination of terror and hate in his eyes.

"But wouldn't you get lonely with a live-in nurse? I mean, think about it. I wouldn't spend time with you." I squinted and nodded at him. "Yeah. Maybe I *should* put you in a home. That way you can do the stuff you'd like. Like listen to the children's choir come sing for you while you drool helplessly. Or be wheeled in front of the TV where you can watch '70's soap operas. I think that's better." I couldn't keep a straight face anymore and burst out laughing. "I'm sorry." I fanned myself with my gigantic, bandaged hand. "I'm sorry. Whew. Sorry for the sarcasm, that is. I'm serious when I say that's your fate."

I leaned forward in the chair. "I never did outsmart you, Howard. Every time, I fell right in your trap. But you know what I did do?" I stood so I was over him and his heart rate sped up a dozen more beats a second. "I *fought*. Harder than you ever could. I stuck my hands into the fire to burn those bindings off. I shot my psycho sister." His eyes were darting back and forth like a frightened colt and I put my bandaged mitt under his chin and raised his head so he had no choice but to meet my eye. "And I rolled a fucking truck down the side of a mountain and right into you." The EKG made another shrill beep and whined like a siren alerting that his heart rate was too high.

I tightened my lips and stared down at Howard. I pictured Claire's body, skeletal by now. The clothes all big around her bones like a kid in their dad's shirt. Howard was right about some things. The world often was black and white. When I was just a girl, I awkwardly ignored my best friend's cry for help. And somewhere—partly because of that inaction—she lay dead in the woods.

But I wasn't even the same woman I was three days ago. I looked at my reflection in the window in the room, bandaged like a mummy. Strong and confident, I straightened my shoulders and a smile crept across my face. I wasn't going to let the memory of the person I used to be get in the way of admiring the woman I was today.

SAN DIEGO, SIX MONTHS LATER

My hands still haven't fully healed. I can move them alright; hold a fork. Tie a shoe. But my sense of touch is numb, and my hands look something like Freddy Kruger's face. A lot of the time I wear long leather gloves and thick round shades to complete the look. After all, I'm rich. I pull off the aesthetic just fine.

Howard is at an assisted living facility. It's nothing fancy. It's just what insurance will cover. I'm not even paying out of pocket. It's a dimly lit place that smells of cleaning chemicals and is staffed with CNA's who hardly get paid more than minimum wage. No one is very attentive, and I don't blame them. Sometimes, I take Howard out in his wheelchair and visit the daycare that's just across the street. Lucky for him, the daycare is run through a church and they have a program where the kids spend time with the disabled from his facility.

They'll do talent shows, sing, and today they're doing a tea party. I have Howard parked at the low table, I let the kids dress him up. They have a bin of clothes for dress-up and I let them don him with scarves and hats like he's a mannequin. Howard's nightmare is being feminized to entertain children. But he makes them happy. I'm making him a better man, whether he likes it or not.

When my toxicology report came back, they'd found flunitrazepam in my bloodstream, better known as Roofies. I had been drugged, and while this excited the police it led nowhere. A few weeks later they found the burned shell of a moving truck on a logging road near Canada. It was last rented to Howard. No doubt Philip had made a run for the border and burned the evidence. But Bea's body wasn't found with the truck. Philip was smarter than to burn her there. And I doubt he buried her close by, either.

284

I think of Bea more than I thought I would. Howard and Miranda are afterthoughts. It's my sister that gets my attention. I can't decide whether I'd killed her in a moment of strength or weakness, but I lean towards strength. If Bea had lived, she'd likely be making my life hell right now. It was weird. I resented my sister. She'd lied to me. Shot me. She'd been content watching me burn alive. But still I wanted to find her body and give it a resting place. Maybe it was because I couldn't do that for Claire, either.

There was an active investigation into the events of that night, but I knew the police didn't have much. They had searched the houses and were perplexed by the bunkbeds, but there wasn't any way for them to know about the actors. They'd all left. And content to keep their money, they'd tell no one. Either Philip found my handgun that Randy lost, or the police are withholding evidence from me. However, ever since they'd found the Benzos in my blood, they'd been treating me as less of a suspect and more of a victim. Even without my expensive lawyers I was safe. They could never prove I crashed into Howard on purpose.

I've been thinking about my time in Carson's Pass because I got a text this morning. It was ominous and left a frown on my face since I'd read it. I pulled out my phone and looked at it again.

"You owe me nothing. But I need your help"

A second text was sent with an address to a ranch in Western Montana. That was it. I couldn't even text the number back. It was already out of service. I couldn't think who it was. Philip? Amy? But perhaps it was just a friend from college who knows I'm rich now. I thought about sending a private investigator to the address, or, I thought, I could go myself. After all, maybe I didn't have the Sherlock brains it takes to be a great investigator, but at least I knew I had the guts.

FROM THE AUTHOR

I do hope you enjoyed my first book. I'm a young author and I love to write, but there's a long way to go before I get to do it for a living. Currently I spend my days trying not to lose my fingers to a sawmill so I can still write at night!

If you liked the book and want to support me, please leave an Amazon review.

Nothing would help me out more.

Subscribe to my mailing list to get updates on new books!

New book coming this April.

J.M.Cannonwrites.com

Printed in Great Britain
by Amazon

21616396R00169